Super-Celeste

The Super-Celeste was expected to require just one hundred metres of runway – less than seven times its own length – to get airborne. Fifteen seconds after take-off it should be able to reach the speed of sound. It should climb faster than the Apollo moon-shots to reach a height of seven miles in well under a minute. The better than one-to-one thrust/weight ratio of the aircraft would enable it to accelerate while climbing vertically.

All in all, the Super-Celeste would have ten times the fire-power of an entire World War II battleship packed in its sleek body.

PETER WAY

Super-Celeste

MAGNUM BOOKS

Methuen Paperbacks Ltd

For Istvan Orczy von Orczy
and the brave Hungarians

A Magnum Book

SUPER-CELESTE
ISBN 0 417 02180 1

First published 1977
by Victor Gollancz Ltd
Magnum edition published 1978

Copyright © 1977 by Peter Way

Magnum Books are published
by Methuen Paperbacks Ltd
11 New Fetter Lane, London EC4P 4EE

Made and printed in Great Britain
by Cox & Wyman Ltd,
London, Reading and Fakenham

PART ONE

JEAN-PAUL PETIT'S LAST day began for him at five in the morning, in a small hotel on the Rue Jacob, Paris. Neither the French Defence Ministry nor Jean-Paul's employers in Euro-Aviat would have liked to know that this was where he was starting any day, let alone the day of the Super-Celeste's first flight. Nor, for that matter, would his wife, Estelle. Though she would have been less surprised.

With such conditions in mind Jean-Paul Petit took care to wake up with the aid of two alarm clocks, rather than a call from the hotel reception. It was not the kind of hotel where you rely on the hotel reception. It smelt of homogenized milk.

The two clocks, gleaming green by the bedside, rang within a half second of each other. From innocent sleep Jean-Paul extinguished both with a single, swift movement.

He lay, open eyed; watched the silence. There were still two-and-a-half hours before the first smear of light would get through the cloud cover above another stinking Paris February day.

He could hear the girl breathing at his side. After a moment he heard a spat of rain flung against the window, like a summons. He frowned, feeling the twist of fear in his gut. Nothing to do with the day's work. Just a childhood memory, returning often when he woke in a warm bed and heard the cold rain outside.

Jean-Paul stretched on the bed; shifted his weight away from the girl, who had burrowed against him. He began to think about the day's work. The Super-Celeste, the aeroplane he would soon be flying, must now be warming in the lights of its hangar at Euro-Aviat's base at Dreux. He loathed Dreux, a boring town, eighty miles east of Paris. All that part of north-western France—flat as a cemetery. Men from the six Euro-pean nations who had been sweating ten years towards this day

would already be attending to the Super-Celeste there. Not a
few of them, he reflected, would also be pissing themselves with
worry about his absence.

Well, he could do without the smell of their tension at this
moment. First flights were dramas for salesmen and directors.
It was Day Three in this test programme that was more interesting for Jean-Paul (level flight at Mach 2) and Day Five more
interesting still (flight with asymmetrical bomb loading). Then
it could become dramatic.

And yet he knew that, at this moment, he was strangely
excited. He could feel the jolt of adrenalin in his blood. The
first flight *was* always in one sense the pilot's day. Which was
why he felt justified in beginning it how he damned well liked,
he reminded himself. For a few minutes today the 23,000-
pound weight of the machine *would* rest in his hands alone. The
35,000 men in Euro-Aviat, *and* the defence ministers of three
NATO countries, *and* the tax payers of Europe, *and* the
President of France would simply have to sit on their arses
and watch Jean-Paul make their hopes and 3,000 million
dollars airborne.

The girl moved in her sleep again and laid her leg over Jean-
Paul's feet. Immediately, he moved it away. He had never been
able to stand anyone touching his feet. It was why he always
bought long-legged girls to sleep with.

As he moved, the silk sheets slid coolly across the hair of his
chest. The sheets were not provided by the hotel. Claude
brought them with her. She always brought them freshly
laundered and unpacked them in front of Jean-Paul while he
watched her carefully. She then remade the bed. There were
other rituals that went with their meetings, which were but
seldom, since Jean-Paul also had a wife and a mistress. Among
them was the shaving of all her body hair, and the way Jean-
Paul would anoint her all over with baby oil.

Still lying on his back, Jean-Paul let himself review the day
ahead. It was a careful, punctilious procedure. It really was
why he took care to wake up very early on the day of a big
event. It was one of the reasons Jean-Paul Petit was the man
chosen to fly today—apart from being the personal protégé of
Henri Levitte.

Within three weeks of his death, a junior official in Brussels would be calculating that M. Jean-Paul Petit had cost two million francs in fees and widow's pension alone.

As he lay looking at the dark, Jean-Paul could sense clearly the feel of this new aeroplane under his hands. One of France's leading psychiatrists had, four weeks ago, interviewed Jean-Paul for *Paris-Match*. "I don't love machines," Jean-Paul had said, while slicing a raw carrot as hors d'oeuvres in a most expensive restaurant. "There is a personal electricity between me and the machine. This is something that can destroy you, but also you must coax and love out of it your survival."

Outside the hotel, in the Rue Jacob, the rain gathered power. At this time of the year, the dead of winter, the shops of the street hung on with more or less hope for the influx of spring tourists. At number 29 a dim and worm-ridden statue of the Virgin, carrying the dead Christ, encrusted equally with gilt and dirt, gazed sadly out of the window glass, which seemed itself to be weeping for her plight.

With neat and conservative skill Jean-Paul lifted himself out of the bed. Without making a murmur on its ancient springs. The air in the room struck chill on his naked body. He was thirty-eight: old for the job. The daily ritual of Canadian Air Force exercises had kept his body tight, flat-bellied, trim. He did not shiver in the dark. The fine, narrow nostrils in his small, precise face sniffed and contracted in displeasure at the scent of the night's events from his own loins. He moved to the bath-room and began to shower himself thoroughly. A range of toiletries lay ready in their black leather case to aid him.

Meanwhile, the review of the day ahead unrolled like a film in his head—a film he could stop and restart when he chose. He now began to concentrate entirely upon the aeroplane. If required, he could have copied down almost word for word the entire, closely typed manual about the Super-Celeste that he had written himself. The manual at this moment lay between the creases of his neatly folded trousers under the foot of the mattress. As he turned the film in his head he stopped at any moment of still remaining doubt, rerunning it, probing it.

The girl in the bedroom woke, and called his name. He heard the soft, Provençal accent and ignored it.

Again, the French government would have been alarmed to know that a detailed specification for this particular piece of machinery was at this moment resting neatly beneath the well-rounded little bottom of the girl Claude. The news would of course have been a delightful gem for the Communist deputies.

Not that the specification contained any information about what the machine had been designed to *do*: the extensive weaponry it was intended to carry. Among these were missiles and guidance systems costing 400,000 dollars apiece that could take on six different targets in a single pass. Nor was there much information about the aeroplane's performance. Until Jean-Paul Petit began today to ease it down the runway on its first gentle flight there was scarcely any performance to inform on. There was, of course, a very clear idea about what that performance would be if all went well—*when* all went well (the alternative was too dreadful to mention).

The Super-Celeste was expected to require just one hundred metres of runway—less than seven times its own length—to get airborne. Fifteen seconds after take-off it should be able to reach the speed of sound. It should climb faster than the Apollo moon-shots to reach a height of seven miles in well under a minute. The better than one-to-one thrust/weight ratio of the aircraft would enable it to accelerate while climbing vertically.

All in all, the Super-Celeste would have ten times the fire-power of an entire World War II battleship packed in its sleek body.

The aeroplane had a simple function in life to serve. It was Europe's final gamble in the increasingly expensive and feroci-ous aviation business. It just had to prove itself the world's best fourth-generation fighter aircraft; against all the competition America could devise.

Jean-Paul patted his cheeks carefully with Arpège after-shave and returned to the bedroom. He was aware that just thirty-five minutes remained to him to walk the three blocks that would take him out of these narrow streets by the Seine and into the expensive hotel where he was *supposed* to be spending the night. He would then breakfast in his room and wait for the call that would let him know the Euro-Aviat car was waiting to drive him to Montparnasse and the train to Dreux.

There had already been disapproval expressed about Jean-Paul's habit of leaving the base to come to Paris. But that was part of the man's profile. He was a civilian, and nothing would persuade him otherwise—not even the great Henri Levitte himself. When his employers became restive about Jean-Paul they had simply to console themselves with various memories about the man's performance.

Like the day he had volunteered to take over a 707 that had been baking in Beirut in the hands of four armed Palestinians. He flew them round the sky for thirty-six hours with only three refuelling stops until they were exhausted, then dropped the machine in a huge bone-jarring dive. It spilled the guerrillas from one end of the plane to the other, giving the rest of the crew the chance to overpower them.

In the public version of these events it turned out that the guerrillas had then managed to poison themselves. In fact Jean-Paul had murdered every one of them with his bare hands, taking each man in turn to the toilet for this purpose. A number of people were extremely displeased at this. The guerrillas were little more than children. And a strange rapport usually develops between captor and captive on such occasions—Jean-Paul's fellow crew members never spoke to him again. Officially the action was (apart from being entirely hushed up) put down to the strain the man had been under. But Jean-Paul had been under no particular strain. He simply did not approve of the guerrillas, and saw no reason why they should waste time and money in prison waiting for some other gang to commit some other crime to get them out.

The girl Claude's dark and soulful eyes widened slightly as Jean-Paul returned to the bedside.

She, too, felt a certain distaste, mingled with fear, for Jean-Paul. In her very small, distinguished clientele she was used to most of the diversions and perversions that the human race has managed to invent.

But with Jean-Paul there was something different again. The man was so silent. As bodies went, she liked his well enough. He was hard, always smelt fresh and scrupulously clean. Only the Saudi cabinet member among her friends was comparable in this dry and immaculate bodily freshness. The man seemed never even to sweat. In their sexual encounter he treated her deftly, gently, unhurriedly and well.

He treated her with the respect he gave to all machinery.

The flicker of fear she felt was perhaps that he might, one morning, simply dispose of the machine as dispassionately as he had employed it.

Without a word he patted her flank and she moved immediately so that he could retrieve his trousers. Then he drew back the sheet from her naked body and looked at her for a moment. She lay on her back and tried to smile. She expected that he would not want her to touch him again today.

But today, it seemed, was a little unusual. There was a departure from the routine. Jean-Paul pulled up his trousers, without removing his gaze from her body. She had noticed about him that he could look into her eyes in exactly the same way he looked at any other part of her body. Today, however, he stretched out his small, well-manicured hand and with his fingertips touched, in turn, her nipples. And as his gaze turned to her eyes she imagined, possibly, there was some hint of regret.

Fifteen minutes later, Jean-Paul reached the dismal foyer. The desk was unoccupied. The bundle of newspapers provided so lavishly by French newspaper publishers to every hotel in the city lay spilled on its counter.

A tray of croissants lay alongside it. The bakers and the newspaper employees were among the very few people stirring outside the doors of Paris.

Jean-Paul lifted the catch, heard the warning buzzer throb deep in the basement of the hotel and quickly closed the door behind him. The rain was heavier now: no longer in flurries but mean and icy. With his small case in his left hand and the croissant he had taken from the desk in the other, he set off up the narrow street.

Behind him, a grey Renault 4L van with only one side-light functioning moved away from the kerb. They have remarkable stability. One can even drive them on three wheels. This particular van was unladen, at present. As it stopped, fifteen yards ahead of Jean-Paul, he was just lifting the last of the croissant to his mouth. The soft, fatty flesh of the croissant was already half soaked in the rain.

He was not able to swallow his mouthful. It lay, half in and half out of his mouth as he sprawled across the pavement. The bullet from a 7.62 SLR, fired at six yards, entered his right eye, exited through his skull, shattered the glass in front of the Virgin and buried itself in the wall behind her.

The two men from the grey van moved without any special hurry. Jean-Paul lay open-mouthed on his face, his well-shaven upper lip pressed into a dog turd.

The men transported Jean-Paul to the van by pulling him into the street by his feet. Helpfully, he still clung to his attaché case. In the van, they put him into a stout white plastic bag, and, before sealing its mouth with a wire clip, they sliced his throat in case their guest might still prefer to bleed to death. Then, with unhurried calm, they spent a few moments studying the pavement. The rain was already erasing the small trail of blood Jean-Paul Petit had time to shed. The remains of the croissant lay on the edge of the kerb, and one of the men carefully turned it into grey paste beneath the sole of his boot.

And then they drove away.

It was still two hours before dawn. The rain, as if to vary a monotonous programme, suddenly changed into sleet. The Madonna in the window by which Jean-Paul had fallen would not find a buyer today. At the end of the street, the Renault paused obediently at the traffic lights.

As the lights changed in the brilliant evening sunshine of Sydney, Australia, Hermann Ackermann's head snapped back and the blue Holden surged forward into the path of the pedestrians still trying to cross the road ahead. Hermann Ackermann shut his eyes. Never in his life had he encountered anything like the way the drivers of Sydney went about their suicidal missions.

"*When*'s your flight?" asked his driver.

Ackermann risked taking his eyes off the road again to press two buttons on his wrist-watch. In the bright sunlight, tiny red figures glowed with the news that the day in France should be just beginning.

"Three hours," said Ackermann.

"You want to be back at your hotel then?"

"No. They can phone later."

"No worries?"

"None at all."

"Touch my wooden leg," said the driver, pushing the accelerator.

The car plunged downhill from King's Cross towards Rush-cutter's Bay. To the left was the flicker of the sails of expensive yachts behind the heavy leaves of summer. A sidelong glance showed the driver, a Queenslander of fifty-one years named Don Gorton, the sweat standing out on Ackermann's head and he discreetly slowed down. He wanted his guest to have a good time tonight. He'd even laid on a big blonde girl for later, if it looked as if the German would be interested. After all, Gorton had things to be grateful for. The Euro-Aviat cheques for ten thousand dollars a year had been coming in for eight years now. And a lot of solid work had been achieved. It was extraordinary, thought Gorton, that this was the first time he had actually met Ackermann. He felt he knew him well. Extraordinary too, that as far as he knew, this was the Bavarian's first visit to the land.

Eight years ago, when Ackermann first started taking an interest in Australia, even the most loyal aides of "The Hun", as he was known throughout Euro-Aviat, thought it was an aberration. In the small community of the world's top aerospace salesmen the idea of hinging the success of Europe's all-purpose fighter on events in the great empty continent looked bizarre. Not that Ackermann told anyone that was what he had in mind.

"Take a look at that," said Gorton, stopping the car.

They were already into the expensive suburbs—the lavishly built project houses surrounded by huge rubber trees, with a kidney-shaped blue pool in every garden. The road had risen to a hill-top between two bays and the whole of Sydney Harbour lay beneath. Distantly, the Opera House lifted its sails with lighthearted grace.

Ackermann peeled his shirt from the baking plastic, dabbed his bald head with the fourth linen handkerchief of the day and got out.

"Exceptionally beautiful," he said politely.

Gorton was slower coming out of the car. That joke about the wooden leg was no joke. Gorton had left both his legs behind in West Irian, ten years ago. It is a place not far from Australia where God never intended mankind to travel anywhere except by walking. The air strips on the high plateau are too small and rough to land anything more beefy than a hedge-hopper. But on the other hand they are too high for a hedgehopper to reach by flying up and over the mountains. So those who needed to visit any of the thousand tribes, each speaking a different language, had to fly up the ravines. The ravines are okay but there's no chance of turning round in them when the clouds come down. Gorton was there when the clouds came down.

He had settled down to a boring life as a controller of NSW intra-state flights, his buccaneer days over—until Ackermann's representatives came to see him.

"See that down there?" said Gorton, taking Ackermann's arm.

Ackermann followed his gesture. A plump, elderly sea-plane rested in the water below.

"That's the old Lord Howe Island plane. That's where we're going: Watson's Bay. I've got a good dinner down there for you."

The harbour waters were busy: fat-bellied ferries were pushing out to Manley with the usual mix of commuters and surfers aboard. Golden young men in tiny dinghies, sitting far out, bounced over the waves thrusting in from the Pacific. Ackermann ran his handkerchief round his neck again, fast reddening in the sun. Gorton waited for him to say something. He was proud of this view.

Hermann Ackermann looked at his watch.

"Mind you," said Gorton, slightly hurt, "I'd probably trade it for a chance to fly the Super-Celeste today. What's your man's name?"

"Jean-Paul Petit."

It was true that, passionately interested as he was in Australia, looking at views was not very important to Ackermann. It was looking at maps and statistics that mattered.

Eight years ago, within a few days of the Super-Celeste going on the drawing board, Ackermann had gone to work. It was obvious that the days of fixing a market simply by massive bribery and corruption were over.

When Ackermann looked at the map of South East Asia, he noticed a number of peculiar things. The first of which was that the great, fat, empty continent really *is* part of South East Asia, whether or not the Australians like to give it a safe page to itself in the atlas. The island of Timor, for example, is closer to the mainland than Tasmania. And Timor was now red: not British Empire red but Communist red. In fact there was plenty of red and it was getting closer all the time. There was Chinese red creeping down through the Philippines, with the pressure of million upon million of Chinese pushing it forward. There was Russian red all over the ocean, with the friendly Russian fleet helping the Tongans build deep water anchorages for the Tongan fishing fleet.

Meanwhile, the American Seventh Fleet had pulled back right out of the map and, as a quickly reprimanded Australian admiral had said: "We couldn't defend Botany Bay on a fine Saturday afternoon."

It was puzzling, to Ackermann. The Australians were sitting on the most important piece of real estate left in the world: stacked with fast disappearing natural resources like gold, oil, nickel, bauxite, uranium and food. Yet they were happy to make jokes about the fact that they had a two-ocean fleet—one boat in each ocean. It seemed that the generation who had had a taste of conscription in Vietnam wanted nothing else than to bury their heads in their golden sands.

Ackermann, patiently, cleverly, started to dig them out. It had been complicated. It had taken time. He had stayed well clear of it. The money that had gone into feature films about Australia in World War Three, into solid academic treatises on defence policy, travelled through well-laundered paths before reaching the film makers, authors and publishers. Slowly, slowly, Ackermann built his market. It was no coincidence that the first flight of the Super-Celeste was timed to coincide with the fortieth anniversary of the raid on Darwin.

"Let's go," said Gorton. "Let's go and enjoy ourselves."

The French police inspector kicked with some anger at a pile of dented cans that happened to be at hand. "What a pile of shit," he complained. "And when is that fucking canopy coming?"

It was still raining. Inspector Jules Mortain liked to do whatever was possible to minimize the miseries of his job. Standing in the middle of hectares of freezing concrete—looking at the empty place from which a large white plastic bag had lately been removed in a white Citroën police ambulance—was no way to spend a February morning. Before yet more important visitors arrived to see what he was up to, he would at least have liked to have a decent little canopy put over the site. At the moment one couldn't even give the impression of efficiency by drawing a neat chalk outline of the position the body had been found in. The rain would have washed it away immediately.

Looking around the scene, Mortain had to admit it was a very good place to leave a body. In the old Les Halles market, people were friendly, they knew each other. They would have noticed someone arriving to dump a six-foot-long plastic bag in full view, for Christ's sake.

In this ghastly creation, the new Les Halles between Paris and Orly, no-one seemed to know anyone else at all. The juggernaut lorries rolled in and rolled out. The fork-lift trucks surged to and fro in noisy isolation. You never heard people singing and whistling at pretty girls in this place. There *were* no pretty girls.

At some time about dawn, it would appear, someone unknown in some unknown vehicle had added the plastic bag to the mounds of merchandise and bustle going on in the dark of the market's peak period of activity. It was a very good idea, thought Mortain.

By the time the day's trading had died down, the bag would stick out like a whole fistful of sore thumbs from the scattered heaps of other produce that had rotted before arrival.

An inquisitive road orderly had been the first to unwind the metal band tightly wound round the neck of the bag. A few pints of dark, already congealing blood had spilled on to his pointed and leaky shoes. By now, at ten in the morning, Jean-Paul Petit was lying quietly in the morgue, receiving his second toilette for the day. And at the air base in Dreux, in offices in Munich, Brussels, Amsterdam, Paris, Toulouse, Rome and Milan a very considerable number of people indeed were not lying about quietly at all.

The death of Jean-Paul Petit had hit the Euro-Aviat Corporation in a three-fold shock wave. The first wave struck at ten am, when the pilot's non-appearance on base led to a check-back in Paris and the discovery of an empty bed in the hotel he had supposedly been at. Euro-Aviat coped smoothly enough with that one. They announced that Jean-Paul was indisposed and began dressing up the reserve pilot, Henri Bosco. Even so, it was bad enough news, and the personnel director, Dassin, already knew his head would roll for letting Petit off base. But it was still manageable.

At 10.45 came the news of the plastic bag in Les Halles. And this news reached Euro-Aviat one minute thirty seconds after it reached a squad of tough-minded, swarthy men who were busy chaperoning the President of the French Republic into a blue Euro-Aviat helicopter for his flight to Dreux.

Without hesitation, they hauled the President off again. Their logic was simple. If someone was gunning down Euro-Aviat pilots, the corporation's security would need a thorough review before the President was put at its mercy. While Euro-Aviat's now embattled front office in the Rue Frédéric was trying to negotiate a face-saving statement that the President was indisposed too, the final blow came down from Henri Levitte himself. No President; no flight.

"This plane *is* France," Levitte shouted down the phone to his managing director. "These bastard politicians wanted to be there. And now these bastard politicians are *going* to be there. We're not putting this thing in the air furtively."

"But Henri—you know what this is going to do. You know the timing. This is a hell of a risk."

"Tell that to the President. Tell him we'll drive him there in a fucking tank if he's frightened."

Jean Perrault, Managing Director, listened to the empty phone for thirty seconds, then swore expressively. According to Henri Levitte, there hadn't been a French president since de Gaulle.

Perrault scribbled a brief note, then took it down to the public relations director, whose team of ten girls was now coping with a battery of telephones warbling like hornets.

"Christ," said the PR director when he had read the note. "Claire," he called, "cut all the phones. Now."

The room went perfectly quiet.

Perrault said: "We may be rescheduling the flight, ladies and gentlemen."

The PR director lit a Gauloise and spread his hands in

eloquent despair. "Just because of the President?" he asked. "Shall I tell them that?"

"No. Tell them we shall be making a statement. I'll still try to change his mind."

"Why don't I just ring up the *Sydney Morning Herald* and tell them the plane hasn't got wings anyway?"

Perrault, a big smiling man, moved swiftly round to him and spoke so the girls wouldn't hear.

"You do your job, Denis," he said. "This is the kind of time you draw your fat salary for."

The PR director stubbed his cigarette. "Sure, M. Perrault. It's just that, like they say on the movies, a lot of people worked very hard to make this day possible. Okay? You reckon Jean-Paul would have liked to see the whole thing given away?"

"I said, I'll try to change his mind," said Perrault.

The woman Claire came in. "Excuse me, M. Perrault, before you go away," she said, "A lot of the press are asking after the . . . personal connection."

"What personal connection?" said Perrault, his voice still pleasant.

The PR director picked up a memo. "You can tell them," he said, "That Jean-Paul Petit is—was—one of the most valuable pilots in France. That he was deeply loved by the entire Levitte family. Into which family he was adopted as a child. After the death of his father, the general, who was a comrade-in-arms of Henri Levitte."

He put the memo down carefully. It had come from Henri Levitte's office. At nine am.

"That isn't what I meant," said Claire.

"And anyone who tries to raise the story of Jean-Paul and Marie-Thérèse Levitte you can remind what happened to the last magazine who printed filth."

"Tough as that?" said Perrault mildly.

"Oh yes," said the PR director. "Tough as that. Anyone who prints any more crap about Jean-Paul and the *patron's* daughter is going straight out of business and into jail. Especially now. Okay Claire, switch on again."

The phones awoke with a single voice and the team got back to work.

Perrault set off to try to tackle Levitte personally. Whoever in hell lay behind the slaying of Jean-Paul Petit, he was beginning to decide, had certainly struck the hornet's nest in its most tender part.

The old house in the Rue Frédéric, with its high wall round a Spanish-style courtyard and fountain, had been the home of the Levitte family, on and off, for almost 150 years. It is now linked to the new, bronzed glass headquarters building by a fifty-metre subway. The boardroom is still in the old house. Few directors or employees, except Jean Perrault, ever trod this coolly air-conditioned passage without a chill grabbing their souls. Today even Perrault, though walking apparently calmly as usual past the ranks of photographs of earlier aeroplanes, felt a twinge of the schoolboy's fear of the headmaster's study.

But today, even Perrault was unable to get past the fearful dragon of a secretary that Levitte kept at his door. In the Old House, the air was heavy with thunder. As usual, it smelt stuffy in here; the massive furniture smelt as if it had been dusted long ago in talcum powder.

The dragon was a little daunted by the fact that, for the first time in her experience, the patron was refusing to see his managing director.

"In that case," said Perrault, "will you please take the following message for Henri." The secretary looked up expectantly. Perrault pointed firmly to the pad in front of her. "I want it typed up and passed to him," he said grimly.

"You'll be seeing him in an hour's time. Didn't you know? There's a full board meeting at noon."

He looked at her in amazement. "But half the directors are at Dreux."

"They're coming in," said the woman. "M. Levitte has sent the helicopters for them." She didn't mention that her boss had told the pilots to bring the directors back in their pyjamas if necessary—if they hadn't lifted their arses out of bed.

"Thank you," said Perrault, "I suppose you were going to inform me in due course."

"It's on your desk, M. Perrault."

"Well, you write this down," said Perrault. "Dear Henri. First may I express my grief and deep sympathy at the news of Jean-Paul's death. I must also record that I have heard the news of the cancellation of the day's events with great alarm. We have learnt that Melvyn Murray has arrived in Sydney and that the timing of a confrontation between the Super-Celeste and the F-24 is now critical. May I ask that an un-official flight be made here in France today to assist our sales situation in this crucial market."

"I'll give it to him," she said.

"And tell me," said Perrault, "Where are the Levitte son and daughter—where is Daniel?"

"I believe *he* is in Flanders," she said, buttoning her mouth. "And Marie-Thérèse is in Normandy."

"Have they been told? Have you tried to reach them?"

"I've had no instructions," she said, looking up at him with ice-hard eyes, in a good imitation of her employer's blankest stare.

When he got back to his own office, his secretary was still dialling Sydney. A pale, pretty girl, she was still white with shock, her fluffy hair falling over her tearful eyes. Many of the young people at Euro-Aviat had been smitten with Jean-Paul Petit.

Perrault gave her wrist a comforting squeeze, sat on the edge of the desk and dialled PR.

"There's a board meeting at noon," his secretary told him. He nodded. "And the police want an interview." He shushed her with a gesture.

"Denis, has this news gone out on the radio yet? Any chance you can get it held while relatives are informed? I doubt it too, but try."

"Listen," he told his secretary, "While I'm over with Levitte, could you try to reach someone at his country place in Nor-mandy. *Not* Marie-Thérèse. Tell them what's happened."

"You mean she doesn't know?"

"I mean that M. Levitte's secretary has no instructions to put a call through."

"That woman is a cunt," said the girl. She apologized. Perrault ignored it.

"And Ackermann?" he said.

"Hotel reception in Sydney say he's out at dinner."

Perrault stood up. "I hope he makes the most of it," he said. He was at the door when she found yet one more note on the desk: "And you have the sympathies of North-West Aerospace. A Mr John Rose rang you."

The name meant nothing to him.

"Keep trying Ackermann," he said. "Tell him I'm trying to get something in the air. I'll speak to him myself if I'm around."

While his phone rang and rang in his empty hotel bedroom, Hermann Ackermann was indeed making the best of his dinner. The fresh air from the sea revived the Bavarian's appetite. Gorton watched with pleasure as his guest set into a second plate of oysters. He decided to leave the bad news until after coffee.

The restaurant, built over the waters of Watson's Bay, was one of the best. The proprietor set off every morning to bring back the fish that featured on the menu. Second helpings were free. Few asked for seconds—not through any quarrel with the food, but simply because the giant platefuls were a match even for Australian appetites.

A young, well-tanned waiter with a chestful of golden hair slammed four more beers in front of them. Ackermann looked appreciatively at the powerful torso, shirt unbuttoned to the waist. Gorton suddenly understood that the blonde he had lined up for Ackermann later was going to prove a wasted investment.

"Well, Don," said Ackermann expansively, "I must say I'm grateful. For the dinner." He flipped an empty oyster shell over the rail into the cool water alongside, and pressed its still live inhabitant between his tongue and upper palate. "And I am grateful for all the hard work."

"Well," said Gorton, "It's not hard to put money in people's pockets. Not in this country, anyway."

"Or anywhere," said Ackermann, looking along the tables stacked with well-fed brokers.

"But I'm not sure how much it's bought you," said Gorton. He decided there was, after all, too much bad news not to start on it now. "Some of our clients, I've found out for sure, are taking money from the other side too." He passed across a brief list of names. Ackermann raised an eyebrow at one of them, then folded the paper and put it in his wallet.

"Of course they have," said Ackermann. "The idea is just to

peg level. Money alone isn't going to clinch things this time."

"I even had an offer myself," said Gorton.

"You took it, I hope."

"Hell, no."

"Well why not?" asked the German mildly, turning his amber eyes on Gorton.

"Actually," said Gorton, "I'm not such a complicated guy. The other thing is: Melvyn Murray has arrived. He's got a lot of meetings fixed. You're going to be hitting him all week in Canberra." Ackermann didn't seem disturbed.

"You know him of course. Personally, I mean," said Gorton.

"He's quite an old friend."

Gorton looked sceptical.

Ackermann picked up his beer and spread out. "Last time we actually did business against each other personally, though— yes, that was in Ankara. I was selling the Anglo-French Sub-Martel and Murray was doing the McDonnell Douglas Harpoon. That was a nice device too, the Sub-Martel—best USGW on the market at the time. You could fire it out of the sea any depth you liked. No smoke. 150 second burn time."

"I thought you lost that deal."

"Sure," said Ackermann, "Murray was giving thirty-five per cent discounts. Still, we had a great celebration afterwards. Younger then."

The bronzed waiter, backing a trolley of gateaux along the restaurant's deck, collided with a table, and a huge piece of confectionery toppled off, to fall with a splat on the floor. Ackermann looked at the cream dribbling through the floorboards and sighed.

"Well I don't know what discounts he's offering this time," said Gorton, "but he seems to have his tail up."

"Of course he has," laughed Ackermann. "If he was selling a lead balloon with a rubber band for a motor he'd be confident. That's what we're paid for."

"And he has a very good package of offsets. You've seen them. They're better than yours."

Lining up the offset deals had been a busy part of Gorton's work for the last two years. You throw a foreign aircraft into the pond of a nation's own aerospace industry and you set up waves that are going to throw a lot of workers out of their jobs.

This is where the labour unions come in. Whether or not the native industry has the capability to build what you now propose to sell them matters little. You have to find them some other work to do, whether it's making seat belts for your 747s or nose wheels for helicopters. If the worst comes to the worst, you have to agree to send them your aeroplane in kiddy-shaped pieces they can screw together.

"Offsets aren't going to sell the F-24 either," promised Ackermann. "Nothing is going to sell the F-24 because that thing isn't an aeroplane, it's a fucking committee meeting. It's a bunch of compromises. Also, it's American. Your memories aren't *that* short here."

"Sure, Hermann."

Ackermann began to puzzle. He knew Murray's style was impressive, but he hadn't expected Gorton to be so easily impressed. What had come with the offer of money Gorton just admitted to?

"Well, maybe tomorrow you should spend some dollars reminding people what happened the last time you bought American," said Ackermann. "I see there's a few people still left off your list of North-West converts. Media people, I mean. Get one of them to write up what happened to the F-111s."

There was no need to spell it out. Back in 1962 Australia had ordered a batch of F-111s from America. And didn't get them for another eleven years, by which time their price had doubled —quite apart from the cost of hiring 24 Phantoms in the meantime at thirty-four million dollars each year. What was worse was the reason for the delay. On December 22, 1969, one of the ill-fated Nellis F-111s had pulled up from an attack in Vietnam and shed a left wing. None of the crew survived the vicious roll that followed, but examination of the debris revealed that the lower plate of the wing pivot fitting had developed a crater an inch across. In the course of the next two years 320 aircraft were grounded and tested, very expensively, at temperatures forty degrees below fahrenheit.

"*Sure*, Hermann," said Gorton, "But isn't that the point? Doesn't that just prove why Australia is never going to buy anything off the drawing board again? Whatever it's supposed to do. We have to see it fly."

Ackermann spread his arms. "By all means. That's why I'm here. Let's go back home and find out."

The two men stood up. Ackermann paid the bronzed waiter, who looked bad-tempered—understandably, since he had just been fired for drunken driving.

It reminded Gorton.

"Hermann," he said, "I don't know how you're fixed, but I just asked a good friend of mine to call round on you tonight, you know? She won't mind if you have work to do or anything."

Ackermann smiled. "That's very kind of you, Don. That's very thoughtful." He clapped Gorton on the shoulder and the two men went out together, stepping their way through a throng of cicadas to the Holden.

The last thing that anyone would have tried to say about M. Henri Levitte, director general of Euro-Aviat, was that he was concerned in running a happy ship. The *coups de grâce* that followed any mishaps in the amazing career of his company were well known throughout the western aerospace world. By noon, as the senior management of the company awaited his arrival in the chilly boardroom of the company's headquarters in the Rue Frédéric, a number of family men with mortgages almost envied Jean-Paul's present tranquillity in the morgue at the other end of the city.

M. Henri Levitte was half an hour late for the meeting, and those who knew him knew perfectly well that this was the lightest of the punishments about to be inflicted. The senior personnel director, in particular, tried to concentrate his mind on the career opportunities likely to be open to him in other industries. It was a joke in the aviation world that some ten per cent of the staff of Euro-Aviat's competitors were M. Levitte's rejects. The French Minister of Defence had on one occasion ventured to suggest to the great man that this was a useful way of diluting the expertise of France's premier aerospace industry to the benefit of its opposition. M. Levitte had fixed him with his most baleful stare and asked the distinguished minister to let him know in writing if the French government required him, M. Henri Levitte, to run his wife's nursing home rather than an industry making the world safe for democracy. It was on such occasions that the defence minister had to remind himself of the close personal friendship that M. Henri Levitte had enjoyed with the late General de Gaulle.

The carriage clock on the marble mantelpiece tinkled the half hour. Dassin, the personnel director, began quietly tearing the piece of blotting paper provided in front of each member of the meeting. No-one spoke to him, in case the door should open and they should even be *seen* speaking to him.

For the hundredth time that day, Dassin tried to work out where that bastard Petit could have been all night, and why the idiot in charge of these things in Dreux hadn't told him about Petit's habits.

The room was really very cold. Another of the old man's economy campaigns, he supposed.

When the door opened, Dassin did not venture to look up. There was an immediate silence in the room. Henri Levitte walked to the head of the table and laid down his papers. Dassin still did not look up. Two moments later he felt a finger inserted under his collar at the nape of the neck. To the spectators it really did look as if their white-haired chairman had succeeded in lifting the unfortunate Dassin from his seat with one finger.

"*You* are dismissed," said Levitte. "You will leave these premises instantly. Any personal possessions you may have here or elsewhere will be sent to you. If you are seen in any of my factories ever again you will be removed by the police."

Having said this, Henri Levitte returned to the head of the oval table and sat down in perfect tranquillity to consider the reports in front of him.

For a man just chopped off at the bowels, Dassin did what he could. "May I make a statement, Monsieur le Directeur?" he asked in a quivering but loud voice.

Henri Levitte appeared to consider this but did not look up.

Dassin continued. "I deeply regret the tragedy that has occurred. I must remind Monsieur le Directeur and my colleagues—"

"Your ex-colleagues," said Levitte. "Dassin. You have already cost this company three million dollars at the very least through the dereliction of your duties. I have no time to listen to your apologies."

"Nevertheless," said Dassin, "I must say that Jean-Paul

Petit has always been a sensitive management problem. One does not treat a man like this as one does mere employees. I may say, sir, that his close personal friendship with members of your own family in itself led me to feel that had there been any reason not to treat him with a certain latitude then that fact would have been brought to my attention."

Dassin had carefully prepared this last statement. Nevertheless, it did not come out quite right. On the other hand, he could hardly say that he knew Petit had been fucking Levitte's daughter.

"Monsieur Dassin," said Levitte. "Do you know where Jean-Paul Petit spent last night?"

"No sir."

"Were you aware that it was your job to know?"

"I should have been informed. Yes, sir. The immediate management at Dreux will doubtless bear the responsibility for that. You appreciate I have responsibility for some 35,000 men in a number of parts of Europe."

"The management of Dreux will follow you into the gutter," said Levitte. "Now will you get out."

At the door, Dassin turned. He later regretted the last humiliation that followed. It was the moment he would remember first on waking for many years.

"May I ask about my pension rights, M. Levitte?"

Levitte looked at him, the dark eyes blazing from his long, lugubrious face. "If you want to sue, the receptionist at the front door will give you the name of the company lawyers."

As the door closed behind Dassin, Levitte turned to the rest of his troops, some of whom were now feeling a strong desire to urinate. "Gentlemen. We are not running a two-ring flea circus. Will you first try to understand—" (at this point Levitte struck the table with his fist; on one memorable occasion he had succeeded in breaking the table by doing this) "—that you will from now on in public smile and tell the truth. The death of this poor pilot matters nothing, *nothing*, to this business. The aeroplane will fly as soon as the President of France finds time to watch it fly. Monsieur Perrault, I have the defence ministers of Belgium and the Netherlands trying to make a meeting with me about all this. That must be stopped. There will be no meetings. No discussion. In the case of one of those countries,

as we all know, any damage to this programme will be politi-
cally welcome for some of those politicians involved. *No discussion.* Monsieur Maherault, I want the engine performance
figures from last week's tests released. Encourage people. Get
out there and encourage them. Is that understood?"

At sixty-eight, Henri Levitte enjoyed, and used, a still powerful and resonant voice. Among the many epithets used about
him the most frequent was that he was a hard man. At the age
of twenty-three he had flown to Australia in a machine largely
of his own design and personal manufacture. In the war, much
of which he had fought alongside Jean-Paul's father, he had
shot down more German fighters than his colleagues in his
German factories still cared to remember with pleasure. In an
increasingly impersonal and vast business such as the aerospace
industry, Levitte had carved and clung on to a highly personal
empire. He loathed politicians but understood them. He was
known to be passionately patriotic and made no secret of his
traditional Gaullism. The men on the benches and at the
drawing boards of Euro-Aviat loved him. When he visited his
establishments he had a habit of bowing his head slightly,
speaking softly and kindly like a charming old man who by
now, of course, must be little more than the father figure of so
vast an enterprise.

His fellow directors went in terror of him. To ensure that this
situation did not in any way discourage people from telling their
management about any little thing that might go wrong,
Levitte took care to employ his closest confidant, the plump
and cheerful Jean Perrault, who now sat at his side. Everyone
dealt with Perrault if they had the chance. Perrault had often
been heard to say that it was high time M. Levitte took a place
in the mental nursing home that his wife ran as a charity.
Foolish people sometimes allowed themselves to talk too freely
to him as a result.

It was Perrault who now was the only man at the table ready
to carry the discussion further.

"Henri," he said, "I am sure people here would like to know
the present position. Everyone will recall the heroic occasion
when M. Petit frustrated a hi-jacking attempt in Beirut. One
must have in mind the possibility that his death is in some way
connected with this. The company is of course sending tributes

to his widow in the normal way and as soon as a date is settled
for the funeral you will be advised. M. Jean-Paul Petit was one
of the most brilliant pilots of his generation and we all feel a
sense of personal loss. Please do not talk to the press. I have a
press conference immediately after this meeting. Thank you."

Perrault turned back to M. Levitte, who had been gazing
impassively at the ceiling. "Henri. You got my note. We have
at the moment three active sales missions abroad. Above all we
have, as you know, Ackermann in Sydney, and in view of the
importance of the market there I am wondering whether the
next flight has to wait. The Australians are not sophisticated
people. They want to see this one fly."

Levitte frowned slightly and waved his hand. "I'm sure
Ackermann can cope. He'd better."

Perrault nodded. He didn't envy the German.

After the directors had left, Perrault stayed on in the chill
room. And Levitte continued to look at the ceiling. The old
man was increasingly given to these brooding reveries, inter-
spersed with violent and decisive action. A secretary, tiptoeing
in, hesitated to interrupt him. Perrault beckoned her over and
she spoke softly into his ear. Perrault nodded and dismissed her.
After a moment he said, "Henri, your son has been telephoning.
He wants to know if Thérèse has been informed."

"Why should Thérèse be informed?" said Levitte.

"I am just repeating the message. He was apparently very
distressed."

"I have told him not to ring this office," said Levitte. "Get
hold of Ackermann, will you?"

Perrault got up to go. On the way out he laid a hand on
Henri's gaunt shoulder.

"I am sorry," he said.

"The bastards," said Henri Levitte.

Back at his hotel, Ackermann was hailed by the girl at
reception.

"Calls from Paris all evening for you, Mr Ackermann.
They're on now. You want it here?"

Suddenly, Ackermann got the first, unmistakable, acrid
smell of trouble. "I'll take it in the room," he said, and walked
fast to the elevator.

He pushed into the room, surprised to find the lights on. A girl was asleep on the bed, flat on her face and stark naked, rosy pink buttocks gleaming between ample areas of tan. She was snoring peacefully.

Ackermann reached for the phone.

"Ackermann," he said, and started to listen. The voice was faint.

After a while he said: "Who in hell would do that?"

He sat down on the bed.

"But Jesus Christ, Perrault, you've *got* to get that thing up. How soon till he gets the President back? *When?* Oh, that's *great.*"

On the bedside table were his pills for hypertension. With one hand he reached out and unscrewed the bottle. The last two tablets spilled out and rolled out of reach under the woman's belly.

"Well, look, Perrault. I have to have *something*. I'll have to release some of the engine tests, *and* dress it up a bit. I'll stay low till Monday, and for God's sake tell Henri Levitte that North-West is breathing on us will you?"

The phone rang again immediately.

"Well, Hermann, how are *you* settling in?" Instantly, he recognized the loud, dry, papery drawl of Melvyn Murray.

"Melvyn," he said warmly. "Good to hear you."

He tried to bend over to see if the pills were visible under the gently heaving flesh on the bed. Stupid bastard Gorton.

"What in hell are you staying in King's Cross for?" asked Murray. "It took me ten hotels to find you."

Suddenly, the hope flickered for Ackermann that Murray had not yet heard. "I'm fine," he said.

"Listen," said Murray, "You and I don't see enough of each other. I mean *anyway* we don't see enough of each other. And before we get into this lot of trouble I've got a proposition to put to you. There are too few summers left for hard-working men like you and me. What we're going to do tomorrow is this. Tomorrow we'll meet up in a really nice civilized place I know out in the country. We'll have a two-day weekend right out of this and we'll go fishing and tell each other stories from our wasted youth. All right?"

Ackermann thought about it. Whether that bit about a

proposition meant anything. Whether, with two days out of Sydney, Murray could be kept out of range of the news from Paris.

"That sounds a very generous idea," he said, "But I need to be convinced there are civilized places in the country. I'm still looking for them in town."

"You don't know where to look then, Hermann. This is one of the most diverse and civilized places in the world if you know where to look. Okay. Hire yourself a car. Then get on your way to a place called Wiseman's Ferry. It's on the Hawkesbury to the north. Ask someone—someone who won't notice. I want a discreet weekend for the two of us. We've got things to talk about."

"What hotel in this place?"

"There's only one."

"All right," said Ackermann. "I'll do that."

"Fine. Oh, and by the way, I was sorry to hear about this weird thing in Paris. That's a hell of a thing to happen."

"Yes," said Ackermann, "I knew the guy too. Good flying man."

"It's a tough enough business without that. I'll see you tomorrow."

Oh, shit, thought Ackermann, putting the phone down. It was stifling hot in the room. From the radio system stuck into the wall by the bed ghastly vapid muzak was still emerging faintly even though the thing was switched off. And down in an alley at the back of the hotel some damn drunk was howling and sobbing as he sorted through the hotel's discarded wine bottles for dregs. What a country.

Then the blonde's snoring got through to him again. He'd almost forgotten her. In general, life was beginning to look perplexing, but there was one small action that was both necessary and desirable at this moment.

Swinging his broad Bavarian hand from shoulder height, Ackermann brought it down with an almighty slap on the bare rump.

Perrault poured himself a large Scotch. The press conference was going to be nasty. To his secretary he said: "Where was M. Daniel Levitte phoning from?"

"He's filming in Flanders, sir. He said he would be driving back to Paris. Sir . . ."

"Yes?"

"He was terribly angry I couldn't get him through to speak to M. Henri."

"That's not your fault. Did he say anything else?"

"He said he didn't know where his sister was going."

"I see."

"She left Caen at ten."

"Well, I think we have to leave these things to the family. And thank you. You've done well."

He allowed himself to pat her slim shoulder and took the lift down to the floor that had been hastily arranged for the press conference.

Predictably, it was a tough one. Perrault and the three senior public relations officers of the company looked as calm and resolute as they could in the circumstances. Euro-Aviat had a reputation for mopping up vast amounts of public money. The autocratic Henri Levitte was no favourite with the press.

"Gallet of the *Jour Communiste*," the first questioner announced himself. "In view of the urgency of the situation vis-à-vis the Super-Celeste and the American F-24, why was it necessary to postpone the flight for an entire week? Has this murder caused you serious worries about other aspects of security in your organization?"

"We appreciate the concern from a Communist newspaper about the success of the Super-Celeste," said Perrault. "Today's flight has been cancelled on advice from the security forces. Naturally we are as anxious as you are, M. Gallet, to know the possible motivation of this appalling affair."

"Is it suggested that the KGB is involved?" a right-wing journalist interrupted. Gallet turned round angrily.

"It is not for me to make speculations," said Perrault. Gallet was on his feet again.

"May I ask whether you have had any expression of regret and condolence from the CIA-backed bureau of undercover operations run by North-West Aerospace in this city?"

"No such bureau exists," said Perrault. "Next question please."

"Is it correct that Jean-Paul Petit lately separated from his wife?"

"I am here to answer questions as a director of Euro-Aviat," said Perrault coldly, "not to peddle dirt."

"Nevertheless," the questioner persisted, "since Jean-Paul Petit was brought up by the Levitte family from an early age, we presume that his death is a personal loss to both Henri Levitte and to his daughter Marie-Thérèse?"

"Jean-Paul Petit's death is a loss to Euro-Aviat and to France," said Denis. "He was a brave man and a distinguished pilot."

And so it went on, relentlessly, until the hour was up.

By mid-afternoon, the second death of the day occurred. Marie-Thérèse Levitte, the Papa's only daughter, was in transit from the family home in Normandy to Paris when the news reached her, brutally, on the radio. Henri Levitte, who could have forewarned her, had not done so.

Marie-Thérèse had met Jean-Paul when she was six years old. He was already being brought up in the family almost as an adopted child. She had loved him since that time, if the truth were told.

Deep behind Marie-Thérèse's long, bony, rather ugly face, now in its thirty-sixth year of experience, still lay a passionate memory of the time two tiny children had walked hand in hand in the golden gardens of the family estate near Blois. And the times—rare but immense—that the adult Jean-Paul had been able to discover something of that lost paradise, to relax for once, to become less of the brilliant machine in charge of other brilliant machines.

It had been a long and useless obsession. Marie-Thérèse had inherited her father's long and melancholy nose, his deep and passionate dark eyes, but none of his determination to get his own way.

Unless, of course, the psychiatrists are right in saying that some people will go to any lengths to make themselves miserable.

It was now fifteen years since the dreadful day that Henri Levitte had discovered his daughter was sleeping with Jean-Paul. He had done so by the simple expedient of opening her correspondence. For Henri Levitte, it had seemed worse than incest.

He had spelt out the options plainly enough. If Jean-Paul wanted to continue his career in the family, and his expensive training as a pilot, then the price was fixed. It included marriage to the first suitable candidate Henri Levitte could summon up.

Well, she couldn't blame her dear Jean-Paul. They'd managed well enough, even so, all the years since, until that disgusting innuendo in the magazine three months ago. God, she'd like to know how they had found out. Life had been unbearable anywhere near Henri Levitte ever since.

Now, less than thirty miles from Dreux, as she drove her cherry-red Fiat along the narrow straight roads of Normandy, between the sodden, vast fields punctuated by the church spires already becoming dimmed in the failing light, it was time for the news bulletin. She pressed the button on the car radio and listened attentively.

When it was over, she slowed down for a moment thoughtfully to allow a Renault 4L van to overtake her. She then accelerated.

When the car had reached 120 kilometres an hour she turned the wheel briskly in her dry, ringless hands, and felled one of the many poplar trees lining the roads of northern France.

The Renault driver who had overtaken her saw the little Fiat approaching rapidly in his rear mirror again before fragmenting on the roadside.

The driver, a small jobbing plumber from Rouen, first noticed the remains of the white Pomeranian dog that had been on the front seat next to Marie-Thérèse and had now arrived fifty yards down the road after its projection through the windscreen. The plumber ran, with palpitating heart, to the burning tangle further down the road. After one gulping look, he returned to his van and set off for the nearest telephone.

In Flanders, Marie-Thérèse's brother, Daniel Levitte, was still urging his film crew to get it over with. They had come to Flanders to find mud and melancholy for a TV commercial, and there was no doubt that they had succeeded. Daniel had deliberately booked this day, to be as far away from Paris and

Dreux as possible. Now he was desperate to get back. When he finally finished the scene, he leapt into his white Porsche and drove crazily homewards. At times the tears running down his cheeks blinded him too much to drive. Then he would stop for a few moments and drink from the whisky bottle under the front seat. He too had loved the dead pilot. He remembered the times the three of them, he, Marie-Thérèse, and Jean-Paul, had spent their secret evenings drinking in obscure Paris bars, chattering like children again. From childhood, all three had been united in their fear and dislike of Henri Levitte. "*You bastard!*" screamed Daniel suddenly. "You bastard, bastard, bastard!" he roared as loud as he could in the speeding car, his hands trembling on the wheel.

Like many sons of famous fathers, Daniel Levitte was born into and had to grow up with a world of power, glamour and glory that was proffered to him with one hand and denied him with the other. A brief staff job with Euro-Aviat ended badly. Privately, no-one at Euro-Aviat had been sorry to see him go. He wasn't cut out for it. In fact, there were many who believed Daniel Levitte was not cut out for anything; that he was more than a little way "round the bend". It was not quite like that. From his earliest infancy Daniel's sky had buzzed with aeroplanes. Aeroplanes designed to kill. He had always been frightened of them, their smell, their noise. He had been a disappointment to his famous father from the cradle. These things happen. In the third year of life, his father had built a model aeroplane of balsa and paper with which to amuse the child. It was powered with an elastic band. If one wound the propeller the band turned and turned and the plane would fly about the room. His father —who had flown across the Pacific, that blue expanse on the globe in the dining-room, in just such a machine—had wound up the elastic as a treat for Daniel while he lay in bed one hot summer evening in Blois. The aeroplane had careered across the long room, buzzing horribly and returned to land in Daniel's groin as he sat on the bed in his blue pyjamas, and had lost a wing.

His father had laughed and said he would mend it in the morning.

Daniel had crept out of bed at ten-thirty at night and smashed the balsa and paper and elastic thing to a nothing and hidden it in the crevice between his toy-box and the floor. In case it should do it again.

His father had beaten him for this.

Daniel wrenched the car into the left-hand side of the road, lights blazing, horn pounding to overtake a *camion*. How dare he not speak to his own son? How dare he not tell him where Marie-Thérèse was?

But then he wouldn't, would he? "France's grand old man of the air. Fucking tyrant." Daniel hoped at least the grand old man would be hurt enough that Jean-Paul was dead. He was like a son to him, wasn't he. More of a son than Daniel had ever been. He'd only adopted Jean-Paul to rub that in. But God knows what Henri Levitte had been thinking since that damned magazine had got on to Marie-Thérèse.

There was still a hundred kilometres to go. Daniel took another swig from the half-empty bottle and stamped down on the accelerator.

Fifteen years of secrecy. What a mess it had been for all of them. And now Jean-Paul, dead.

By the time Daniel arrived at his apartment he was three-quarters drunk.

It was no coincidence that the woman now listening with alarm to the fumbling steps approaching their apartment door was called Celeste. Henri Levitte had not been content to let Daniel have this beautiful woman to himself any more than he had let Marie-Thérèse have Jean-Paul. To Daniel's fury Papa Henri had lavished nothing but charm and affection on Celeste's sleek little head. The whole process was designed to suggest, subtly, that the father—had he but been younger—would have outpaced his son in this performance as in any other. The very manner in which Henri accepted the fact that the two lived together unmarried was, thought Daniel, designed to show that father didn't care a damn about his son's place in the dynasty. Daniel's mother had added the fact of their open fornication as one more cross in the long list she bore. The fact that Henri did not support her in her protests was only to be expected.

When Henri Levitte, two years previously, had named the new aeroplane after the girl Celeste, Hortense had wept all afternoon.

Henri had been brusque on the topic. "I do not propose to call the machine the Flying Hortense," he had told her.

Celeste heard Daniel's key stabbing angrily at the lock and hastened to open the door. He looked bad. His curly black hair was stuck flat to his skull with rain and cold sweat. His dark eyes shone in the pallor of his blurred face.

It was plain to Celeste that, however she was going to break the news of his sister's death to her lover, he would need sobering up first.

She did this with all her gentle and loving efficiency. As he stood trembling in the middle of the vast living space they had converted beneath the rafters, the rain dripping from his shoulders on to the expensive Persian rugs scattered on the waxed wood floor, she began to remove his clothes, unbuttoning his shirt with her slim fingers, slipping the sodden jeans down his thighs and lifting one foot at a time, as if undressing a child, until he stood naked and swaying in front of her. Then she wrapped a huge white bath towel about his shoulders and led him by the hand to the bathroom.

Celeste had an instinct for such things. Since she had been brought to France, at the age of eighteen months, with nothing but a cotton shirt and a luggage tag round her neck, this child of a Vietnamese peasant woman and an American marine had learnt to treasure any love and attention the world might give her. Fortunately for her, her inheritance from her native land went a long way beyond the luggage tag she still preserved in a silver box. At the age of eighteen she was the most beautiful and successful model in Paris. *Miel au soir*, one editor had called her; honey in the evening. It was a tribute to her beautiful skin, her mysterious expression—something hidden and dusky in her amazing green eyes, and her gentle yet animal body.

She now gave Daniel a revolting concoction of salt, water and mustard and assisted him to vomit in the basin, one gentle hand on his damp forehead.

Then slipping her own dress to her ankles she pressed him gently into the shower and let the hot water play over them as she held him close.

Gradually, Daniel felt the world coming into focus again. He began to be extremely conscious of Celeste's breasts pressed against his chest as the warm water sleeked its way over their two bodies.

By the time she had dried him, holding his still shrivelled penis encouragingly in her warm hands for a moment, Daniel Levitte was very nearly a sober man.

"I'm sorry, Celeste," he said, "I've had a hell of a bad time." She nodded and smiled.

He shook his head, went weakly to the bed, tore back the covers and crashed down on his back. She came to lie alongside him, her hand rubbing his chest.

When his own had stirred to stroke her breasts she felt that the recuperation had gone far enough. Briskly she sat up and squatted, naked and cross-legged, on the bed beside him.

"Daniel," she said urgently, "something terrible has happened."

"I know," he said. "Jean-Paul is dead."

"Something else. Your mother rang. Your sister . . ."

Daniel went rigid. He stared straight at the ceiling. "Tell me," he said.

"Her automobile crashed. I am afraid she is dead."

"When?" he cried. "When was this?"

"This afternoon. Your mother is terribly distressed. She must see you. I think your sister died at once. It has been on the news."

Daniel could feel the tears beginning to run down his face, without sobs. He kept his lips tight together and felt his nostrils contract.

She knew well neither to say anything nor try to comfort him.

He seemed to stand like that for a long time. She watched him, the tears welling freely in her own beautiful eyes. Naked and drunk and sick he had been so like a little boy, a handsome but rather frail little boy. Now something seemed to happen to him. As if he had become taller. Without a word, Daniel went to the wardrobe and with great care selected a dark and discreet suit. He then proceeded to dress. She watched him. When he was ready, he came to her and for a long moment he held her small, rich body tightly in his embrace.

"You were wonderful to me," he said. "I will be back later. I must go to my mother."

"Of course," she said. "You won't drink any more, please?"

"I won't be drinking any more," said Daniel in a chill voice.

As he walked steadily down the street to where their car was parked, Daniel Levitte, even in his grief, found this new anger in his soul a strange and rather frightening thing to deal with. Quite suddenly a whole lifetime of confusions seemed over. He realized he was no longer afraid. Not of Henri Levitte, nor his factories, nor his aeroplanes, nor any part of the vast, ravening beast with its stink of kerosene and noise and destruction. It was all death-dealing and evil, but he was not afraid of it any more. It had *always* been death-dealing and evil—it had corrupted Jean-Paul into a machine. It had kept Marie-Thérèse and Daniel beneath its huge, tearing claws all their lives. He clenched the car keys into his fist until they bent.

Well, it would soon be over. Before he had left the apartment he had known what to do.

As he drove slowly towards the Rue Frédéric, Celeste was engaged, on his instructions, in what would be a long session of telephone calls. His instructions had puzzled her, but that didn't matter. Her task was to discover where an American called Melvyn Murray was and how he might be reached for an urgent and personal conversation.

At the present moment, however, Melvyn Murray's employers had preoccupations of their own. The rival to the Super-Celeste, the variable geometry wing F-24, was airborne again. Though for public consumption, the first flight was scheduled for the following week, the Americans had plenty of open space and plenty of good reasons for a discreet preview.

"Thirty thousand feet coming down to one eight zero," said the pilot, Nathan Zucker.

High in the blue sky over Texas, the fighter looked like a tiny, ghostly, silver arrow.

The men on the ground were not watching her, though she was held well on frame in the colour TV screen above them. They were sitting, chins on their fists, watching the wizardry of the North-West telemetry station in action.

"When you're ready, Zucker."

There was plenty to watch. Every item on the plane's control panel was duplicated on the ground control panels. Every manœuvre in flight was recorded in all its implications on a stack of pen traces. The ink lines swerved this way and that across their endless page.

"I have total flame out," said Zucker.

Now it was quieter. Until now, behind Zucker's voice, throbbing the way your voice does when your brain is vibrating in your skull, there had been the remorseless hiss of the engines. Now the engines were off: Zucker was flying a glider. Naturally it is interesting to know if they are going to start again.

Of course, in theory they are going to start again. In theory the computer has told you exactly what is going to happen in every eventuality. For example—just how the plane will feel flying if you happen to be in a roll with four 1,000-lb bombs under one wing and you lose the power of one engine. Or if you have 8,000 lbs of bombs aboard and lose both engines.

There are a lot of variables. And somebody has to go up there and find out if the things that are supposed to happen are actually going to happen.

"One seven zero knots. Losing a thousand feet in a mile," said Zucker.

Part of his job was to keep talking. That all went on the record too. Because of course what the pilot thinks he is doing may be different from what he is actually doing. Either because he has got it wrong or the machine has got it wrong.

It wasn't likely Nathan Zucker would get anything wrong. He was a damned good pilot. But he wasn't too pleased at pushing into this test programme at the speed they were going. He knew it was the sales situation that had put on the pressure. He knew enough to keep his opinions about the salesmen to himself.

If Zucker, an avid student of World War II fighter-plane films, could have his way, he would resolve the long battle between the F-24 and the Super-Celeste in a simple classical dogfight between the two. Preferably over the Straits of Dover.

The men on the ground, all at the same moment, leant back slightly in relaxation as the engines lit again.

"That's fine, Zucker, get up again."

Zucker climbed again, going through the sun. The sweat trickled on his neck. Ahead of him was the dark blue, the rim of space.

The next thing would be to roll the plane around a bit.

This was where the difference between reading meters on the ground and reading the same meters in the air became more noticeable. On the ground you hadn't the distractions of having your whole body switched in and out of 2G—getting your weight doubled, trebled, halved in a matter of seconds. And if the plane started to yaw the men on the ground wouldn't be having their heads banged from side to side while they decided what to do about it.

"Coming up to two turns now," said Zucker. "Then a stall."

He was by no means sure about this plane yet. He wasn't as bothered as the theoreticians were about the fact that the Super-Celeste was supposed to outmatch it in action radius, weapon load, electronics and ground attack capability. That was all theory. You could still have a machine that lacked a pedigree on paper but actually knew how to fly—a *pilot's* plane. Like those funny little Fireflies the British had at the start of the war.

Zucker went into his spin.

"Sweet Jesus Lord," said the negro, sweeping the concrete outside the telemetry station.

For suddenly the little arrow in the air was wrapped in a pall of white smoke. He dropped his broom. In some of these manœuvres, you get fuel pouring out of the air intakes. It's not serious, unless you have a good combat reason to stay invisible. Zucker got it back.

"Two turns now, about as much as I can get on," said Zucker. The pressures on his body squeezed his voice up half an octave. The roll rate meter spun round again. It was going fast. It is best, for any pilot, not to look out of the window too much. You get disorientated. You can vomit. And the way vomit can spread itself about in a spinning cockpit is wonderful to see. The barred shadows of the cockpit structure swept across the control panel: that can confuse you too.

"Ah, shit," said the man at the end of the line of panel watchers on the ground. Zucker was level again now. It was okay. But it wasn't good.

"Look at that." The ink traces in these last five seconds had taken on the appearance of a graph on the Wall Street Crash.

"Side slips off the top."

"What speed?"

"About one five zero."

2*

"Okay."

"How much aileron?"

"Ten control."

Well, there would be plenty of time to analyse it all later.

"Thank you Zucker. I think that's going to do."

"So do I. One low level pass okay with you?"

"If you want."

Zucker was already forming the private opinion that this plane was a bit of a pig. He wouldn't be surprised to find it had pulled a few rivets this trip. Below him, the dusty brown wrinkled landscape surged past. You could see the base and the colossal white folding doors of the hangars. Zucker lined up the telemetry office in his gunsights and tore downhill towards them. It must have been fun to come down like this in a Spitfire and shoot up an airfield.

The negro sweeper dropped his broom again as the fighter ripped the air off the roof of ground control. The controllers gave no visible sign that they were at all put out by the fact that the two most expensive pieces of machinery in North-West's possession—the plane and their office—had just come within thirty feet of each other.

"You do that again, Zucker, and I'll have your balls for breakfast," said their chief quietly.

The sweeper picked himself up and waved happily at the retreating twin glow of the engines. He felt pretty pleased about Zucker.

It was as well someone was happy. Naturally, no-one was going to admit it, but if things went on like this, thought the chief, someone *would* have to devise some special measures to get this thing sold. He picked up the phone and pressed the button that would encipher what he had to tell the people in Washington.

By the time Melvyn Murray left Sydney early on Saturday morning, driving through the used car lots that lined almost endless suburbs, the flight of Nathan Zucker (who had been given the biggest bawling out of his flying career) was detailed to him. Not good. But all the more reason for the trip to Wiseman's Ferry.

However, Ackermann very nearly cancelled this weekend.

He'd spent the first hours of Saturday morning on the telephone, trying to raise the defence department in Canberra and reassure them that the flight delay was regrettable but trivial. He could raise almost no-one. His secretary assured him that, with the temperature hitting 30 degrees centigrade in Canberra on a Saturday morning, no-one in the town would be caring a fuck for aeroplanes. Ackermann looked at her in amazement: a fresh-faced, blue-eyed Amazon, six feet tall and foul-mouthed as a soldier. Extraordinary race. He decided to join Murray after all.

He got the girl to hire him a big blue automatic Ford Fairlawn and found his way, like Murray, away from the farthest suburbs towards elemental horizons. Strangely enough, he began to enjoy the drive. He liked maps. To get to Wiseman's Ferry he took a long road through Central Mangrove, enjoying for the first time in his life the feel of a dirt road disappearing under his rear axle. When he arrived, Murray was waiting.

"I'll tell you why I brought you to this place," said Murray. "It was built by a pirate, a man just like us."

It was true. The place lay north of Sydney on the way to the rich coalfields of Newcastle. At this logical crossing point on the vast brown Hawkesbury River a Mr Wiseman had established a staging-post in the early 1800s. Even today, the long verandah of the Inn was the main landmark in a one-street town—despite its superb restaurant the Inn was a place from a lost world. The tall brown men standing at the bar drinking their schooners were the descendants of those Irish convicts whose riotous horse races had shattered the calm of the hills above Hawkesbury 150 years previously.

Today, the calm was shaken only by the water skiers on the Creek. Before dining, the ample shape of Hermann Ackermann had felt young and hot enough from his drive to plunge into the vast river itself. The water was warm as silk. Melvyn Murray assured him it was free of sharks, snakes and all the other nasty things Ackermann had been warned of. Ackermann had swum systematically fifty yards from the bank, while Murray's pale, languid and crinkled face diminished to a dot on the vivid grass. The smell of barbecues from a camping site came level across the deep and tepid water.

"Maybe," said Murray, "if I had been simpler and younger

and more clever I would have settled for a farm in a place like this."

Through their evening meal, the two men talked of nothing but old times, the excellence of the food, and—for Murray's part—the attractions of the long-limbed girls who brought it to them.

It was not that Ackermann didn't enjoy the simple pleasures —but he was just as good at waiting for his old opponent to start talking as his old opponent was at staying conversational.

Finally, over brandy, Melvyn said, "You and I should have done this more often." Ackermann revolved his glass and nodded, smiling.

"Don't you think," said Murray, "how nice it is, that no-one on God's earth knows where we are. Our masters are flying about in the northern hemisphere with billions of dollars set against each other and we are sitting here like two civilized human beings at their expense."

"That's very true," said Ackermann.

It was true, and it also didn't mean a damn. As both of them also knew.

"Well," said Murray, "Here's to the last great domino game. Come on, Hermann, I'm going to take you for a short walk. I'm sorry about your pilot. Bad news."

The two men, one slim, one fat, both in their fifties, left the restaurant without causing notice. They walked downhill towards the ferry. If anyone had noticed, they would have passed as family men from Sydney, possibly accountants on a fishing weekend—their wives doubtless back in the trailers in the park.

Neither of these two had wives. Murray was in between his third and fourth. Ackermann was not that way inclined.

By the ferry they stopped. A tranquil sky crowded with stars lay low above their heads, full of constellations strange to Ackermann. The cable, across which the ferry pulled itself, slapped like a heartbeat on its wooden housing as the steel fibres resisted the tug of the huge river. The cicadas hammered their warm song into the velvet dark.

"Hermann," said Melvyn Murray, "I brought you here because I like you. We've worked together too long. We are neither of us too young. I have a serious proposition to make."

Ackermann rested his left foot on the thrumming cable, to feel its pulse.

"It is a very nice gesture," he said. "It is a lovely place to come to."

Murray laughed. "Ah *shit*," he said. "Yes it is. But I'm serious. Hermann: I have to win this one."

"You may well," said Ackermann.

"Damn well," said Murray.

The two men looked across the silent river. On the other side, the ferry was piling up motor traffic and would soon pull itself across the sleeping water.

"Listen," said Murray, "the best plane won't win. I don't know how many of these savages you've met, but for sure they'll buy into our machine. They must. They don't understand quality. I've instructions to undercut you on any price you like. You know the discounts we go into. Let alone everything else. We're going to sell them this thing if we have to give it away. It's your fault—that's the domino you set up."

Ackermann knew. Whoever sold a plane here would sell it to NATO through the 1990s. Sell here and the unit price would come down. That was the game he had set up.

"We'll sell it for butter and wool if necessary," said Murray.

"So you've no problems, Melvyn," said Ackermann.

"Well," said Murray, "I don't want to take advantage of your disadvantage. I am simply telling you. Through no fault of yours, you are beat before you start this time. Last time you were beat after you had sweated pints of blood and fat—and maybe, looking at you, you could stand doing that again. But why the trouble? Hermann . . ."

"Yes?"

"I'm being absolutely sincere, Hermann. I don't need to do this, but on the other hand I can do it. And we've worked a long time against each other, and I remember the good times in Ankara too."

"I see."

"You *are* a fucking Hun, Hermann. You really help me. What I am saying," said Murray patiently, "is *this* time we do a deal against a foregone conclusion. For your sake. For nobody else. Just once on the level. I like you."

"Tell me," said Hermann.

"What do we do this for, any more?" said Murray. "I mean: you and I have been smashing around the world for, what, two decades now in this game. We were nobody's friends when we started, but my Christ, I'm not even friends with myself any more."

"They do say that's the more difficult thing," said Ackermann.

"Anyway. Sure as hell neither of us is going to be doing this ten years from now," said Murray. "You know ten years from now we're going to be sixty?"

"Sobering thought," said Ackermann politely.

"Yeah. And what's more sobering is that *one* of us isn't going to be doing this job ten *days* from now. Whatever your crazy Henri Levitte thinks, Hermann, if your Euro-Aviat loses this one, the blue miracle in Europe is for the scrap heap. You're working for the last of the feudal dynasties. And the man's son is a wino."

"When did you meet *him*?"

"I've met him," said Murray. "Doesn't matter. What I'm saying is that if we lose this then about sixty thousand Americans lose their jobs, which is not going to happen. And maybe the President loses the next nomination, because as you know he's put more money against Congress into North-West than anyone knows—and *that's* not going to happen either. Or North-West goes back to building bicycles, which was where they started. So did I. Can you believe that? You're talking to a bicycle salesman from Omaha."

Perhaps, thought Ackermann, Murray was just drunk.

"Maybe I'm hitting the mid-life male menopause," said Murray. "I even start thinking if this world *needs* more armaments. But I'm certainly thinking that you and I haven't cleared our futures, anyway. Okay, you've had a pile of money, I've had a pile of money. You've probably put away more than I have. And sure they won't actually put the loser out of the pension fund. But when you think of the millions we've been handling all this time! Have we, even now, got one million ourselves out of it? Supposing you and I had taken the percentage on turnover the manager of the local deli takes on daily trading: would we now be sitting on this fucking lost continent at the age of fifty on a summer night?"

"I thought you said you'd like to buy a farm here."

Murray hit his fist on the rail round the cable housing.

"Now, shit, Ackermann, you listen to me. I've got a million dollars for you. It's stacked in a bank in Jersey—Europe Jersey, not mine—and it's in the name of Jules Stein and Estate, and you're the estate. *That's* what it's worth, Hermann. The number of the account is back home in the hotel."

The night hung on the river like a second skin. Slowly, slowly, the yellow lights on the ferry at the further bank hauled towards them with a *putt, putt, putt*. As the boat took up the slack of the cable, it ceased to slap against its track and the night gathered just the soft background of cicadas and the far-off engine.

"And what do I have to do for that?" asked Ackerman.

"Nothing, Hermann. Just that one of us doesn't need to make a star performance this week."

"Well that's what puzzles me," said Ackermann. "If it is just that, you wouldn't have all this money to spend."

Murray was watching the ferry. The boat was here now. It slid on to the rich mud alongside and both men turned to see the few automobiles easing off on their way to the lonely properties in the valley. It was the last run of the night. Suddenly, Ackermann felt the hair rise on his neck.

He knew that there were few things the Americans would stop at this time. That they kept agents throughout Europe in expensive villas to beguile passing politicians. That their slush fund ran to millions. That—so it was said—an entire Paris call-girl racket was funded by North-West.

"No," said Murray, "not me. But I honestly don't *know*. That's the point. It *is* personal. *I* don't know who killed Jean-Paul Petit. Let's go home."

As they stepped back into the dirt yard of the hotel Ackermann said: "By the way. There was a call for you from Paris. Daniel Levitte. You were fishing."

As the fat old servant, who had been with the Levitte family for twenty years, opened the door to the family apartment in the Rue Frédéric, Daniel could see his father across the hall through the half-opened door of his study.

The rest of the apartment seemed to be almost in darkness.

"Oh Monsieur, how terrible it is. How terrible."

Daniel patted her gently on the shoulder.

"Where is Maman?"

"She hasn't moved from her bed. The doctor has seen her. I have sat with her."

"Has my father been with her?"

The maid allowed herself an eloquent shrug.

The contrast between the brightly lit study and the dim rooms surrounding them was more than a matter of the light. His father's sanctum was cold, hard-edged, lined with trophies of the Euro-Aviat successes. There were few photographs of loyal employees, but many pieces of machinery, and of course the entire propeller of the aeroplane in which Henri Levitte had crossed the Pacific.

His father was speaking on the telephone. The two men nodded to each other as Daniel passed the study door. Daniel went straight into his mother's bedroom. Here everything was in disarray. The expensive soft furnishings in opulent old-fashioned French style were scattered with clothes, papers, pictures. Before collapsing on her bed, Daniel's mother had spent thirty minutes in an hysterical frenzy, tossing things out of drawers until she found the tiny silk shoe that Marie-Thérèse had worn as a baby.

She now lay on her back, her hair straggled over her collapsed and once beautiful face, the tranquillisers beginning to blur the outer edges of her pain. She clutched the silk shoe in her right hand like a talisman.

Daniel sat down on the bed with her.

"Maman," he said, "Maman." She reached out and took his hand, but continued to look at the ceiling.

"My little baby girl," said Hortense.

Daniel was still his father's child. The dark room, the smell of face powder hanging in the air, overturned in the hysteria, the woman on the bed clutching the silk shoe were both tragic and also somehow ridiculous. He wished his mother could manage a less theatrical grief.

"She was such a *good* person, Daniel," said Hortense. This was not particularly true. Lonely, frustrated, damaged by her father's interference in the only chance of love she had ever known—but not notably good.

There was a strong knock on the bedroom door.

"Daniel, can I speak with you?"

Daniel felt the *frisson* of fear he had known since earliest childhood—when his father would return from work and be informed by his mother of the children's misdeeds during the day.

"I will be back," Daniel promised his mother, and stood up to meet Papa Levitte.

"Come in my study. I suppose your mother is still prostrated." They went into Levitte's room.

"Sit down."

They sat opposite each other. The older man rested his head on his hand. He had not been able to avoid a disgusting telephone conversation with the Belgian Defence Minister—a swarthy ex-miner who, in Levitte's book, was a Communist. Levitte felt the man's commiserations on his daughter's death were like a smear on his clothes and had cut him off short. He had watched the Belgian defence ministry for two years shifting their fat arses one way and another on the question of the development budget that nation had promised the Celeste programme. He knew that any real disaster to the plane would have them tumbling off their fence into outright opposition in no time at all.

"I appreciate that you have dressed suitably," said Henri Levitte, looking at Daniel's unusual dark suit. "You are going to have to be a support to your mother."

And so might you, thought Daniel.

"Absolutely inexplicable. The police will be coming. The papers will be speculating. They are even wondering already if the car had been tampered with. It is an impossible thing to have happened at such a time." Daniel Levitte just managed to stop himself saying "At any time." Instead he nodded.

"Poor Marie-Thérèse," said Henri, "I know I did everything I could to make her life happy. I have done everything I could for both of you." He shook his head. Daniel felt his fists tightening on either arm of the wing chair. He decided that he should get this over with as soon as possible.

"Father," he said, speaking in measured phrases, "I feel that this tragedy should be the time that brings us closer together. I want to do something about that if you will let me. I know the burden you are carrying, with the aeroplane at this point. I know people are going to wonder if the family is weakened by this—they are going to see the aeroplane and all this together. So I have something to ask you. When will the Super-Celeste fly now?"

"Next Friday."

"What I want to ask you . . . 1 suggest it would be good for the world if everyone could see us standing together on this occasion. I would like to be a passenger on that first flight. I think it would create confidence."

Henri Levitte looked at his son as if he had never seen him before. Before the younger man had finished speaking Henri Levitte had analysed the idea very carefully. It would prostrate Hortense all over again of course. It might give a few idiots the idea that Daniel Levitte was, after all, back in the business of being heir to an empire.

"*Have* you ever been up in a thing like this? The pilot has enough to do without handing out vomit bags."

So his father didn't even remember the times he'd been up.

"Oh yes. I wouldn't let you down."

Yes indeed, thought Henri Levitte, it could be a useful gesture. He stood up, and for the first time in ten years the two men embraced. Henri Levitte kissed his son on both cheeks. And Daniel Levitte returned his kisses, his lips dry against his father's cheeks.

Just before dawn, Melvyn Murray, dragged from his sleep by the owner of the Inn, made his way barefoot across the gravel to the telephone in the main building. The smell of stale beer hung like fog. The innkeeper was grumbling so loudly at this interruption to his sleep that Melvyn Murray could not catch the name.

"*Who?*"

"Daniel Levitte."

"You'd better prove that to me," said Murray, after a moment. He pushed a ten-dollar bill at the landlord and waved him away.

"Okay," said Daniel. "Two weeks ago you and I went for a long walk by the Seine and you made a proposition to me. You thought I might like to work in the Apple business again."

Jesus Christ, thought Murray, so there *was* something in that meeting.

"Go on," said Murray.

"This is a personal thing," said Daniel. "I am the one person in the world who can stop our apple getting to market. For keeps. Think about it and you'll realize that. All I want you to do is this. I know your firm has got agents in Paris. It's night here now. Tomorrow morning, that's Sunday here, I want to meet one of those people. At the Capitol restaurant opposite the Gare du Nord. By noon."

"I'm not sure what you mean about agents," said Murray. "I haven't heard of any agents."

"Yes you do. Your Dirty Tricks people."

"You'd better shut up, son. That's not how this firm does business."

"Well anyway, Mr Murray, that's what I rang to say."

The line died.

Jesus Christ, thought Murray again. These hysterical Frogs. He'd suspected something peculiar at the time. It had been at a fund-raising ball for a NATO dependants charity—a charity that was doubtless one of the many front organizations run by North-West's Special Relations people for their own mysterious purposes. Yes, he had no doubt of that. What *was* the name of that little bugger who had pushed him into meeting Daniel? *Rose*, that was it. One tried to keep clear of people like Rose, but it was one of the unspoken rules—you had to co-operate with Special Relations. It had seemed harmless and idiotic enough. He'd been told that Daniel Levitte was on bad terms with his father. He'd been told to offer him a job: money, travel. That's why they went walking afterwards. To sound him out. Let him know North-West was available, Rose said.

Murray hadn't done it with much enthusiasm. Daniel had not seemed to take it with much enthusiasm. In fact he seemed nonplussed. Murray was nonplussed now. He didn't like it. Why was Daniel telephoning *him*, the other end of the world. In no way did he like the games Special Relations got into, nor the people who played them.

Around any operation involving the movement of huge amounts of money and power—not excluding the American

Presidency—a number of strange individuals cluster like flies round manure.

In some ways, they are the descendants of those rough and desperate men who came by night so readily to the bidding of Shakespeare's villainous kings. Like the murderers hired by Macbeth: men reckless of what they did to spite the world. Some of them, men "so weary with disasters, tugg'd with fortune that they would set their life on any chance, to mend it or be rid on't". Others, just greedy.

However, since those days, a certain amount of sophistication had come into the business. In Shakespeare's day, the first thing that happened to most hired murderers after a successful mission was their own death. It was all too easy to demonstrate the link between the paymaster and the operative.

In the last few centuries, both sides of the business have learnt the essentials of survival—and these are: for villain and paymaster to stay as far apart as possible.

It was thus that the Mafia godfathers could place their hands on their hearts, in the full light of congressional committees, and declare they were olive oil merchants.

It was for such reasons that, for example, the Watergate tapes were so baffling to the uninitiated reader. Mr Nixon and his closest friends had invented a private language in which things that could not be said were said. Stretching all the way downhill from the White House were layers and layers of people whose task it was to pass information down, stage by stage, and to take good care that information did not come back *uphill*.

Melvyn Murray was only telling the truth when he denied knowledge of any agents. He, like anyone else on his level of the aerospace industry, took good care not to know about such things. True, one could not help understanding a certain amount. On a few occasions, one got personally involved against one's will, only on higher orders.

But personally, you stay clear. Melvyn Murray knew that two members of the Euro-Aviat board received retainers from North-West Aerospace, and collected their fees from the same fund and bank he had just proposed to Ackermann. That's okay. Ackermann knew it too, doubtless.

In such matters, the borderlines between malpractice and proper business are highly blurred. Maybe, in the bad old days of Ghenghis Khan, if you bought a blunt sword out of public funds, for payment of a private rake-off, you'd get strung up for treachery. The relatives of those who'd gone into battle and died as a result would have come looking for you. In 1982, the okay thing was to resign all your company directorships. Give it a few years and you could start creeping back. But if you were clever you would want to be retiring with a fortune about that time anyway. The pilots who'd flown in perfect formation into a hillside that shouldn't have been there stayed dead anyway.

Melvyn Murray preferred to stick to his job of selling aeroplanes, rather than get into the grey and muddied waters that he knew lay below him.

He'd told the truth to Ackermann. He told the truth as he knew it. The same attitude of mind would be found at every, ever-darker level of those waters below him.

There is one flaw in such a situation, as Mr Nixon had found to his cost. However well laundered the money might be (through Mexican banks or innocent but carefully instructed accountants) as it passed downhill to the lower levels, the price of innocent ignorance about what one was actually paying for could be high.

For the men at the bottom of the heap remain in essence the strange characters they have always been. "Ay, in the catalogue ye go for men," Macbeth had sensibly pointed out to his hired murderers. As "demi-wolves are clept All by the name of dogs."

Such men are motivated by, and find their job-satisfaction in, different directions from the rest of us. They do not work to please their employers—any more than a paid informer expects gratitude from the police. They do not work to a job specification: no-one wants to take the responsibility of giving them one. They work within a budget. They work alone. They work within the limits of directives set out in vaguely phrased conversations in obscure meeting places. They work to please whatever passions and psychopathic urges drive them personally.

In the struggle between the North-West Aerospace corporation and Euro-Aviat about this particular aeroplane, the word that had come down to these unloved individualists had been unusually clear.

It was this: "Anything goes."

Melvyn Murray went back to his room, found his address

book and returned as quickly as possible to the task of putting Daniel Levitte in touch with the person he wanted to see. He didn't like it. It was not his responsibility. But it was a job to be done. He was also intelligent enough to see *why* he should do this. He had a fucking aeroplane to sell.

To do so he put a call through, not to Paris, but New York. Melvyn Murray had no idea who it was that Daniel Levitte would be meeting. Nor, for that matter, did the man he spoke to in New York. But the message was on its way downhill.

PART TWO

THE NEXT PILOT of the Super-Celeste already knew what it was like to be blown out of the sky in an exploding aeroplane.

It had happened a long time back, but now, at two-thirty on the Sunday morning in Dreux he was dreaming through it again. In his bed at the air base at Dreux he had no wife to nudge him awake. He had to sweat and moan his way through the nightmare alone. Euro-Aviat was not going to let another pilot out of its sight any night this week, even in legitimate feminine company.

Their employee, Henri Bosco, clutched the rim of his blanket in his sleep as yet again he climbed to 42,000 feet and rode the Sabre over the nearly pure white disc of the sun. That part of the dream was the longest; the moments before the wrenching shock of the engine exploding behind him and the horrid limpness of the steering column as chunks of metal sliced through the controls.

Sitting in a heap of hurtling, dead machinery, jumping now like a wild horse, he was miles high in a sky so cold that in a torn suit you would freeze to death in two minutes. Flames stripped down the sleek sides of the fuselage behind him: he could just see their spiralling trail if he churned his neck muscles round until his helmet was jammed against the canopy. At any second, another blast could rip his body and the rest of his plane apart. He braced himself against the centripetal forces that instantly spun the blood away from his heart. And beyond the thin remaining shell of the broken machine lay a wind strong enough to smash your skull to soup, air too short of oxygen to breathe.

In his dream Bosco wrenched his oxygen hose from the plane's supply, pulled the green apple on the oxygen cylinder attached to his parachute pack. Breathing again, he lowered his seat and pulled his feet back into its stirrups, then wedged his arms inside the armrests of the ejection seat. With a prayer, Bosco pulled up on the armrests and saw the brief flash as the canopy jettisoned away above his head.

For a dreadful pumping second the air in his lungs expanded in the thin atmosphere and pushed the oxygen mask away from his face. The wind now hammered into the open cockpit and the sudden expansion of his pressure suit turned his body into a heavy, rigid block. Forcing himself upright, he squeezed the trigger at the end of the armrest and was catapulted with the force of a 37-millimetre cannon into the freedom of the sky.

It was usually at that point that Bosco managed to wake up, spinning nauseously over and over waiting for a second explosion from the gas cylinder at his lap belt to free him from his seat.

Tonight he didn't wake up. He went on falling at 120 miles an hour, the burning plane, from which he was now free, streaking ahead in a mass of flame and silver into the sun.

On the real occasion Henri Bosco spent one minute fifty seconds in free fall through the thickening air before it was safe to open a parachute. To open it earlier would have meant three ways of certain death. The parachute would have been ripped to shreds instantly or killed him by deceleration—or thirdly the trip would have outlasted by ten minutes the oxygen in his cylinder and the time needed to get to breathe proper air. But in the dream, the trip went on for ever. In the total silence of a parachutist swinging in a cloud. When he woke up from it he always cursed the fact of having had to go through this dream yet again. Despite the number of jumps he had made before and since, only this one came back to haunt him.

The nightmare was like a worm in the gut, hidden and irremovable. Bosco knew perfectly well that a mature, veteran pilot shouldn't *have* such a nightmare—or, if he did, should disclose it to the Euro-Aviat psychiatrist. But he despised these people who pried into the mind. He was confident he could keep a calm front to his world; not a nervous tic, not an ulcer on the horizon. It was *his* problem, his only problem. He could live with it.

After this particular nightmare this Sunday morning, Henri Bosco blamed the menu of the evening before.

The fat and cheerful M. Parrault had been delegated by

Henri Levitte to take personal care of Dreux and all its staff for the coming week. Between now and Friday's first flight it was simply a matter of lifting the morale of the corporation after Petit's death, feeding the press with optimistic information, and trusting that the back-up pilot was as competent as he was supposed to be.

Perrault had started this task even before he left Paris. He had telephoned Dreux and assured an anxious management that no-one was going to follow the unfortunate personnel director, Dassin, into the gutter. One had to allow the old man his rages. He had found his goat and scaped it, joked Perrault. Now let us get on with things. Perrault had suggested a small working dinner party at the Hotel Lion Noir. He would arrange the menu himself.

The management at Dreux breathed again. Though they knew that Henri Levitte and M. Perrault played a "hard-man, soft-man" routine between the two of them, it was always more pleasant to deal with Perrault nonetheless.

Perrault chose the menu with care. The main dish was Duck in the Manner of Rouen, one of the classic dishes of Normandy. It involves strangling a duck, pressing it in an interesting manner and then cooking it slowly in its own blood.

The point was not lost on the management at Dreux.

Before dinner, the official party had taken a walk around Assembly Point Three. In this long building—nearly a kilometre from end to end and entirely air-conditioned, lay two completed Super-Celestes, and ten in a herringbone pattern of assembly, their dismembered bodies still bandaged in tape and protective wrapping.

To watch the place being lit up fully was in itself an event. Rank after rank of neon flickered to life from one end to the other of the vast corridor. When, at the far end, a security guard patrolling with two Dobermans hushed their barking with a shout, both bark and shout echoed through the roof girders and gantries like summer thunder.

Perrault, as he always liked to say so disarmingly, was "only an accountant". With the pilot Bosco alongside him, Perrault lifted the blue cotton drape from the aeroplane to pat a fat hand on its cool, glossy metal.

It remained, as ever, a startling and impressive vision. Apart from the black painted radome to which the plane tapered wickedly, the entire machine gleamed in its colour of Euro-Aviat blue. It had the sleekness of a fish, dramatized by the dark apertures of the air intakes and the twin gun ports. Even without the wingtip missiles that would soon be mounted like arrows upon it, the plane looked menacing in repose.

"We all of us have a great responsibility," Perrault had said. "I am honoured to be standing here now with a man like Henri Bosco, who will bring the machine to life. May I make a sentimental remark, if you like, at this point. When I stand here at this moment you must believe that it is not the billions of Eurodollars involved in this project that is in my mind. As you know, that is my job, to take care of such things. But I am not thinking of that at this moment. I cannot understand what it will be like to fly this aeroplane"—here he laid his arm over Bosco's shoulders—"because I am not a pilot. But all of us, very different people, are involved in this machine. When I look at it I see something very beautiful, very aesthetic. Even though this is an instrument of war. We are already, in our own way, at war as a commercial enterprise.

"This 'commercial warfare' is not sordid. It is part of the human race. We fight in one way or another all the time. What I am saying now is that I believe"—here Perrault drummed his fist gently against the Celeste—"all of us here know there is more at stake than our pensions, our mortgages, our jobs. This machine is going to triumph. So far as this week is concerned, our fight *is* against our allies, the Americans. We mustn't be ashamed of that. Everyone here knows what is happening in Australia this week. We should not be ashamed about fighting against our American allies. It is our job to do so. I want all of you to bear in mind that we have five days in which to begin to prove to the world that Europe is still the place where the best aeroplanes in the world are designed and built."

It had been a good speech, though not in Perrault's style. In fact Henri Levitte had written most of it himself. Afterwards, Perrault had made a point of accompanying Henri Bosco personally to his own car and driving to the restaurant together.

The replacement pilot now turned on to his left side and went through the routine of relaxing his muscles towards sleep.

In Paris, his predecessor was not to be left in peace for the night. Alphonse Magritte, the seventeen-year-old attendant at the morgue in the Rue Alphonse Daudet, fought back his desire to vomit. The morgue, in between the old meat market of Paris and the last surviving music hall—a handy form of address that the police had learnt not to give to next of kin—consisted of a marble slab that dated from the fourth republic, a rank of huge filing cabinets in which lay the bodies. And a cold smell of disinfectant. Young Magritte was tired of the family jokes about his name and his business address. Jean-Paul Petit was Alphonse Magritte's first corpse. He was the only corpse on the premises. The stinking *clochard* in Drawer One had gone out yesterday. Magritte, a pale young lad from Lille, had by now pulled Jean-Paul out of his drawer on six occasions, and at each one the persistently open left eye—the right was covered with a three-inch square of gauze—upset him as much as ever. He had decided, already, to get another job.

Indeed, it does take some getting used to, the steadfast gaze of a dead man. It was now six am on Sunday morning. Through the bars of the high window in the mortuary—the architect had designed the place as a prison, out of habit, back in the 1870s (having done so many such buildings throughout northern France)—the bells for the first mass tolled through the dark.

And now that fanatical young detective from the 18th arrondissement wanted Jean-Paul pulled out again—to take a scraping from the inside of his thigh. "What are you looking for?" the mortuary attendant asked him. "Sex," said Derivat.

The young mortuary attendant was not the only person annoyed by this young policeman's zeal. Nobody would easily like someone so keen to better himself as young Marcel Derivat was. Not least because he might prove himself faster and better than his diligent superiors.

Marcel Derivat, indeed, saw himself as a man with a mission. He was only three years older than the mortuary attendant from Lille, but he knew he had a long way further to go. He also knew that the death of Jean-Paul Petit was of huge concern to his superiors. At the long examinations of the contents of Jean-Paul's attaché case, wallet, pockets—and previous resting place in the white plastic bag—Marcel had to play the humble and most junior assistant.

He had watched the senior policemen come and go. He knew they were puzzled about the analysts' report on the famous white plastic bag. It seemed that the bag had once contained a consignment of hops as used in the manufacture of English beer. Marcel Derivat had also witnessed the tussle with the French Ministry of Defence, who had removed the private dossier on the Super-Celeste that had been found untouched in the briefcase.

Now, at this hour in the morning, Derivat felt, rightly, that the day belonged to those with energy left for the task. His superiors, clever though they were, at such a time felt the need to sleep.

The young detective, however, had two tasks still left for the night. The first was this scrape for the Forensic Lab at Montparnasse. They would do the job, not for him, but under the impression it was required by someone in authority. The second was to take a walk through Paris. In the address book carried by Jean-Paul, Marcel had noticed a name: Hélène Jacob, 22. There were many names in the book, without telephone numbers—rarely with addresses, and the police were checking them all. But it struck Marcel as unusual that one would write down a girl's name and age. Leaving the morgue, but with the plastic phial in his jacket pocket he strolled through the empty streets towards the Seine.

It was with a very great deal of personal pleasure—a feeling that a large and successful career lay ahead of him—that Marcel Derivat arrived outside Number 22, the Rue Jacob and saw in the window the discreet printed sign announcing the Hotel Hélène. He noted the telephone number down on his pad and slipped it cheerfully back into his hip pocket.

At Wiseman's Ferry, a long Sunday afternoon was already nearly over. In the trailer park, families were packing up: a week of toil all too close ahead for the husbands; a week of usual suburban languor for the wives. Murray and Ackermann were also packing up their weekend. They were, apparently, two middle-aged men among so many others getting ready for the week ahead. They had spent the morning, as Murray had promised, fishing the wide brown waters—they were out early while the mists lay so cool and heavy on the valley you couldn't imagine the burning heat ahead in the afternoon.

"That was good," said Ackermann, "that was a good two days. I didn't imagine I would be drinking a fine German hock in February and 27 degrees. As for the rest: thank you, Melvyn. We'll run into each other in Canberra this week."

Melvyn took Ackermann's plump hand in both of his. "Sincerely, Hermann," he said, "I'm glad you understood. There's a reception tomorrow evening—anniversary of the Jap raid on Darwin—you'll be there?"

"Of course I'll be there," said Ackermann. He pressed Murray's hand with real comradeship and gratitude. The details of the numbered account in the Channel Islands' Bank were in his wallet. He stripped off his jacket and settled himself into his car for the drive back to Sydney.

Murray had told Ackermann that he was about to leave for Sydney too.

In fact, he was going straight from here to Canberra, on a long and punishing drive through the south and central table-lands of New South Wales.

He didn't know Ackermann's schedule, but he hoped to stay ahead of him by a few hours. And would need to.

In Canberra, he knew, it was going to be bad. He didn't trust Ackermann. He wished he'd slept better. He could have done without being disturbed by Daniel Levitte. That was a nonsense he couldn't count on. Even if Ackermann accepted, Murray knew that he would be up against it in Canberra. Something else again from the technical superiority of either machine. Something other than money—or the discounts and extended credit terms and offsets and reciprocal trade treaties. Something bribery and corruption wouldn't solve either.

It was the fourth factor. The one that hangs around any aviation deal. Straight politics. Worst of all, Australian politics (some of the roughest and oddest in the world). All in all, it was going to be great in Canberra.

He headed south. The Holden gradually cooled as he lifted into the Blue Mountains, and out of the valley. Such a vast country. Difficult to believe it needed anybody's aeroplanes to protect it, either F-24 or Super-Celeste. He stopped at a roadside apple seller, bought a kilo of Granny Smiths apples, and chewed as he drove.

"Don't," said Celeste, "don't. Please don't."

They lay, in bed, apart.

"Don't what?" said Daniel.

"Lie there like that," she said, "my edge-of-the-bed man."

It was an endearment between them.

"It's nearly dawn, Celeste," he said. They could hear the bells tolling from the church towers for early Sunday Mass. He had lain awake most of the night. Working at it. Working out the last details. Yet you could say he was happy. The feeling of that moment of decision in the evening before had not left him. The cold prickle of the hair on the back of your neck. It comes to poets as a poem suddenly gathers itself into words: the strange feeling of arrival; of creating and of being created.

He had lain there thinking of his dead sister and his dead friend, while Celeste, at times, when she too woke, squeezed her arm about his shoulders and raised her head to kiss his cheek.

Now she ran her right hand down his stomach, pausing to make the muscles flutter above his groin, laid her hand across his cock and began to stroke him alive there.

"We have to go to Mass in two hours," said Daniel. Crisping her fingers she drew her hand up and down so that only the tips of her fingernails touched him.

"We should make love," she said. "Why shouldn't we make love for them both? Please, Daniel, it would be right. It would help." Daniel took her hand and raised it to his lips. He rubbed his nose and upper lip across the back, then, between finger and thumb, felt his way to the small cage of bones in her wrist. He loved to feel the way they moved. He found the pulse and let it beat against his own fingertips.

In this attic, high above Paris, he had been very happy. In summer, in the early morning at this hour, huge yellow linen blinds kept the sun from the studio windows—so that always, even on a dull day, one felt the sun was out there. Or they might run the blinds up and lie naked on the huge bed beneath.

"Don't go into the dark," said Celeste softly. She snuggled her body on top of him, lay there with her head curled into the crook of his neck. Daniel stroked the curve of the base of her spine. She pressed herself gently on to him.

Sadly, but sweetly, they made love, for the dead, for each other.

Then in silence again they dressed and made ready to join the rest of the family at the memorial mass for Marie-Thérèse.

"I have an appointment for midday," said Daniel.

"Who with?"

"Just some business. Something that has to be done."

"You mean," she said, "something to do with the man I found in Australia for you."

He would not look at her. They sat opposite each other and he looked only at his coffee. He had never evaded her before. "I love you, Daniel," she said.

"I love you."

"What does it mean, Daniel? What are you going to do?"

"I'll do whatever has to be done," he said. "I can't discuss it."

She shook her head sadly, but knew to keep silent. For the moment, she would let him work it out for himself. All his life, as she knew, her Daniel had been pushed around by people anxious to make up his mind for him. Whatever was going on now, would have to go on.

After Mass, the family stood on the steps of St Sulpice for the photographers. Henri Levitte had found it useful to exchange the religion of his birth for Roman Catholicism, as had many Jews of his generation. His wife Hortense leant against him. Her face was still smudged and slack with drugs. Henri Levitte stood stiff for her to lean on, both hands at his side. Daniel stood two steps higher. Celeste, her arms wrapped about herself in the cold, two steps below them all.

That was the way the family group came out in the next issue of *Paris Soir*.

"I wanted to go to see the Grandfather," said Henri, "but someone will have to look after Hortense. Someone must tell him. I've had the nurses take his radio away." For the first time in years they were beginning to talk like a family again.

Grandfather Levitte was eighty-eight years old. His room in a private nursing home in Neuilly cost Henri Levitte 300 dollars a week. The old man had refused point blank the offer of a place in Hortense's own nursing home, the charity she ran.

"I'll go," said Daniel. "Celeste and I will go." There was time before his appointment at the Capitol, he decided.

"Thank you," said Henri. He was surprised, still, at this new co-operation from his son. He took Daniel by the arm and led

3

him away from the women. "Will you both dine with us tonight? Are you still wanting to join the flight? I'll have to make arrangements today."

"Of course," said Daniel.

"You won't chatter with your friends about it, will you? I don't want it all over the papers yet."

Daniel restrained himself from his normal angry reaction: his father was expert at introducing small insults of this kind into his remarks.

"Of course not, Father."

The Levitte Rolls, in its characteristic Euro-Aviat shade of blue, drew up at the foot of the steps.

"Daniel," Hortense said feebly, as he stepped to open the door for his parents.

"Yes, Maman."

"Do try to explain to him about the Malvern water. It is really quite impossible."

"Yes, Maman."

In a country filled with medicinal springs, the Grandpère Levitte had for twenty years insisted on drinking a daily bottle of Malvern water from England. There was now no way to import it and the old man had taken it as a personal insult. Daniel waited a moment for either of his parents to say something else, *anything* else. Some word for the Grandfather other than the detail about his tonic water.

He allowed himself to slam the door shut behind them.

Grandfather Levitte, in his time, had also been a formidable figure. He had been a scholar—a professor of classics at Strasbourg. His son had turned to aviation and "trade"—that is how the grandfather had termed it anyway. It is the way things go in families. Henri Levitte had been his only son, just as Daniel was Henri's. And Henri Levitte had found his own father no easier to please. Perhaps the analyst who had discovered that episode, deep in Daniel's unconscious, about the model aeroplane that had struck him in the groin would have liked to know that long, long ago, when Henri Levitte was a child, his own father had told him the story of Icarus.

However, between the grandchild and grandfather there had always been affection. They had no need to fight themselves out in any classic Freudian complex.

Grandfather Levitte now sat by the window in his chair. It was fifteen storeys up. "I don't want to die in the sky," the old man had complained. But he was of an age to be outvoted. It was his punishment for refusing point blank to go to Hortense Levitte's own nursing home. He couldn't stand his son's wife at any price. He often dreamed of that rich and rambling farm near Strasbourg with its vines and chickens. That was the sort of place to end one's days, with one's children's children—and even, by this stage, their children too round the foot of one's chair. *Here* there was polished plastic flooring, wall to wall at the foot of his chair. Nowadays, chickens arrived in small, bite-sized pieces for an old man's false teeth. Even his books, tidily arranged on shelves as he had insisted, were now too high to reach. Still, he knew most of them by heart. He could rehearse his beloved Seneca for hours to himself: the long unvisited hours. His hands lay loosely on his rug, their skin flecked with the huge freckles of old age.

Celeste kissed his forehead.

"You are wet, my child," said the old man. He smiled up at her, the dark Levitte eyes suddenly bright in the gaunt skull.

The few drops of rain that had sprinkled from Celeste's honey hair lay on his own grey spikes like dew on winter stubble. It was refreshing in the overheated room.

"Daniel," said the Grandfather, "what has been happening? The nurses are hiding something from me again. They have taken the radio away and say it needs mending. Cannot I afford a new radio?"

"Yes, Grandpère. There's bad news."

"Has that stupid aeroplane fallen apart?" he asked with a gleam of childlike malice. Celeste knelt down at the old man's side and took his huge, feeble hands in her own.

"There is bad news. About Marie-Thérèse," said Daniel. He clenched his left fist. It was a magic from childhood. He had checked with the nurses that the old man's blood pressure would be up to taking it.

"Is she dead?"

"Yes," said Daniel, after a moment.

The old man looked out of the window. Celeste squeezed his hands.

"She had a motor accident," said Daniel. "There would have been no pain."

"It is the way it would end," said the old man. "Come here, Daniel, come here. Sit by me."

Daniel pulled a chair across. Grandfather Levitte was now between them, the rug over his knees.

"I've always feared for you both. You and Marie-Thérèse. We have not been a happy family. You understand that."

"It was just an accident, Grandfather."

"There is something else," said old Levitte, "something else to it."

"The funeral is on Tuesday," said Daniel. "We will all see you afterwards."

"We are so sorry, Grandpère," said Celeste.

The windows, double-glazed and sealed throughout the year, rattled as a 747 hidden in the cloud-cover outside began its descent to Le Bourget.

"My dear little Celeste," said Grandfather, "you must look after this grandson of mine, Daniel. We all need good wives, we men. *My* wife was a fool. Your mother is a fool too, Daniel. Yes, she is. The Levittes usually marry fools who spend their lives weeping instead of keeping us in order. I gave your father a bad time as a child, Daniel. So what happened? He gave you and poor Marie-Thérèse a bad time. Three generations of Levittes."

He bent his head to the girl still crouched at his side.

"Now you, Celeste, are the woman we should all have married. You are. Don't blush. But I don't think you do blush, do you, my little Asian grandchild. And you are, though this boy won't marry you yet."

He laid his hand on her head.

"Someone to make the men in the Levitte family feel good inside themselves. Then we would have been kinder to our own children."

"You must be calm, Grandpère," said Daniel.

Daniel felt lost. The Levitte family never spoke intimately to each other. Occasionally they made emotional speeches. Daniel had to believe this was such an occasion.

"Do you know the only time you ever made me sad, Celeste?" the old man said. "It was when you gave your name to that stupid aeroplane of my son's."

"It wasn't my choice, Grandpère," said Celeste.

"The Levittes never give anyone a choice," said the old man. "The women we need are the ones who won't accept that."

Daniel stood up. He went to the window and pressed his forehead against the warm glass. The noise of the 747 abruptly ceased.

"Do you know why my son wanted to give that machine your name? Because he loves that machine more than he loves Daniel and Marie-Thérèse and his wife. That is how strange we are. He was marrying you to his machine instead of his son. Do you understand anything of this?"

"I know it," said Celeste. Daniel turned to look at her. Never in his life had he heard such things. He clenched himself against all of it. He had *decided*.

"Poor Henri sent me a brochure, a prospectus, of this machine of his. The aeroplane with your name. It is on the table there. He was so proud, poor man. As if he were telling me about the birth of a child. Go and get it for me Daniel."

Daniel picked it up. It was true. He had never seen the document before. His father had not shown it to him. On the cover there were two pictures. There was a smiling profile of the "Grand Old Man of Aviation" and there was the blue dart of the Super-Celeste cut out against the menacing sky.

The words on the cover were few: "Super-Celeste. Europe's Own Fourth Generation Fighter."

"Tell me Daniel," said the old man, "what does this mean, the Fourth Generation?"

"It's about the kind of aeroplane it is," said Daniel. "Aeroplanes grow out of each other. I mean, what one learns from one you put into the next. The American F-16s were the Third Generation. The Super-Celeste is the Fourth."

"Well you know what I think about it," said the old man. "I have been too loyal to poor Henri your father, maybe. If we are talking of fourth generations it's your child we need, Celeste. *Your child.*"

He coughed, wiping his mouth with the back of his hand.

"And don't think I'm going to say I'll never live to see him. I can live another ten years yet. Poor Marie-Thérèse."

For a whole minute nobody moved.

Then the door opened and the old man's personal nurse came in: fat, sidling but authoritative.

"I think you should leave M. Levitte now," she said in an ugly Bordeaux accent.

Celeste got up, took the old man's head between her hands. Then kissed both cheeks.

With Daniel he shook hands, formally and with surprising strength. "Don't waste it, Daniel," he said. "Don't waste it."

Daniel took a table in the Capitol café at twenty minutes before noon. Like so many places of refreshment near the world's great railway stations, the Capitol had declined from its high minutes in history, when gilded first-class passengers had disembarked among its mirrors and palms after the best international travel available. Today, the expensive people flew between anonymous airports and anonymous meals in plastic trays.

But the long mirrors, the tables covered in fresh linen, the old-style leisure of lukewarm coffee served in fat and shallow china survived.

Daniel sipped a coffee and Calvados: the apple brandy of Normandy with which many in northern France still began their day's work. The last sip you poured into the last of the coffee and its mixture of sugar and grounds. A powerful and warming start.

Daniel did not look up as the man sat down opposite him. He poured the last fragrance of his Calvados into his coffee and drank it. Then he looked up. He knew at once, as he had expected, that the man in front of him was not the man he yet needed to see.

Vic Wild, deputy director of North-West Aerospace's Special Relations office, was not sure if Daniel Levitte matched the photographs in the file at all. The press cuttings nearly all showed a wild and rather rumpled young man, usually accompanied by clinging socialites—photographs taken at parties and film festivals. It was quite a substantial file. North-West's Special Relations office was staffed mostly by ex-CIA men like Wild, and the CIA passion for making files on almost everything had persisted.

In SR there were respectable front men, and Wild was one of them. He was kept busy enough on routine matters—the "contributions" to political parties in far-off lands; the hiring of "consultants" among government officials, the "entertainment" of visiting delegations. Vic Wild, with his totally forgettable face on top of a totally discreet suit, was an expert in what is known in West Africa as *Dash*, in Latin America as *La Mordida* and in Italy as *La Bustarella*.

He sat down and looked at Levitte. This man didn't look like the spoilt only son having an emotional tantrum. He looked a serious customer, decided Wild. A weak man, perhaps, but well groomed, sober and calm. A good-looking man too, better than his photographs.

"Right," said Daniel, "this is the position. I want some help in a personal matter. There's no need for me to spell it out, is there? You know who I am?"

"I got a message," said Wild. "It's a little irregular, but we can only listen."

"Then listen. The flight is now going to be on Friday. So you've got a bit longer. There'll be a press announcement tonight. Now, you know who I am: and I'm telling you that it's arranged I'm going to be on that flight. I'll be at the base from Thursday. What I want from your people is this. I want to talk with an explosives expert. Someone who can get me a small device."

Wild caught the waiter's eye and ordered a coffee. A large black one. He breathed deeply a few times: he had a theory this got more oxygen to the brain and helped one to think.

"Look," he said, "you need help, young man. But not from me. We are in a serious legitimate business, you know. I know this dead pilot was a friend of yours. You've been under a lot of strain. But we don't do things like this. We don't *do*—things like this."

"All right, all *right*," said Daniel. "I don't expect you to say anything else. That's why I'm not telling you any details. You don't have to know. All you have to do is this. By the end of today or tomorrow I want somebody—somebody who knows how to make a bomb by Thursday morning. Here's where I live—" he passed a piece of paper across the table: Wild refused it with a quick gesture. He already knew.

"Nobody's going to get hurt," said Daniel. "Except Euro-Aviat." He hoped he was sounding convincing. "I promise you that. But I don't want your man trying to make any conditions at all—I know what I want and I want him to be free to do what I want."

Wild shook his head. "I'm sorry M. Levitte, but this conversation has got to stop. The idea that we would help you in a thing like this is unimaginable—"

"And so on and so forth," said Daniel roughly. "Don't bother to wait for your coffee. Just get that man to call on me. And it's nothing to do with Jean-Paul. *If the man you send me killed Jean-Paul with his own bare hands that doesn't matter a fuck to me.*"

"I still want to recommend a psychiatrist to you," said Wild. "What in hell put this thing in your head? You don't think we had anything to do with *that*, do you?" He spoke softly and with real urgency. This was a hell of a dangerous thing.

"Don't bother yourself about my state of mind," said Daniel. "You and I don't have to meet again. If you do it right, even the man you send me won't know he's working for you. And I'm not going to tell him. Even if I did there wouldn't be any evidence I wasn't inventing the story, would there? It's perfectly workable. I've thought about it on and off for years. My father makes planes and I make films. I invent stories. And if you want to know why I want to do this I'll tell you. I've had my father up to *here*."

"You're crazy," said Wild, "I'm sorry." He stood up.

The two men looked at each other for the last time. Daniel nodded dismissal.

Wild walked briskly out of the swing doors and into the grey noon. He felt alarmed but despite himself, intrigued. If the truth were told, Vic Wild was bored of being middle-aged and plump —bored at spendings days on the telephone fixing fees for the younger sons of Iranian air-force chiefs of staff to act as consultant architects for 700,000 dollars. A good straightforward wrench in the guts of the opposition's works was a great deal more satisfying. Only last week, he remembered to his disgust, it had been his lot to arrange a night's sexual entertainment for a visiting African general. As a young man, Vic Wild had fought in Vietnam. Now he was paid to be some sort of pimp. The machines themselves were straightforward, wicked weapons of war. It somehow seemed a lot healthier to be into blowing one of them up than messing about with slush funds.

There were times when Wild wished he was young enough and fit enough to be one of the few real adventurers that SR occasionally passed the word and money to. Like that young Englishman—the one whom he had seen with that fantastic sleepy Provençal girl Claude.

Wild hoped his director, John Rose, would feel the same way. He hastened back to report to him. He wondered what Rose would make of it? The trouble was, you never knew with Rose.

In ten years of working in their rather specialized end of the aerospace business, Wild and Rose had become so much a partnership that they carried the shared nickname of the "Little Flower" : a name rather remote from their trade. Yet Rose was —as everyone knew—a man of pure and shining integrity in his naughty world. By which is meant that his loyalty to North-West Aerospace was total. It is a desirable quality to have in an employee paid to pass unaccountable sums of money to bent customers. Rose administered his slush funds with all the virtue of a Baptist Church accountant. When, four years ago, he had left North-West Aerospace to join an American rival in the same line of business, Wild had felt that something irrevocably wrong had happened to the moral fabric of the universe. Indeed, it *was* unthinkable. One year later Rose had quietly returned to his old office, his orderly mind well stocked with useful information about the opposite number. The entire exercise had been planned that way.

Rose's loyalty to his company showed up, too, in his passion for any official convention or party run by the firm. He would fly the length of Europe to have the chance of joining in any corporation jollity that might be going. He knew every senior executive in the corporation by his first name. The fact that most of them avoided his dry but warm hand at such occasions did not put him off. He knew and respected his own special and unsavoury reputation in Special Relations. In all his years in Europe, whether in Milan, Paris, Brussels or Amsterdam, Rose never ate anywhere but in the steak and hamburger bars that brought the subtlety of American cuisine to Europe. He called the French Frogs. But not in their hearing. When he wanted to be, Rose could pass perfectly well as anyone's Frenchman. In his mid-forties now, Rose, the ex-CIA code expert, mostly looked like an international, harmless, tortoise-faced accountant.

3*

Sometimes, thought Wild, that wasn't the real Rose at all. But surely if you'd worked day in and day out with your partner you would know him.

Something about John Rose's eyes bothered Wild. They didn't belong to the face: they were jet dark and hidden.

North-West Aerospace's Dirty Tricks department, known to the trade as the Special Relations department, was known to the world as Design for Aviation et Cie. The main office, off the Champs Elysées, was open and airy and full of drawing boards —suggestive of openness and light. Indeed, from this office came the letter-headings and advertisements for the technical press that told the world how large and great North-West Aerospace was in the air. Occasionally, Rose and Wild would take an active interest in the official business. It was Rose who had coined the phrase The Final Freedom Fighter, to describe a useful fragmentation bomb that had been developed by one of the subsidiary companies and which had killed many thousand peasant women in the course of the Second Korean War.

Today, as Wild made his way there, the drawing boards would be unattended, and only Rose would be waiting in the soundproof office behind, which was checked for bugs each week. Rose would be there, behind his black leather desk, poised at his special post, the last frontier of respectability. The man anyone in North-West Aerospace could be seen talking to, but beyond whom, you knew, lay men you wouldn't care to meet. The word got passed down to Rose and from Rose into the dark.

FIRST CONVERSATION TAPE 3DQ78 13.00 hours PARIS
WILD: Hi. I met him.
ROSE: Sit down. You want a Scotch?
WILD: No. Fine, fine. I'm fine.
ROSE: Let's get it then.
WILD: You know, it's crazy, but I reckon he could do it. He's going on the first flight. He wants to lay an egg on the plane. Doesn't like his papa. Not any more. Would you believe it?
ROSE: Jesus! And you froze him off.
WILD: Don't worry. One hand on my heart, one hand on my balls. *But* . . . but, but, but.
ROSE: Told him we were clean.

WILD: Oh so clean. Listen, Rosy, he hadn't got a tape on me. He's a screwed up young man. But he's not mad. He's not drunk. But *maybe* he justs wants to find whoever hit Petit. It could be that.

ROSE: You put it to him?

WILD: Oh sure, sure. He says not.

ROSE: Just between him and papa.

WILD: He just wants someone who can fix him up for Friday.

ROSE: Friday.

WILD: Someone who can get me a small device.

ROSE: Which you killed stone dead.

WILD: Not our line of country. Nor is it. Is it? Wasn't it you put Daniel and Murray together at that party thing?

ROSE: You're so right, it isn't. Vic, what's he going to do with it?

WILD: Couldn't ask.

ROSE: I mean pre-flight? I mean if someone's going to get hurt we're already in a position.

WILD: He said no one gets hurt. And no connection. Which is right, Rosy.

ROSE: Yeah, but look at this. He gets what he wants—not from us, *somewhere*. Then he fucks it up. Then he talks. And some damn waiter remembers you.

WILD: So I wasn't there.

ROSE: You can count on that?

WILD: Not a fingerprint.

ROSE: Photo then. Someone with a camera. Someone who heard him phone Murray.

WILD: Okay. So we tell Papa Levitte now.

ROSE: Yeah, we do that and your man does nothing and we look really good idiots.

WILD: Well then, that's exactly what we say. We say Okay. We get a message to meet this loon so we meet him. He's a nice young man in a breakdown so I say to him "Get yourself a good shrink" and he weeps a bit and says "Okay. I forget it, thank you Mr Wild. I promise to be a good boy." And then— how about this Rosy. Just to show how much we care, on a personal basis, we think: who can help this poor young chap? Now there's that lucky bird he lives with.

ROSE: Super-Celeste with legs.

WILD: That's right. So we write to her today. Here's a copy. "You want to look after your man," signed anonymous friend.

ROSE: Could be. Could be.

WILD: Would make sense. More sense than over-reacting and telling the police or papa.

ROSE: Listen. I'm taking a Scotch, if you aren't.

WILD: Okay then. Will do.

ROSE: Jesus! That enough? If he did that, they *would* be right up shit creek. Can you imagine?

WILD: I can imagine. Especially if he did it properly and blew it up in flight. If that thing went to pieces in the air it would be a billion dollar bang.

ROSE: If it was in the air. No one would ever know. Apart from the usual suicide notes.

WILD: He might not write them. He really is serious.

ROSE: Anyway. Not going to happen. If we weren't nice people Vic, this could be really sweet Jesus *it*. Sort of thing would really impress those stupid Australians.

WILD: Not up to us anyway. Who do you talk to now?

ROSE: Straight back to Murray they say. When he is in Canberra. Ring him tonight. *You* ring him.

WILD: Okay I'll tell him. He'll say the same thing.

ROSE: That's right. But Wild: North-West is up against it in Dingo land. I've heard.

END TAPE ONE

"I'm sorry, Murray," said Senator Mackenzie. "But you are up against it. *Are* you up against it! That President of yours doesn't help either, does he?"

Murray could have wished Mackenzie had said "*We* are up against it." Senator Mackenzie's five-bedroomed Norwegian wood house in the Snowy Mountains had been imported there to try out this style of building in the Australian climate. In other words, it had been just one of Senator Mackenzie's little presents from North-West Aerospace.

Mackenzie, Murray's top contact in the Federal Government, was his first call on this Monday morning. It had been a long drive. The dark had come down earlier than he had expected —he still wasn't reckoning on the lack of twilight. And in

Canberra the sun seemed to have a special battering power all of its own.

With all that ocean to play in, why in hell had Australia built a capital away from the water?

"Let me give you the position as of now," said Mackenzie. "Quite apart from your lovely President saying he wants to start kissing China's arse again."

"You don't have to believe it," said Murray.

"Yes. Well we're stupid like that in this country. We tend to believe people mean what they say. Anyway. More important is the missile lobby. Are you meeting anyone in CSIRO this week? Well, if you do you'll find out. Let's put it straight for you. The Defence Review Committee meets next week. Right? Here in this building. Now most of those people want nothing but missiles anyway. They just want two well-hidden missile sites between Alice Springs and Darwin. One labelled Peking and the other one Ho Chi Minh City."

"I know that," said Murray, "and you're getting them. From America may I remind you. But you're not saying Australia isn't going to buy aeroplanes."

"Surely we'll buy aeroplanes. I can tell you it's going to be five hundred machines. For starters."

Melvyn cried, "*How* many?"

"Five hundred."

"And the committee is really planning a decision next week? Why wasn't I told? Why didn't *you* tell me?"

"Only heard myself yesterday," lied Mackenzie.

"Jesus," said Murray. "Look, Mack. Is that on the record yet? In ten hours, for that sort of money, I can get you pictures of the President of the United States breaking up Chinese laundries with his own hands."

"No way," said Mackenzie. "Could be six hundred by next week, anyway."

"You are getting to be a warlike people," said Melvyn. "That's nice for me."

"Thank the Reds," said Mackenzie. He stood up and took Melvyn to the window by his elbow. From here one could see clear down Commonwealth Avenue and across the lake, the Captain Cook Memorial jet pushing 450 feet up into the sky from its waters. "You haven't been here before, have you?"

said Mackenzie. "Look at it. We've got 300,000 people in this place now. Seventy embassies. Fifty suburbs. Three universities. And sixty years ago there was nothing but ten aborigines and a few sheep. We move fast. Now we're into the war game and we're going to move fast on that. We've got to be free to move the way we want to."

"Mack," said Murray drily. "Sit down and stop speaking for the Peoples of Australia. You and I are trying to sell an aeroplane. *You* and *I*."

Mackenzie sat down, pressed his desk phone and called for beer.

"Okay," he said. "I'll start again. If we buy American planes then we're tied up with America for ten years. Now that's going to be an embarrassment if we decide to go it alone and start knocking pieces of South East Asia off the map on our own account. Europe isn't going to make that sort of trouble for us. Europe will sell an aeroplane to anyone who can fly it and pay the bill. You know that. They always have."

"That's not true. They put an embargo on the Mirages for Israel after the Six Day War. What the hell do you mean about knocking off pieces of South East Asia?"

"I didn't say it."

"You just did. You mean you're planning to *attack* South East Asia? You must be joking. When did Australia do things like that? How many votes will you get for that sort of adventure?"

"More than you think," said Mackenzie. "But okay: not enough. Not yet. But when it comes, we want to do it our way. We want 600 planes now. Next year we may want another 600. And we don't want to have an American Red-happy congress saying we can't have them."

"Shit," said Murray coldly. "*Now* you tell me. You mean your people are just waiting for that French plane to hit the air? Jesus!"

"That's politics," said Mackenzie.

"Well, politics can change," said Murray. "We're talking about war. We can hit your politicians pretty hard with the facts. We are going to be *cheaper* than the French. We are going to be one *hell* of a lot cheaper than the French. Also we've already got a machine that flies. Between ourselves, we've been in the air for three weeks. I've got a lot of print-outs on the performance. Do you want them for your friends?"

"And next week they'll have a lot more print-outs from the French. Is that man Ackermann in town?"

"No idea," said Murray.

"What are those. Dirty pictures?" asked Mackenzie. Murray had laid a dossier of pictures on the desk.

"So it can fly," said Mackenzie. "Well that's nice."

"The great Australian people," said Murray, "can be told pretty loud they are making a mistake if you choose Europe. We can undercut any price the French lay on."

"Well," said Mackenzie, "the politicians don't want you to have the time to do it. Listen, Murray, I've got a list of friends and relations for you to see. But frankly, you have to face the fact that the only thing that is going to impress the great simple-minded Australian people between now and next week is the thud of the Super-Celeste flying into the Eiffel Tower on its first flight. And even that would only delay matters."

The ice-cold Fosters arrived, brought by another Amazon in blue denim. The two men drank in silence.

"You at the reception tonight?" asked Murray.

"Along with the rest of the world. We spend our lives going round these things."

"I'll see you there," said Murray, "and listen Mack, don't think like a loser. We are not going to lose this one."

"That's nice to know," said Mackenzie.

Murray had the man at the marble-floored entrance get him a taxi and spurred the driver back down Cotter Road to his hotel at Weston Creek. On the way he began scribbling telexes.

Whatever else he needed by way of luck between now and the Defence Review Committee meeting next week he certainly needed some encouraging public words from the President of the United States. He worded his telex strongly enough to let his readers in Dallas know just where the blame for the present disaster would lie. So strongly indeed, that he trusted fervently no-one had got on to the brand-new code he'd been issued with. There was the money for Ackermann to fix up too. And *that* looked like being a total waste of time.

Before he could start transmitting, the phone rang at his desk in the hotel suite. It was a direct call from Paris.

SECOND CONVERSATION TAPE 4DQ78 22.00 hours
PARIS

WILD: Melvyn? Hi. How are you hearing this? Good?

MELVYN: Yeah. Is that King?

WILD: No. I'm with King. Victor Wild in Special Relations.

MELVYN: Oh, yeah, yeah. Look I'm pretty tied up, Vic. Will
you put that money out for Hermann though? I've been
through the motions there. I'd say it won't work either.
We're in a fuck-up out here.

WILD: I've really got to talk, Melvyn.

MELVYN: Yeah, fine, okay then.

WILD: I went to meet the boy. The one who rang you. Son of
King Frog.

MELVYN: Oh Jesus, *that*—

WILD: Yes, well look Melvyn, I don't know where I'm put on
this one. He says he wants to break up Daddy's apple. He's
serious Melvyn, he means it.

MELVYN: You mean he's some sort of nut. Look, Wild—this
isn't my bag of worms, you know that. I met this creep two
weeks back. He's some sort of lost soul. You handle it.

WILD: Yeah, but this is something he *could* do, Melvyn. I just
want to tell you that. Maybe he could keep the apple on the
ground. That would help, wouldn't it? He doesn't like his
Daddy, you know?

MELVYN: We can't get mixed into that sort of thing.

WILD: We don't have to, do we?

MELVYN: Damn right!

WILD: I told him that. I said he should see a shrink.

MELVYN: Well that's fine, Vic. Look, I've got a fuck of a
situation here. These bastards are going to make a decision
next *week*. And it's not going our way. That's the kind of
information I need to know in advance, not crazy schemes.

WILD: We don't cover Australia, Melvyn. You know that.

MELVYN: You gave me that mother-fucker Mackenzie didn't
you? These people are springing the trap on us, Wild. I
thought we had a clear six months.

WILD: Well, I'm doing my best. I'm just telling you. That boy's
going to be on the base and no-one's going to look at *his* pant
pockets.

MELVYN: You've got to handle this in Paris, Vic. I'm right out here in fucking Canberra for Chrissake.

WILD: I know that Melvyn.

MELVYN: He really could get in there and mess something up? You think that's what he really wants to do?

WILD: That's the point, Melvyn.

(*pause*)

WILD: You still on?

MELVYN: Yeah, Yeah. Look, Vic. I don't want to know any more about this. You tell him that from me, from all of us. There's no way my part of the firm ever plays about the screwballs like that. If *you* do, get to it.

WILD: I told him that. That's the way we'd play it. I know that. But look, Melvyn. He means what he says. He could make his own arrangements.

MELVYN: Good.

WILD: If he gets into this thing—and he really is set on doing that—the big day isn't going to happen. You know it's Friday.

MELVYN: *Good.*

WILD: Well?

MELVYN: That would be very nice. In fact that could be about all we've got left. But it's still not my option.

WILD: That's the way I thought about it. There's a lot of people he could talk to, to get what he wants.

MELVYN: Let's hope he finds one of them then.

WILD: You mean that?

MELVYN: Of course I fucking mean it, Vic, but it's not anything for us.

WILD: It would help if it happened though.

MELVYN: Sure it would help.

WILD: Okay Melvyn. We should leave it like that. I know you don't want to get involved.

MELVYN: None of us is going to get involved. If he gets himself organized that's fine.

WILD: Thanks Melvyn. Be in touch. Good luck out there. What's the weather?

MELVYN: Thirty degrees.

WILD: Jesus! Okay then. I'll see you.

MELVYN: Yeah, and you tell Rose I'll see him in hell if we lose Australia. Tell him I put the proposition to Ackermann.

WILD: He didn't bite?

MELVYN: He put it in his fat mouth and stuck it behind his dentures. Listen Wild: if I ever find out he *knew* how things are here in Canberra before me I really will get you two closed down.

END TAPE TWO

Melvyn Murray shook Vic Wild out of his head and started telexing. He wanted political muscle. He wanted public release of the facts about the flights from Dallas. He wanted a new budget for an order in the region of 600 machines and a delivery date signed in blood from the President of North-West Aerospace himself.

And when he had done it and lay back in his chair to sweat some more he also knew what he was beginning to want even more than any of these. For Daniel Levitte to meet whoever it was he wanted to meet. Just to buy a bit of *time*. He knew they could still swing it then.

In Paris, Rose and Wild played the tape back. There was certainly nothing for Wild to say. Rose looked at the tape machine as if it could tell them something else. Neither man mentioned Murray's recriminations. They were used to mopping up insults when things went wrong. Finally Wild said: "Well there it is, Rosy. Back to the path of virtue. This is where the buck stops and gets buried in the ground, as the man said in the parable."

"You sent that letter to the girl?"

"Telling her to look after him. Sure. Certificate of posting too."

"Well then?"

Wild said: "How are the Walloons?"

The Special Relations office had been busy in Belgium fomenting trouble in the trade unions in the Flemish-speaking areas. Unrest in the machine-tool industries in Belgium helped the deal back in the seventies, still did.

"Breaking each others skulls," said Rose shortly. "I hope."

"They say you can't make an omelette any other way," said Wild.

"Look Vic," said Rose, "time for us to go home. I know what

you are thinking. Now you stay right out of it. Don't stick your neck anywhere near it. That's an order. This is way outside our country."

Wild looked sadly at Rose. Poor old tortoise, he thought. Rose would tuck his neck back under his shell. But he promised to do as he was told.

"I'll see you in the morning," he said.

"Thanks Vic," said Rose.

Vic Wild had been wrong about Rose once before in his life. At the time of Rose's "defection". He was wrong again now.

In his dark office, one pool of light on the black leather desk, Rose sat on for five minutes. He knew he was at the point of his career he had been expecting, one day, would arrive. The moment when a decision lay on him and his conscience alone. The whole weight of North-West Aerospace lay above him in the sunlight. Like a pyramid upside down on a point, a single point: Rose and his decision.

He reviewed where they were. The position was clear. Daniel Levitte had been told off; a letter sent anonymously to the girl as a cover story if necessary. Nothing on tape that wasn't as clean as you would expect in the circumstances. As for the other matter. The imminence of a decision in Australia: it wasn't his fault. But he regretted being unpopular with Murray. He liked to be liked by the big men in the corporation, however indifferent he pretended to be. He'd like to do something to repair the damage.

After ten minutes urgent, private thinking, Rose left the office, drove to the Seine, walked three blocks to a telephone kiosk and put through a brief call to a London telephone number.

Rose listened while the phone rang.

"Yes?" said the Englishman when he picked it up.

"Message for Jimmy Jones," said Rose.

"Okay, go ahead."

"Mayflower," said Rose.

"*Who?*"

"100,000 francs. Usual pick-up. Tomorrow."

It was supposed to be the end of the conversation. But it wasn't.

"You said Mayflower. I don't know who you are. I know a girl called June Flower. Who are you?"

The Englishman heard the phone click and listened to the buzz. Now what in Christ's name had gone wrong?

So far, Crispin Bridge had worked five times for North-West Aerospace. He had only met Rose once, before the first time. Two years before the first time. For two years after that, the monthly credits totted up nicely in a Bilbao bank account. Then the first job had come through in a brief phone call. *January Flower*. The size of the fee. The pick-up.

The pick-up place had also been arranged. Simplicity is best in these matters. A poste restante in a busy central Paris post office. In the envelope had been the money and the name of the man that needed seeing.

All the arrangements were very simple. It is nearly always a good thing. It now looked as if they had been somehow *too* simple. The next job had been coded *Feb Flower*. The one after that *March Flower*.

As jobs went, they had been simple as well. *January Flower* was taking a car full of dollars into Andorra, over the Pyrenees in between two avalanches. The customs post hadn't even been manned. Crispin Bridge had driven unchallenged through walls of snow from which fir trees stuck like used matches. *Feb Flower* was stealing three files from Euro-Aviat's design office in Milan. (North-West had a man who was prepared to tell them where they were, but not take them out himself.) *March Flower* was a trip to Moscow, where Crispin Bridge had watched a fine production of *Spartacus* three times and come back empty handed. *April Flower* was to break both legs of a man who had been stupid enough to try to draw a connection between North-West Aerospace and a call-girl system. It had been on that occasion Bridge met the girl Claude. She worked for the call-girl system.

But *May Flower* had been different from all that. *May Flower* was the one he had been expecting all along. It had never been promised, but it was the one in the offing. His clients, he was sure, hadn't hired an ex-SAS man without a job like this in mind.

So what in hell did it mean to get a call coded *May Flower* again? After all, Jean-Paul Petit was not going to need killing twice.

Crispin Bridge was thirty, built like a heavyweight boxer in his prime, and lived quietly in a council flat on the Pepys Estate in Deptford, in south-east London. By himself. For anonymity, you could not better it. Last spring an old man had been found dead behind his front door in this tall block above the Thames. Had been there for nine months. Hadn't paid his rent; hadn't answered the plumber who had come twice to see the overflow. Hadn't answered the social worker's knocks (three times) nor the neighbours (five times). If you wanted a perfect place for a quiet life, a council flat in London in the 1980s was the right place. On the stairs at the end of a long concrete balcony, by the lift that broke down once a week, some kid had written "Fuck the World" with a blue aerosol can. Someone else had struck out "the World" and replaced it with "Palace" (a local football team) but the message still summed up the spirit of the place.

In works of fiction, men like Crispin Bridge appear as more talented, more interesting than in fact they are.

In the real world, men like Crispin Bridge are hired not to be interesting but to do a few tasks well, resourcefully and fast. The sort of tasks anyone who had done a spell in the SAS during the last bloody days in Belfast had mastered.

Since Belfast, Crispin had felt that knowing how to kill with his bare hands, climb ten-storey buildings, break into any building invented (with gloved hands) were useful skills. He also spoke idiomatic French. The SAS liked their men to have a range of talents.

For two years after his "retirement" from the SAS (he had shot his own patrol leader in circumstances that passed as an accident just sufficiently to avoid court martial), Bridge had been a long-distance lorry driver, taking clandestine military loads on the gruelling run to Ankara. He'd bought his own huge Volvo camion and made good money until the day the Turkish bandits had shot out four front wheels on a mountain pass. He thought the owners of the load would be more than annoyed, but they'd been impressed by the way he had dispatched the bandits who had come swarming up the cab of the overturned lorry. Very impressed. Eventually he had been invited to Paris to meet Mr Rose personally.

Now as he walked up and down his two-roomed flat, with its

huge view of London's empty dockland, he began to feel angry with Rose.

He knew that if he rang Rose at his home in Paris, Rose would refuse to speak. He knew too, that one way or another, he had now been landed deep in trouble.

There were just two options, so far as he could see. Either the *May Flower* job had come from Rose, and Rose was now pretending it hadn't—which could only be to land him in the shit. Or the *May Flower* job *hadn't* come from Rose; which meant someone unknown was *certainly* landing him in the shit.

Crispin Bridge stopped pacing, and had started to pack a case when the phone rang again.

"*April Flower* or *May Flower*," said Rose, "this is us. As in Andorra for January."

"It better be," said Bridge. "Are you safe?"

"For one minute."

"Okay. *I've done May Flower.* That's what it's about. You know that?"

"So *who* was *May Flower?*" asked Rose.

"The flying man," said Bridge.

"Jean-Paul?"

"Yeah: Mr Small. I got the *May Flower* message and I came and did it."

"Not for me," said Rose urgently.

"Listen," said Bridge. "Of course it was from you, Rose. It has to be from you. Maybe you need to say it wasn't. And I ask myself *why?* I'm asking myself hard."

"I promise you," said Rose.

"Well I'm coming to Paris now to start finding out."

"You *won't*," said Rose. "People could be looking for you. I'll check out a few things, be in touch."

"You hold on a moment Rose. I am in Paris tomorrow morning. Now do you want me walking in your front door or at the place we met last? Of course people are looking for me—I want to find *them* first."

"Okay," said Rose, "this one time. But come quietly. There's more in this mess even than you dream. We'd better meet."

"Good."

"Ten am at the place we met last," said Rose, "remember?"

"I remember." Bridge smashed the phone back.

Rose must have told someone the system. If he wasn't lying. *He* hadn't, had he? Had he, some way? He reserved that for a few hours' thinking once he had calmed down, and meanwhile went on packing.

There are two ways to deal with a plague bacillus once it has broken loose. You either run and hope it won't catch up with you. Or you start going about systematically stamping on every contact the bacillus ever dreamt of having.

In the SAS the training was to get straight in and start stamping. With luck, there would still be time to run afterwards.

One thing Bridge knew full well. He would be out of his flat in half an hour and on his way to Paris. And not direct to Paris either, but air to Brussels and train to Paris. Crispin Bridge used European flights the way his neighbours in the flats used buses to Deptford High Street. He was in fact out of the flat in twenty minutes.

He locked the door by the Chubb lock he had put in himself and sniffed the air of the long grey concrete balcony. Cold and sour and still.

Perhaps there is something that makes men like Crispin Bridge unusual. At this point he did not feel he was leaving home, perhaps for ever. He was simply travelling.

All the way out, cat-napping when he chose to—against the airport bus upholstery or the ageing cushions of the Euroshuttle plane to Brussels, Bridge worked out how he could have got himself into this. Anything he'd said to anyone, anywhere to give away the *May Flower* code. He remembered there had been some unusual factors in the last job. Not the least that it was the first that required a killing. But little things as well. The same poste restante, but a letter with more detail—specifying the use of Claude, the hotel and a detailed description of Jean-Paul Petit. But what is supposed to be usual about jobs like this? Rose always took care not to use the same typewriter twice. The money had been in the envelope (bigger denominations than before, he now remembered, but still good old-fashioned mixed number money). The only key to unlocking Crispin Bridge was the code *May Flower*. And that is all.

Now, for all he knew, the moment he stepped off the plane at Brussels they would be there to arrest him. At least.

It was Monday, February 19, eight in the morning. At Dreux, the countdown towards the Super-Celeste's new flight began now. And Bridge was riding the early morning commuter train from Brussels—the back door way into Paris on a train so stuffed with Common Market officials that frontier formalities were not observed. Two Belgian delegates to the European Beef Commission stirred in their doze opposite him as he unzipped his case and took out his breakfast. Bridge was something of a health freak. He drank a can of vegetable juice and munched through three sesame seed biscuits as the train slicked over the points at the outermost industrial suburbs of Paris.

As he approached Paris, Bridge knew from his pulse he was working into just that state of anger he needed for survival. Men like Bridge are quite wrongly labelled psychopaths, or "cold-blooded". Men like Bridge are the ones who stay alive and stay employed. They use their anger for commercial ends. They work between two boundaries: almost all of the time they are more calm, more passive in the true sense of the word than most of us. They never suffer from depression. They take with indifference situations that would make the rest of us panic, or like the young man in the morgue, vomit. That state of mind explains the leisurely pace with which Bridge and his friend had hauled the body of Jean-Paul Petit into the Renault van.

The further perimeter is anger. Not "cold-blooded" killing but exactly the same anger any ordinary, long-suffering wife uses when she finally takes the carving knife into the gut of the husband she has detested for twenty years. But with one difference. Men like Bridge allow this sort of anger to flower— you need both passion and precision in a killing.

For the first time in his life Bridge found himself with three good reasons to be angry at once.

He was still angry with Rose. During the night he had come round to giving up, for the moment, the idea that Rose was responsible for the disaster. He was prepared to believe the *May Flower* message wasn't from Rose. That somebody else wanted Jean-Paul dead. But that still must mean someone with Rose had let loose enough information to get him tricked this way. Secondly, he was angry with the way he had been tricked. To do a killing for an unknown client was just so stupid it couldn't be true. Thirdly, he was angry at the thought that the

French police, with or without his unknown client's help, could by now already be burrowing after him through a whole network of private contacts in Paris he would now not be able to use again.

As the train slowed into the suburbs, Bridge took his case and slid the window open at the end of the carriage. A cold wet wind slapped into his face, but he hung out to watch for the lights of the next suburban station. Then, with his back to the compartment wall in the train corridor, he stretched his arms high as if shaking off fatigue and curled his fingers round the alarm release.

The platforms were already crowded with the first commuters. In their pleasure and excitement at the chance of climbing aboard the express that suddenly stopped half way down the platform there was no problem for Bridge in joining the throng disappearing into the exit tunnel.

He jumped aboard the first bus likely to move in any direction and watched the door carefully for any sign of anyone following him into Paris. At the first stop he got off and walked three blocks before he found a taxi. Then he sat back and relaxed as the driver circled his way round Paris towards Montparnasse.

There was still plenty of time, before his appointment with Rose, to make one dangerous but necessary visit. The first *May Flower* briefing had been very detailed about the girl Claude. It had assured Bridge that Claude would be spending the night at the Hotel Hélène in the Rue Jacob, and indeed she had. Bridge had seen her go in. And he had seen Jean-Paul Petit joining her two hours later. So one thing was certain: Claude would have something to tell him about how she had got into these arrangements. Not that she would be likely to know much. Behind that glossy southern skin and wide dark eyes, as Bridge well knew, lay a very small intelligence.

He stopped the cab near the hotel she was last at. The one she established herself in when she had to go freelance after the *April Flower* blackmail job.

It was now going to be just a matter of luck as to whether the police were already interested in the affairs of Claude.

The sight of the usual fat Algerian at the foyer was reassuring. Bridge stepped inside the Hotel Musée. Two American tourists were arguing the toss with the proprietor—the hotel acted as an overflow for the sleazier tour operators who had double-booked their clients too successfully. There was usually one row a week as some hapless mid-west school-teacher suddenly woke up to the fact she was living in a brothel.

Had the police connected up with Claude successfully, it would not be likely that the proprietor would still be lolling behind his desk, listening with half an ear to a complaint not about the hotel's morals but its plumbing.

Instead the man would be either in the basement of the police station or lying low in his squalid Algerian village.

Bridge stepped briskly to the desk, interrupted the two Americans without ceremony and said "Good morning."

The Algerian went on picking at the crevices of his ear with a matchstick and then sucking it. His only acknowledgement was to lift a few of his chins upwards to give Bridge a glance over.

"I'm looking for the girl Claude," said Bridge.

The Algerian began to look at Bridge with care.

"What girl is this?" he asked.

"She's a prostitute. She lives here. You know that."

"You think this hotel is some sort of brothel?" asked the Algerian politely.

"I *know* it's some sort of brothel," said Bridge. "Now where is she?"

The Algerian sighed and stood up. He moved slowly round his desk as if throwing Bridge into the street was going to be as easy as throwing the suitcases of the girl Claude had been. He had done that just last night, when the police had come showing photographs of her.

Bridge waited easily until the man had actually begun his stupid, ponderous effort at making a rush.

The Algerian, to his surprise, suddenly found himself with his back bent double against his desk and his ears pinned to the woodwork by two powerful fingers and thumbs.

"You're not going to need to clean your disgusting ears much longer," said Bridge. "Because I'm going to pull them off one by one. Okay?"

The American ladies were retreating, mewing like cats, to the stairs.

"Now tell me where Claude is."

He released his victim, who clutched his ears to discover if they were still attached.

"I don't know," he said, "I swear I don't know. I threw her out last night. The police were looking for her. They came with a photograph."

"What police? What station? Did you hear any names?"

"No."

Bridge jabbed him in the stomach. "Think," said Bridge.

"There was a kid they called Marcel Derivat," gasped the Algerian.

"Good. Where from? What station?"

"How would I know?"

"Come outside with me," said Bridge. "Come now, just walk easy or I'll kill you at once." Two other residents joined the Americans on the stairs. It was time to move.

The Algerian did as he was told. He felt, wrongly, he might be safer in the street anyway.

"Now," said Bridge, "you know where this Derivat works or you wouldn't know his full name, would you? He gave you his name so you could contact him." He had an immovable grip on the man's left wrist and was beginning gently to bend his fingers back.

"Oh God don't!" screamed the Algerian. "He's from the station in the 18th, Rue de Naples. He's only a kid."

"Good," said Bridge, "and you're not telling them anything are you?"

"Of course not. I threw the girl out—they were just checking hotels. I don't know where she went."

"All right. I'll believe you," said Bridge. Carefully, he applied just enough pressure to break the man's little finger at the second knuckle. A bus was passing, to mask his shrill scream of agony.

"Now you stay quiet and remember nothing," said Bridge, "or I'll be back to finish you." He let the man go, sprang back into the hotel to collect his case, and walked briskly away down the street.

So the police were already looking for Claude. That was just beautiful. It meant, for certain, as he knew anyway, his career in Paris was over, even assuming he got away with this one. He just hoped Rose would be properly terrified enough by the news about Claude to give him the help he now needed.

Rose was already waiting for Bridge in a dirty, yellow-painted room that was three flights of narrow stairs above a ruined fruit merchant's premises near the old Les Halles. The merchant had clung on to commercial life ever since the market had moved out of Paris by looking after occasional surplus goods that arrived by water and at night. He had been glad to rent out the upstairs room to M. Guy, the cocoa merchant, who required a quiet place for conversations a few times a year. M. Guy, otherwise Rose, had explained that the cocoa business was occasionally involved in "matters of discretion". He was prepared to pay quite well for a room no more then two metres square and equipped with nothing but two metal chairs and a grimy deal table.

Rose was not terrified. But he was tired, and suspected, rightly, that before Friday arrived he would be a good deal more tired. It went with the job. It sometimes happened that pressure would arrive on Rose from both of the worlds he operated in. There could be a crisis in the world "above ground" and acute problems in the world "below ground"— and when that happened he could neither delegate nor explain to either side his other preoccupations.

At least, this week, both pressures concerned the same event: the flight of the Super-Celeste.

When, at six in the morning, the phone at his bedside had rung, he had just been beginning to doze. The call was from North-West Aerospace in Dallas. And Rose was most impressed by the fact that it was from David Callaghan, Director of International Sales. "How good to speak with you," said Rose, "we met at the D-Day celebration at Caen in June, remember?" Callaghan did not remember, but assured Rose how well he did. He knew the little man's enthusiasm for the corporation. "Rose," said Callaghan, "we're getting into a tough situation in Canberra. Murray has been telexing us for every kind of help we can get him. He believes we're up against an almost fore-gone conclusion—against us. Trouble is too that there's a possibility of a really big apple order involved. Let alone the domino position."

"Well, we're on the edge in Belgium," admitted Rose. "And

I agree with you, David. If Australia goes, it all goes. It sounds like the battle that wins the war to me."

"Well, we think so too. And all we need is time. We'd had no indication the Australians were so near to making up their minds. Murray seems to think that's your fault, but there it is. We have a hell of a lot of pressure we *can* bring in if we have time. That's why I'm suddenly interested in your help."

Rose noted, with resignation, how, as usual, people like Callaghan were not interested in the SR Department until an emergency came up.

"You mean this proposition from the young man?" said Rose.

"I mean that. We have to talk a bit carefully here, Rose."

"I understand that. You've had an up-to-date position?"

"I have indeed. And the feeling here, which is why I am phoning you, is that we don't actually want to stand in the man's way."

"Really," said Rose.

"It's an exceptional circumstance," said Callaghan. "Obviously no-one must get hurt. That has to be made plain. Could it be done and absolutely certain that no connection was made?"

"I couldn't recommend it any other way," said Rose carefully.

"All right then, Rose, I'll have to leave this one with you. If you feel you can help. Meanwhile I'll let Murray know and if anything changes during the week we'll take the pressure off you if we can. You've no idea how much rushing around we are doing in the States. Did you know today is the anniversary of the Jap raid on Darwin?"

"No," said Rose.

"Neither did I. With luck, the President will be presenting a gold cup or something to one of the survivors, if we can find one."

"There's a lot at stake," said Rose. "Listen, David. You can rely on us. I have already had this one in hand for twenty-four hours. Things are moving on it."

"Well, that's fine, Rose. Look after yourself."

"I will."

After this conversation, Rose decided there was no point at

all in trying to find some sleep. He got up and took his solitary breakfast while working through the morning papers. There were several articles to mark for his cuttings files. In the popular press, pictures of the Levitte family on the steps of the church headed stories giving the family's point-blank denial of any connection, romantic or otherwise, between the dead pilot and Marie-Thérèse Levitte. This was described by a family spokesman as a typical and gross innuendo and an insult to long-standing family friendships. It admitted that a possible momentary loss of attention while driving could have been the cause of Marie-Thérèse's death, which coincided with a news bulletin. As for the newspaper which had dared print this stuff, legal action was being taken. Rose smiled. He put a blue tick on this press cutting.

Then there were features on the Super-Celeste: news of the latest successes in the engine trials. A profile of its new distinguished pilot, the veteran Henri Bosco—with the suggestion that it had always been a matter of chance whether he or Jean-Paul Petit would fly the plane first. In a large aviation concern the final choice of pilot always lay between more than one equally distinguished pilot. And so on.

Finally there was news that the police were making dramatic progress in their search for Jean-Paul's killer and were almost certain that the matter was linked with Arab terrorism. An Algerian terrorist movement was mentioned by name, and the hi-jacking episode in which Jean-Paul had played so effective a part was described.

Rose read all this with attentive deliberation. Then he saw the first serious news of the day. The pictures of Claude. The description of her as a girl from Marseilles whom the police wished to interview in connection with the Petit murder.

Rose certainly remembered the girl Claude. He studied the plump face reflectively for a moment. Then he went to his wall safe and took out the file on *April Flower*. He took out several more pictures of Claude, and also a picture of the man that Crispin Bridge had attended to in the *April Flower* assignment. What was it Bridge had done to him? Smashed both his knee-caps? Rose had thought that a little savage when he'd heard of it, but he had left it to Bridge's discretion as to how much dissuasion was necessary.

After reading the file through, Rose replaced it, took a wad of money from the safe and locked it up again. Then he set off for Les Halles.

Bridge got there soon after. He asked the proprietor of the fruit warehouse for two packets of Disque Bleu—no, make it three. The proprietor had converted his street-level frontage to a tobacconist's The request for the Disque Bleu, put that way, was his signal to show Bridge without question to the dark stairs at the back of the shop.

"Sit down," said Rose, when he arrived. "Do you know this girl?" he passed the newspaper cutting across to him.

"Yes," said Bridge, "I've already been looking for her. And she's gone."

Rose looked at him thoughtfully. He was glad Bridge had admitted knowing Claude. Wild had seen the two together. Rose wondered how intelligent Bridge was. There seemed to be something slightly vacant about his large blue eyes and blond hair, but perhaps one always underrated blue-eyed blonds of either sex.

"You are in a great deal of trouble, Bridge," said Rose, "if what you say is true. You'd better start by telling me everything about this Jean-Paul Petit business."

"Or you should start by convincing me you don't already know," said Bridge.

"I don't have to," said Rose, "there's the evidence." He indicated the picture. "It's not likely, is it?"

"So who else wanted him dead?"

"Well, that we have to find out. Faster than possible. Look, Bridge, I'm prepared to be very frank with you. We are *both* in trouble. Now you tell me, and I'll tell you."

Bridge thought about it. There seemed nothing to lose.

"Okay," he said. He lit a Disque Bleu. Rose laid out a sheet of paper on the grimy table. He looked like a small-town American lawyer helping a client make his will.

"How did you meet this girl?"

"On the *April Flower* job."

"And you've been sleeping with her since."

"What else is she for?"

Rose looked at him with distaste.

"All right," said Bridge, "let's start at the beginning. You remember the *April Flower* job. You're not denying that came from you?"

Rose nodded.

"The message was that a man called Muhammed Hassin was trying a touch of blackmail and I should go and ask him about it and then discourage him for keeps. So I went along and told him we'd do everything reasonable to help him out. You know the scene. I didn't mention North-West—I just told him I was from the people he wanted to see. We had a good greasy meal and a friendly evening together and when the girl Claude called in this Hassin introduced me and said she was a very special piece of cunt. Which she is. Hassin's big piece of blackmail was a bunch of fuzzy dirty pictures showing Claude and a client. I gathered that much. They looked as if they'd been taken through a hole in the ceiling. Obviously I couldn't ask Hassin who he was because otherwise he would have been on to me. So I just took Hassin home and told him he could sell his pictures to the Pope if he wanted to and when he got restless I took him off at the kneecaps. Does that fit with your facts?"

Rose nodded. "Who was the guy in the dirty pictures anyway?" asked Bridge.

"Jean-Paul Petit," said Rose.

"Christ," said Bridge. It had in fact crossed his mind.

"Exactly," said Rose. "Now let me tell you about this Hassin. He *was* in the management of a call-girl ring. With which we do have connections, I admit. Obviously he didn't know those connections for sure—no-one does except one man we trust—and still trust. Hassin for some reason—which I'd better find out—seemed to feel these particular pictures were worth taking and tried to get a price from our man for them. We just couldn't understand that bit. The girl certainly wasn't sleeping with Jean-Paul Petit on our instruction. Our man knew she worked privately as well. Most of them do, it seems. She could have met Jean-Paul at some party or other. Maybe Jean-Paul went along with people in the aviation business we *did* have an interest in. That seems the most likely to me. I guess the girl was at some reception in tow of some guy we'd fixed up. We knew Hassin hadn't really got on to the girl's connection with North-West, but he was beginning to get close by choosing this pilot as a target. Too damned close. So far as we were concerned, he needed discouraging. That's why we called you in." Rose looked at Bridge with dislike. "I should have been warned then too," he said. "You really overdid it."

"It's a hell of a job working for you Rose," said Bridge. "You never know what's going on."

"That is supposed to be the idea," said Rose. "But maybe you're right. I'm a victim of my education."

"In the CIA," said Bridge. Rose let this pass.

"I'm going to look forward to catching up with Hassin again," said Bridge. "Then you'll see."

"Never mind about that," said Rose sharply. "Why in hell did you keep going with this girl afterwards? I thought you were a clean operator."

"I like her. She's a top-class prostitute on your books—or used to be, because I assumed you'd get rid of her soon after, which you did. So all it meant to me was that I had a clean lay in Paris. Doing you a good turn too. Hassin would know I was keeping my eyes open in his direction."

"Or could have come round and found you with your pants down."

"Listen," said Bridge, "with or without my pants down I can take on people like Hassin before breakfast. Hassin will be on crutches for the rest of his life, and frightened to death the rest of his life too. When I hit them, they stay down."

Bridge wasn't all that bright, decided Rose. A simple, straightforward hit man with limited imagination.

"Well," said Rose, "somebody in this mess didn't stay down. Why are the police looking for Claude?"

It was still difficult for Bridge to realize that Rose really didn't know.

"She spent the night with Jean-Paul Petit—his last night, I mean. I'm not adjusted to the idea this is all news to you still. Look: let's go through the Petit business. I got a *May Flower* message at the usual post office, right? Must have been six weeks back."

"But no phone call first."

"True, but our arrangement was I'd call in regularly anyway. The briefing said Jean-Paul Petit was going to be spending the night, by arrangement, with Claude at the Hotel Hélène in the Rue Jacob and I was to take him as soon as he got out in the morning, early. Now why shouldn't I believe that? There's the *May Flower* code. There's a perfectly reasonable target. There's the girl Claude—I *know* that girl's too stupid to do anything she isn't told. *And* there was the money. I'm not sure I still don't believe it."

"Bridge," said Rose patiently, "you really think we'd kill the pilot of the Super-Celeste on the morning of the first flight? You have to be very naïve."

Bridge shouted, "Why shouldn't I think? What is it you people make? Kiddies' pleasure boats?"

Rose inspected the palms of his hands, which had collected a shine of black dirt from the table. He began to rub them on a clean linen handkerchief. Well, he could see Bridge's point. "So you called at the post-office, found a letter for Mr Mayflower and went right ahead. I have to believe you."

Bridge studied the newspaper cutting. "It's the way we do business," he said.

"You saw the girl go in?" asked Rose.

"That's right. And I hit Petit when he came out. I had some hired help, but someone I trust. What's this in the paper about Algerian terrorists? Was that bastard Hassin Algerian?"

"Moroccan, I believe."

"All the same. I'd say the police are right then. That makes sense."

"I doubt it," said Rose. "My God! It's unbelievable. For two reasons," he added. "Algerian terrorists do their own hit work. They're good at it. Anything as sophisticated as setting you up would be way beyond their style. Secondly, there's the question of the *real May Flower* job. The one I called you about last night. Now listen, Bridge, listen carefully. I'm breaking all my rules telling you this. I'm telling you simply to let you know how vital it is you get out of here and back on a plane to London immediately. You'll get paid for this job—exactly as if you'd done it. You'll continue to draw your monthly money for the next three years. But you and I won't be in touch except to let me know any change of pick-up place for the money."

"Sure," said Bridge, "that's fine. I work for money and I work to stay alive to earn more money. Now tell me."

Rose wasn't convinced by this assurance, but pressed on. In as little detail as possible, he told Bridge about the urgent desire of Daniel Levitte to meet someone who could arrange an explosive device for Friday. "Had we gone ahead with it," said Rose, "we'd have had to insist the job was done on the ground, no-one hurt. Quite easy to arrange."

"Then why not go ahead with it?" asked Bridge.

Rose sighed. "Look Crispin," he said. "Persons unknown get you to kill Euro-Aviat's top pilot on the dawn of the plane's first flight. Whoever they are, they must know you work for us. So far as both of us can see, they are either bungling the security of all this or letting the story bit by bit to the police at their leisure. God knows how else they're looking for this girl Claude so soon. Next, we are invited into the business of wrecking the plane itself. Now somehow, *somehow* there's a connection in there."

"You say this Daniel Levitte made a personal approach to you?"

"There's no doubt. We met him. We froze him off. The idea was to make sure someone met him casually, no connection with us."

"And you say Levitte was great mates with Jean-Paul Petit? Maybe he wasn't. Maybe last week he wanted Petit dead and this week he wants to blow the plane. He's the man we have to see."

Rose looked as if he was thinking about it. Certainly someone would have to see Daniel Levitte again. "Well," said Rose, "I'm not saying that has to be wrong. There's another connection you may not have heard of. According to well-informed sources, the pilot was sleeping with Daniel Levitte's sister."

"There you are then," said Bridge.

"*Where* are we?" said Rose. He seemed irritated at chewing the thing over with this hired killer.

"It's some sort of crazy family affair," said Bridge calmly, as if that was some brilliant elucidation. "The answer is for me to get to see Levitte and find out."

"The answer is for you to leave Paris," said Rose sharply. "If you want one of the more obvious explanations, try this one. Daniel Levitte has reasons to fix Petit we don't know of. Somehow he works out a way to get you to do it for him. Then he comes to us with the proposal we've got now. As soon as we bite on that hook he winds us in on both raps. Maybe or maybe not he kills you on the way."

"Sounds reasonable," said Bridge. "All the more reason I go and have a talk with him and find out. You already *have* bitten on the hook."

"Not irrevocably."

"I suppose not," said Bridge bitterly, "you can wriggle off. I can't. Look at it this way. Levitte is not going to have a case on either counts until I actually plant him with explosives. So the best way of keeping him quiet this week—and to find out if he's doing what we think he's doing—is to go along and meet him. It might turn out you're wrong. It might turn out Daniel Levitte really does want the machine blown up. And if it does turn out that way then you've got between here and Friday to arrange a convincing background story putting these Algerians into the hot seat. As soon as the plane blows you can have people ringing the police claiming responsibility."

Rose looked at the ceiling. In one corner a burst pipe had deflowered the layers of paint into something like a scab.

"I know you think I'm pretty dim, Rose," said Bridge, "but I've learnt a few things. Back in Belfast we played 'Whose bomb?' with ten players at a time. There were Prot bombs and Catholic bombs and SAS bombs: I know that game inside out."

"Dangerous game," said Rose.

"We're already in."

Rose shook his head. "Can't do it, Crispin. Go back to London."

"Listen," said Bridge, "you know bloody well. It's me they are after. It's my life. *I* killed that man. You expect me to go back and wait for them to find out?"

"I'm paying you to get out. Here you are. Here's the fee for the job I'm not asking you to do." He took the packet of money out and laid it on the table. Bridge watched him count it out, Rose's dry little fingers flicking the large notes with the neatness of a bank cashier.

"You're left-handed," said Bridge. "Goes with your sinister job."

Rose ignored the joke and passed the packet across the table. Bridge took it and pocketed it.

"Fair enough," he said. "Right. I'm self-employed again. But suppose you gave me a number I could ring. I mean I might want to stay in Paris and look at the Mona Lisa or something. You must have an answering service we can trust."

Rose wrote a number on his pad and passed it across. He said: "Don't go wild Bridge."

"Right," said Bridge. "And I'll give you one thing, Rose. If I *was* going to stay in Paris. Just suppose. I'd get two little bombs made for Daniel Levitte. One would work and one wouldn't. I know about the bomb game."

After Bridge had gone from the dirty little room, Rose stayed on for a while. He rubbed his hands on his linen handkerchief again and smiled. So far it was all going well.

In Dallas and New York, North-West Aerospace accountants had greedily worked out that the latest hearsay order from Murray in Canberra would be worth an initial 2,500 million dollars to whichever company got it. They had telexed Murray the new unit price he could offer on each plane—the "flyaway" price, firm and guaranteed. In Washington, equally urgent calculations were in progress to find a formula whereby Australia could, if necessary, pay for American planes by way of a trade deal for butter and wool. That was more difficult. Until now, without the imminent loss of the order in sight, the US government had been set rigidly against playing about with the balance of trade in this way. But ultimately, it was a powerful and persuasive weapon. The European Community had long since cut itself off from the Australian agricultural market—the last thing Europe could now do was swap planes for butter. It was still a card in the Americans' hands.

Australia's main export markets now lay strongly with Japan, so far as food and wool were concerned. Australians were again watching the spectacle of Japanese buyers dominating the Melbourne wool sales—with a mixture of pleasure at the high prices paid and alarm at the implications. For Japan was understandably edgy at the speed of Australia's rearmament. The weaponry being aimed against Red China could, with trifling adjustment, be aimed against Japan. There were many Australians who were aware of the continuous and growing military presence of Japan and who were anxious about Australian indebtedness to that market in economic terms.

It was no coincidence that, inspired by violent activity from North-West's media experts, television companies and newspapers throughout the West were suddenly finding space to remind viewers and readers that today, February 19, was the fortieth anniversary of the Japanese blitz on Darwin back in 1942.

Given time, North-West's executives were still confident they could work on these and other angles to make a convincing case to Australian public opinion. But time was exactly what the Australian government had taken care to see America did not have.

Melvyn Murray realized increasingly by the end of his first day in Canberra, after two hours in the Department of Defence offices, how thoroughly he had been conned. These weren't—as he had suspected already—preliminary talks at all but preface, to a brisk presentation of a final decision. Once made, it would be no use America protesting, or offering deals in butter or wool, or revising into a soft line towards China. The Australian people would simply say: "Why didn't you do that in the first place?" For some reason unknown, the Australians were determined to buy the European plane.

Only in Australia could such a governmental policy have been kept so well hidden from the Americans. In Europe, America had so many lines of communication with all the governments of the Community that every shift and shade of opinion was mapped out far in advance. In Australia you had to depend on a few tough and secretive politicians, dedicated—no matter how many Norwegian country properties you set up for them in the bush—to Australia's own emerging interests in world power games.

Murray was powerfully inclined to head out to the Snowy Mountains and burn Senator Mackenzie's property to the ground personally.

He didn't need the global sales director, Callaghan, to tell him to stay in and fight. There was nothing else to do. By tomorrow he would have ten senior executives from Dallas at his side to help him. And Callaghan had assured him that every senator in the aerospace lobby—even the ones retained by the other two rival American firms—would be working flat out to use political American pressure against Australia before the meeting of her Defence Review Committee.

And tomorrow could be too late. Murray, fretting at his hotel suite desk, started thinking about Daniel Levitte again. Okay, it had seemed a crazy idea when he first heard it. Would anyone be motivated enough to do such a thing against his own father? Murray thought about it. The more he thought about it the more possible it seemed. History was full of examples of sons going to great lengths to do their fathers down. His own children, when he saw them, never seemed to miss a chance to score off *him*.

He turned his mind to Ackermann. By now that fat Hun would have flown, in air-conditioned comfort, from Sydney to Canberra. Probably had a large bunch of orchids and a love letter from the fucking Australian premier in his room. Well, he couldn't be angry with Ackermann. Was there a chance that he would really take that bribe and go?

Murray threw a large Scotch into a glass and six cubes of ice after it. Not a chance he decided. And even if he felt like it, what way could Ackermann sabotage his own strong position now? He checked the time. Well, he'd be finding out soon enough. In two hours he, Ackermann, and everyone else in the aviation business in Canberra would all be together to remember February 19, 1942. The day the Japanese hit Darwin. He hoped they would remember damned well what happened at Darwin. And if they *weren't* remembering well, then Murray would start reminding them. For what had happened at Darwin proved very plainly, to Murray's way of looking at it, that Australia should celebrate its memory by buying American.

It was seven in the evening. This time, forty years ago to the minute, Admiral Chuichi Nagumo and Commander Mitsuo Fuchida were steadily and in complete radio silence beginning their final approach to a point 220 miles north-west of Darwin. They were a formidable pair. Just seventy-four days earlier, these two men had led the attack on Pearl Harbor.

Despite that lesson, Australia's "front door" town, high up in the tropical north, lay totally unsuspecting and unprepared as the fleet of seventeen ships approached. On the four aircraft carriers, *Soryu*, *Akagi*, *Kaga* and *Kiryu*, 188 aircraft were drawn up for the attack. Another 54 land-based bombers from the Celibes would follow them in. Out of the total armada of 242 planes, only two would fail to return.

The attack came in the morning. The fleet turned into the wind, and 36 fighters, 71 dive-bombers and 81 level-bombers headed south. They were less than one hour's flying time from their target, and still Australia knew nothing of what was to come.

Only as the high-level bombers swept in overhead at 18,000 feet did the pathetic wail of sirens rise above Darwin to meet the scream of the bombs raining down. The 45 ships at anchor in the beautiful harbour took the first full shock of the onslaught. Nine were sunk outright. Men plunged from exploding vessels and flying boats and swam towards the jetty. But the bombs had smashed it in two. Oil and water from the jetty's broken supply lines sprayed the clamouring survivors with a choking and inflammable deluge.

Then the long line of dive-bombers came in from the south-west, hurtling into the boiling pall of black smoke now rising from the harbour. They released their bombs, then flew on over the town, hammering gunfire into the scurrying civilians and air-force personnel.

There was little time or opportunity for heroism among the citizens of Darwin. Even when the second wave of land-based bombers came in, later in the morning, there was little to be done against them. The air-force base was smashed in this wave of attack: the aircraft burnt on the ground and the hangars flew into fragments of twisted metal.

Civilians and military alike took to the bush. The dirt road southwards, leading nowhere but to the burning interior and Alice Springs became crowded with a traffic never seen before or since. As they went, the panic-stricken citizens looted the shattered stores. Later, the army itself was to loot the Qantas office at the Darwin Hotel. Qantas staff were held at bay with a broken bottle while troops tore their way through parcels awaiting transit.

Ironically, many of the parcels ripped open were gifts from soldiers to their families in the south.

Not surprisingly, the memory of this débâcle—and of the

equally humiliating attack on Broome that followed it—had been one of the things most Australians preferred to forget. Not only had there been a totally devastating raid to account for—but the panic of a whole city as it fled in fear of the Japanese landings. A few had been heroic, like the men who had dodged their way, between falling sticks of bombs, to bring out the flying boat Camilla. Otherwise there was nothing to be very proud of in Darwin.

But now, this February of 1982, forty years on, the Australians had good reason to resurrect the Darwin anniversary. Back in '42, in the whole of the southern seas, Australia had not a single land- or sea-based aircraft to give cover to its fighting men.

Now, with China gathering like a storm cloud on the northern horizon, it made sense to remind the inhabitants of the huge, still empty continent.

In Paris, Crispin Bridge was not on his way back to London. Instead he decided that before calling on Daniel Levitte he would (as he had given Rose fair warning) attend to two other urgent matters. The first was a long telephone call to a Mr Terence MacSweeney. The second was to visit Muhammed Hassin. He didn't find him at his old address. But he found him not far distant. With two smashed kneecaps, Hassin was in no shape to move far, and an enquiry from the young, blond insurance agent after a crippled Moroccan led him swiftly to the address he needed.

With a kindly gesture, Bridge gave the children playing in the dank courtyard a few francs to go and play elsewhere. He didn't need an audience. The men would all be out at work, he knew. And the women would stay behind their doors. He was deep in the ghetto area of Paris now: among concrete flats not too much unlike his own residence.

Hassin opened the door to him, then made a desperate effort to shut it in his face. In doing so he fell backwards and writhed on the floor like a broken-backed beetle. Bridge helped him up and shut the door behind him.

"Now why don't you sit down, Hassin," said Bridge. "You need to get all the rest you can."

The thin-faced Arab, already garishly scarred by pock marks long before Bridge had attended to him, went into a convulsive shuddering. The room stank of something sweet, like ageing ice cream.

"There you are," said Bridge, helping Hassin into a chair by picking him up off the floor and letting him down gently.

"You kill me one time," said Hassin.

"Yeah. Well let's hope I don't have to kill you a second time. Now you sit quiet and we'll have a little talk, Abdul. You make a noise and I'll start on you from the sharp end. Understand?"

Tears of pure terror ran down the Arab's face.

"Now," said Bridge comfortably. "Forgive the suitcase, I'm not moving in. I'm just trying to be the first professional hit man to go to work with a suitcase. Now listen Abdul, the last time you met me you were trying to sell some dirty pictures. Remember? Now at the time, I confess it, I didn't know who the man was. Only what I've learnt today is that it was a pilot, a flying man, you know? Jean-Paul Petit."

The man gave another shudder of horror.

"No, listen, Abdul, I'm explaining. Don't twitch about. I've got a bit of a problem now, Abdul, because I killed that pilot man. Right? Did you know that? And the police are looking for that nice bird you introduced me to. So I thought I'd better come to see you to get some explanations."

Hassin flung himself out of his chair and rolled on the floor at Bridge.

"Don't tell me these things," he begged. "Why you tell me these things? You kill me if you tell me these things."

"No, no, no Abdul," said Bridge. "But I'm not picking you up again. You stay down there if you want to. Now tell me. Where is Claude now?"

"Hotel Musée."

"No, she isn't. I've been there."

"I promise you. That's all I know."

"Okay. I believe you. If Claude's one jump in front of the police she ought to be two jumps ahead of you. Second thing. Who gave you this idea of taking pictures of Claude and Petit?"

The Arab slewed himself as far as he could from Bridge by pulling himself over the floor on the palms of his hands.

"Some detectives came. They said it was a domestic thing. They showed me pictures of this young man in air-force uniform. I said I could get pictures."

"What sort of detectives?"

"Private. Like in divorce cases."

"So you got the pictures and they paid you."

"That's right, they paid me."

"Then you recognized who the man was and you thought you might make some more money out of it by blackmailing your employers. That it?"

Hassin was silent. Bridge stirred him with his toe.

"That's right," said Hassin.

"Well that makes sense, Abdul. Then you wouldn't have got crippled. Now. One more thing. And look Abdul—" Bridge took out his wallet and leafed out three 1,000 franc notes. "I want you to help me; and I want to pay you for it. Couldn't be fairer than that could it? Here. Take it." He bent down and pressed the money into the Arab's hand, closing his fist round. "There you are. Now, all I want to know is this. Since I left you last time, did those detectives come back? Come on Abdul, you tell me. Then you can keep your money. Did they come back?"

The cripple sat upright. He held on to the money, but held his arm out stiffly towards Bridge as if too fearful to claim anything.

"Yes," he said, "they came back at once."

"And they said, 'Where's that nice girl Claude? Now that she's been sacked.' That right Abdul?"

"That's right."

"Jesus Christ all fucking almighty!" said Crispin Bridge. "You Muslims are an ignorant lot. Didn't I tell you loud enough?"

"What you mean, what you mean?" shrilled Hassin.

"Don't worry about a thing. I'm going to leave you in peace," said Bridge. He bent down, unzipped his case and took a piece of paper and a felt-tip pen from one of its twenty pockets. "Now," he said. "Look. In the newspaper cutting here they are talking about an Arab terrorist gang. See? The Arrow of the Prophet. See the words? Now. Is that anything to do with you?"

"They are all madmen, people like that. I am an Arab but I am French. This isn't anything to do with me."

"You're sure about that," said Bridge gently.

"Oh yes sir."

"Well, that's what I figured. Now this is the last tiny thing and you can keep your money and hit the jackpot. Never mind, it's just a phrase. What I want you to do is to write those words in Arabic. 'The Arrow of the Prophet.' Write it three times."

"Why? I know nothing of them."

"Just interest, that's all. Just for me. Look at all that money. I'm sorry for you, Abdul."

"Muhammed," said the man, with a sudden spark of aggression.

"Whatever," said Bridge. He laid the pen and pencil on the floor. "And don't write anything else, Abdul, because if you do I'll come back and do you a real mischief."

Muhammed Hassin looked up at him. He took the pen as Bridge smiled encouragingly and wrote the words neatly in Arabic script at the foot of the paper. Three times.

"Very nice," said Bridge. Then he opened his case a stretch further and took out a small gun.

"Don't worry, Abdul," said Bridge. "You won't feel a thing."

The man screamed and writhed farther away across the linoleum floor. Bridge knelt beside him and took his head by the hair with his left hand. The man suddenly relaxed all his muscles, as if desiring death.

Bridge very slowly lifted the gun towards him until the muzzle was against the end of the Arab's nose. He watched the man's eyes as they rolled in and out of focus around it. Then he put the muzzle hard against the Arab's flared nostrils and turned the gun twenty degrees in either direction. Hassin moaned. He felt Bridge's hand tighten against his skull, gripping the hair. Then Bridge let go of him and he fell back on the floor, his eyes tight shut.

Bridge shot him through the left ear. The man slowly coiled up into a foetal position on the floor and died. Bridge retrieved his money and replaced it with part of the scrap of paper. He slipped the other fragments of Arabic script into his wallet, while listening keenly for any reaction to the sound of the shot. Then he repacked his suitcase and left.

Celeste, this Monday, was at work. But nothing was going well. She had received an anonymous letter that morning. Any anonymous letter made her skin crawl. She had had her share. Often they were accompanied by pages torn from the magazines she modelled for, hideously disfigured by the sexual fantasies of the letter-writers. Vic Wild had done his best to sound solicitous, but she had an instinct, did Celeste.

Though this letter began differently from most, the same feeling of menace came across. It claimed to be from a friendly party who had reason to know Daniel was under a great deal of strain and recommended she persuade him to have a talk with his doctor or herself.

All night, again, Daniel had been lonely, unapproachable, lying awake. There was nothing to do but occasionally stroke his forehead or kiss his cheek.

And now there was this modelling session. She had walked straight into a nightmare.

The picture editor had at first been delighted to see her. She looked sad, but mysterious. In the depth of winter her golden skin was pure magic. She looked as if she had a secret. The features editor wondered if she was pregnant. Though she was not, he was also right. The meeting with the grandfather had much affected Celeste. She had begun to think Daniel might outgrow his father if he had a child himself.

At the back of the studio a huge blow-up of the Super-Celeste was in position. The image, taken as if the plane was flying straight at you, gave the machine a fat, ugly, ferocious perspective. The floor was stacked with mock-ups of missiles and bombs. The idea was that Celeste display herself amongst this weaponry wearing what looked like a faded army battledress, unbuttoned almost to the waist. And carry a gun. And look "Heroic. We're trying to get the feel of a Soviet Army poster." They had even brought a small, skinny Vietnamese child of ten whom she was to "mother".

All of it, thought Celeste, was obscene, crude, impossible. Never before had she walked out on a session. Hideous though the clothes were, they were from one of the top houses, and the proprietor was fluttering about in frenzied display of his own personality. A deal of money had changed hands to make this session possible. (Euro-Aviat Syndication had taken its cut by allowing Celeste to model in association with the plane. It had not been explained to her, when her name was bestowed on the plane that a contract would be drawn up on her behalf by the Euro-Aviat publicity machine. Papa Levitte had not told her he would be making money out of the gift he had made her.)

After twenty minutes the proprietor of the battledresses said, "Now *please* darling. Do try to look ferocious."

· She laid down her gun and said: "I'm sorry. I can't go on with this."

"Why not?"

Celeste breathed deeply. And for the first time in her life started answering back.

"Because it's obscene. The clothes are obscene. The idea is obscene. It is obscene to bring this child here."

"Now listen my darling," said the fashion-house proprietor, "you don't talk to me like that." The picture editor interrupted, "Celeste," he said, "do you want to go home?"

"Yes," she said.

"I'll get you a car."

A heavy silence fell across the studio. She disappeared into the changing rooms and left the proprietor bleating.

When the picture editor returned, after putting Celeste into her cab with a warm hug, the man was still bleating.

After a little while the picture editor interrupted again. "Listen Marc," he said, "don't try that kind of 'she'll never work again' crap. That girl's never walked out on anything before. This time she has and she's right. The clothes are pissing awful. The idea *is* obscene and I wish I had her guts to say so first. Now you can get *me* fired. I'm taking this poor brat home too."

Celeste, to preserve her make-up, stayed dry-eyed all the way to the apartment. Then she paid off the cab, ran up the stairs, and flung herself into the attic and on to their bed. She began to sob. They were sobs of rage. "Pigs!" she cried, "pigs!"

"How about a nice cup of coffee?" said Crispin Bridge.

She caught her breath and choked: "Who are you?"

"I let myself in. I'm looking after Daniel for the week. Who are the pigs?"

He stood there so calmly, so much as if he had every right to be there, that Celeste was unable to speak.

"*How* did you get in?" she asked.

"I opened the door. Been here for hours."

"I locked it."

"I know you did. But I've got this trick of being able to open doors when it's cold outside. I'm not a burglar."

"Are you anything to do with that letter?"

"I don't think so. What letter?"

"I had a letter. It doesn't matter. You'll have to come back later."

"All right," said Bridge, "when shall I come back? Can I have a cup of coffee first? I'll make it. You go on beating the bed." He strolled off into the kitchen. "Nice place," he called from the kitchen. "Where's the coffee though?"

She followed him to the door and watched him busy with the coffee pot. "How long have you known Daniel?" she asked.

"I haven't met him yet," said Bridge.

She looked at him in amazement. He started opening cupboard doors looking for the coffee. To her surprise she found herself telling him it was the third cupboard on the left.

"Thank you," he said. "Can I telephone Daniel?"

"Yes," she said, "*I'll* telephone him. I'll do that now."

But she didn't move while he measured out the coffee. And when he had done so he turned to look at her in the doorway. The man had wide, pale blue eyes and looked at her with complete openness. It was the way he looked at everybody. Though Celeste was not to know that, she found something in the way he looked at her totally bewildering, yet somehow familiar. (Later she was able to define its familiarity: it was like looking at the eye of a camera.)

"What do you mean, you're looking after Daniel?"

"Well," said Bridge. "It's a big week. Don't want another thing like that pilot, the one who got killed."

"You mean Euro-Aviat has sent you?"

"No. Daniel's idea."

"Do you think he's in danger?"

"Could be. Both of you. If you're his girl."

"I suppose we *could* be. I hadn't thought of that. What a pity you *weren't* looking after Jean-Paul. Did you know *him?* He was a very close friend. You're a sort of bodyguard are you?"

"That's about it. Where is Daniel now?"

"I'm sorry, I'll ring him."

As she dialled his film studio, Bridge said: "Just tell him the chap he wants to see is here. Maybe I wasn't supposed to tell you about looking after him. And I don't want to get the sack before I start or I'll lose my week's wages."

She smiled at him. She felt reassured. It was a relief to know this large, calm, blond Englishman would be around until the flight. She sipped his coffee—lavishly too strong—while waiting for the phone to connect. Everything was going to be all right. She was glad the man was here. They kept a little hearth in the attic still, and she set a match to the fragrant logs already piled in its iron embrace.

"Everything is going to be all right," Murray informed Senator Mackenzie. The two men stood side by side in a latrine erected in a corner of the lawn. The reception was in full swing. The evening had taken the edge off the heat, but the humidity was colossal. Cicadas hammered away in the velvet dark between the grounds of CSIRO and the freeway. "You can pass the word we're ready to do a deal on butter and wool."

Senator Mackenzie smiled patronizingly. He shrugged.

"Well?" said Murray impatiently. "Isn't that one of the main stumbling blocks? What's the matter *now*?" A drunk RAAF lieutenant staggered in, and the two men left as if they were not acquainted. Melvyn Murray, known in most nations for his cool and collected approach, began to feel himself fraying at the edges. He watched Mackenzie strolling away to join the group round the Australian Prime Minister, whose huge laugh had been heard pealing across the scene all evening.

Ackermann, he noted, was not only safely arrived in Canberra but deep in conversation with the secretary to the Defence Review Committee. With a grim little smile, Murray set off to join them. A knot of RAAF wives were in his way and he elbowed two of them aside to get at his quarry. "And thank *you*," said one shrilly, as the grey-haired American pushed on.

"The tragedy was, of course, that the Japanese only entered the war because you Europeans cut off their oil supplies," said the Defence Secretary as Murray joined the group.

"Do you really think so?" said Ackermann. "*Hello*, Melvyn. I'm sure you two know each other."

"Glad to see you Melvyn," said the Secretary. They'd met earlier in the day, but the Department of Defence man had this much finesse at least, noted Murray.

"Have a good trip in?" Murray asked Ackermann.

"The usual thing," said Ackermann politely—but with enough edge to let Murray know he knew about the *unusual* drive to Canberra the American had made.

"Get you another drink," said the Secretary, and stepped off to the booth. Ackermann revolved towards Murray. The man was obviously pretty drunk, Murray realized.

"What do you imagine is taking place?" said Ackermann. "I am being treated like some kind of beauty queen." He gave a simpering little laugh. "You must believe me, Murray, it's all totally unexpected. But I'll do my best. You can see I'm doing my best to drink myself to death. Will that help?"

Murray clapped him on the shoulder. "May the best politician win is all I can say," said Melvyn. The Defence Secretary returned. Murray now understood why there was a latrine specially built on the very lawn of the reception, outside the gleaming dome of CSIRO: these Australians were serious drinkers.

"Surely," said Ackermann loudly, taking up the conversation where it had broken off, with all the precision of a drunk. "The Japanese went to war from natural native malice."

"Easy," said the Secretary softly, "we have a hundred Jap guests here tonight. We don't want to make life unpleasant for the horrible little yellow bastards." Ackermann tilted his head back to laugh.

"Jesus Christ," thought Murray. He downed the drink that had been brought him.

"So far as I remember," he said acidly, "Europe's main contribution around here was to lose Singapore. I know the guns weren't *really* pointing the wrong way. I'm thinking about the British digging trenches. Yes? And then they thought paratroops could land in the soft earth so they filled them in again. Yes? And, what was it? They requisitioned 1,200 bicycles in mistake for 120."

There was an embarrassed silence.

"Leave me out," said Ackermann. "In those days I was on the other side anyway." He tipped his head back and laughed.

"I don't think you're being fair," said the Secretary. "After all, the British were defending an island the same size as the Isle of Wight. How long would the Isle of Wight have stood out if the rest of Britain had been occupied? Singapore's problem was a water problem. Half the water for Singapore came from South Jahore—fifteen million gallons a day. And the Japanese had got to South Jahore. And the other half came from the island itself out of two reservoirs. I know, because my uncle was running them. Four out of every five of those gallons was going to waste. Because the Japanese were on to them. How in hell could the British have gone on fighting that kind of fact? They had a million civilians in Singapore. Children were dying in the streets."

"That's war," said Murray, briefly. "Churchill told Singapore to fight to the last man. And they didn't. They didn't fight. There were 140,000 troops in Singapore and the Japs came in with 125,000. I'm not saying that's a good thing or a bad thing. My job is selling planes that kill men, women and children. Now I love men, women and children. As a human being myself. I also think my job is worthwhile. I don't think the British should have given up Singapore without a fight. And with all due respect, I think you Australians need to remember who did fight in the South Pacific. It wasn't Europe. It was America."

The Secretary raised his eyebrows. "Excuse me, I must rejoin the Premier. Most interesting to meet you, Murray, and doubtless we'll meet again. Do remember, won't you, to be polite to our Japanese friends. We are only reminding Australia about Darwin to let them know why we need to spend a lot of money on aeroplanes next week. But we have to reassure the Japanese we're not defending ourselves against *them*. That's why it would be very tactless to buy aeroplanes in exchange for the butter and wool we now sell to Japan." He drifted away.

Murray crunched a piece of ice from his glass savagely. So the bastards were even going to fight on that front too.

Ackermann smiled happily. "I always thought of you as a tactful man," he said to Murray.

"Don't be too smug, Ackermann," said Murray in sudden, rash anger. "Even the Australians aren't going to buy a plane that hasn't yet got off the ground."

On cue, a loudspeaker hit the dark, warm night with a cough and a hum.

Murray and Ackermann listened to the Australian Prime

Minister's speech with care. "We are about to make a decision in this country," said the Prime Minister, "that will confirm our ability to protect this continent. Australia has never been an aggressor in international conflict. *Lebensraum* is the last thing any Australian would think of fighting for. But it is prudent and right that we have the power, by land and sea and air, to protect our Federation."

The Premier still towered above the crowd. He was in his seventy-fifth year: a huge and still dominating figure, bronzed and gaunt. In his old age the campaign to re-arm Australia had been his own personal and ferociously held mission. The fact that inter-continental missile sites were about to be dug deep in the arid interior was his own achievement. Murray watched from the shadow of a eucalyptus tree as Ackermann strolled over to the Premier and was introduced.

"And how is Henri?" he heard the Premier say.

He could catch nothing else of the words spoken. But it was enough. As soon as Ackermann bowed out, Murray caught up with him, ostensibly to make his farewells.

"Tell me," said Murray, "does this man *know* your Henri Levitte?"

"Oh yes," said Ackermann. "I think they both used to fly aeroplanes. What was that man who flew round the world—no, he sailed round the world and sailed to Australia—no, *flew* to Australia?"

"Chichester?"

"That's the name. Yes, they always knew each other. It's what you call caramaderies. No: *camaraderie*. Way back from the old days of string and paper aeroplanes."

Murray tried to pierce through the alcoholic fog. "What you mean is that the Premier of Australia and Henri Levitte are old school pals."

"News to me," said Ackermann, vaguely, "news to me."

"I don't believe it," said Murray, "I simply don't believe it. By the law of averages something has to start going right soon."

Celeste still kept a watchful eye on Crispin Bridge as she waited for Daniel's studio to answer.

"May I speak to Daniel Levitte? It's Celeste."

Daniel's day had gone no better than Celeste's. With so little time, he thought, this was a pitiful way to spend it. For the twentieth time too, the girl in front of the camera held her hands over her breasts and tried to look surprised. At each attempt her surprise diminished and Daniel's increased. Even by accident, he thought, she ought to get it right once.

The idea was that by eating *Minbisc* a woman would suddenly find herself losing more than her excess weight. It was not a startling idea, but it would do. Daniel was explaining it again when he got the call to the phone.

"The man you want to see is here," said Celeste. Daniel felt his heart grip in a spasm. It was beginning, then. The real thing. The contact had worked.

"Why are you home?" he asked, "who is he?"

"Can you come back: now please?" she asked.

"I'll be there."

"Daniel, this is all right, isn't it?" she said urgently, "you want him to stay until you come?"

"Yes. Don't bother him with questions."

He could be like his father too, she thought.

Making brief excuses, Daniel told his team to get on with it. They were used to this. In fact they were relieved to see him go. As soon as the door of the studio shut behind him his partner, Lagrange, walked straight up to the yawning actress and gave her a good clout on the bottom. She began to look wonderfully surprised. Daniel, in Lagrange's opinion, was far too nice a man to make it as one of the world's greatest film directors. No wonder the outfit was down to making cut-price TV commercials in Flanders in winter.

Daniel drove, fast and dangerously on the wet streets, to the apartment. At a traffic jam he bent down, to get out of the sight line of any passing gendarme and took a gulp from his hip flask. Then he turned the radio on. It was a pop song with the refrain "We shall not pass this way again." He stubbed the sound out and swung into the back streets around the Opera. He wondered how to get Celeste out of the place for an hour or two. His heart pounded, his stomach churned and he was disgusted at these signs of physical cowardice. Well, his body would have to look after itself. Nothing would stop him. From this moment he would shut his mind against any second thoughts: they would be no more than the twitchings and protestations of a frightened body. Yet he enjoyed this battle against his own weakness. For the first time in his life he felt he was taking action, that everything was becoming clear. As he got out of the car the very air seemed harder, more real. The icy rain stung against his cheek and he welcomed it.

When he opened the door to the apartment, Celeste hurried to greet him, pressing her stomach against his in the way they liked to embrace. Over her shoulder he saw Bridge. He was smoking another Disque Bleu.

"I came home," said Celeste. "It was so awful there today. *He* had let himself in."

He patted her shoulder.

"Let me have a word with him," he said.

"Do you want me to go out?"

"I'm sorry, yes."

She shrugged. "Then I'll go out. What's the matter, Daniel?"

"Nothing. I'll deal with it."

As she put on her Siberian wolf coat she said: "We'll eat out tonight, Daniel? Or shall I collect some meat and make us a rikstafel?"

"We'll have to eat in," said Bridge.

She looked from one to the other, then left them.

"What did you mean by that?" Daniel asked Bridge, amazed.

"I explained to your girl," said Bridge. "I'm your bodyguard for the week."

"I want you for one thing," said Daniel, "then I don't want to see you again. And *I* make the arrangements."

Bridge smiled at him.

They faced up to each other. So this was the man who wanted to blow up his father's aeroplane. Well, he looked crazy enough, thought Bridge. Wild may have thought the man was sane, but Bridge had worked for missionaries before—that was the word for them. People eaten up with a private grievance and too feeble to rid themselves of it alone.

"You'd better start telling me all about it," said Bridge.

PART THREE

SEVEN HUNDRED MILES from Dallas, Texas, a great eagle woke from his open-eyed sleep. The ledge he occupied in the canyon was beginning to warm in the sun. Instinct told him of the thermal currents now pushing up from the canyon floor, a thousand metres below this perch. It was time to go hunting. The mineral-bright, hooded eyes flashed hungrily. The powerful tendons in his legs clenched to hold his grip on the rock as the wings spread like sails in the wind. The heavy, burnished bird squirted a jet of white faeces over the rim of the ledge and opened his beak.

Yes, it was time to hunt. In a muscular spasm he shook his golden and white feathers into a smooth and polished shell. The still fresh air began to course around the powerful body. For a second he crouched, feeling the rising wind against his breast, and then lifted over the narrow ledge on the eddies and thrusts of the canyon.

Arguably, it was from this decision to fly, at this moment, by this eagle, that the entire fate of Daniel Levitte and two international aerospace companies was determined. And perhaps— since they too were dealers in the air—this was the luck they deserved.

Ten minutes before the eagle had lifted into the rising air of the ravine the North-West pilot Zucker had taken off for a low-level exercise: this time, *not* over the telemetry station. No-one had told him to stay clear of the canyon, however. It hadn't occurred to anyone to tell him—with the entire desert available why should anybody try to fly *under* it, which is what dipping into the canyon effectively meant.

After the last trip, Zucker now had a small continuing, enjoyable war going with his masters. He knew perfectly well that to dip below the horizon for a few seconds would bring Ground Control out in a green sweat as he disappeared from radio contact. Nor did he intend admitting it afterwards—let them check the system hand over hand, thought Zucker.

Below him he saw the canyon: a puckered operation scar across the huge brown belly of the desert. He pulled up into a howling climb fifty miles beyond it, then flipped the plane over and dropped back into his approach. Deliberately he made the descent steep enough to confuse his monitors into thinking it was a routine approach to a low-level pass.

Ahead, the scar unfolded into the rock and shadow—each equally solid from the air—of the Yellow Canyon. Zucker had planned it out the night before. There was a six-kilometre straight between the jagged sandstone walls and he had no need to worry about turbulence in a machine like this. He would be below the horizon for five point five or six seconds: just enough to wet the pants of the wise men back at the base.

The scar in the ground spread up to meet him as he dived. The dark blue shadows on the starboard flank seeming to jut out like rocks themselves. Ahead, and 4,000 feet below the rim of the desert, the river flashed like a snake's belly.

It would be easy, easy.

Zucker tipped into his final swoop, beginning to pull out of it the moment before the golden walls of the canyon either side drew up around him. Up to his very last moment of life he was pulling gently on his controls and died with a small smile of satisfaction on his face.

Bird strike remains one of the stupid, intractable problems of aviation—and becomes only more intractable, more devastating the swifter man flies. Even a sparrow becomes a bullet if you hit it hard enough.

The eagle had a mass several hundred times that of a sparrow. The sudden roaring in the sky told him of the plane's approach to the canyon: and in the last seconds before the collision the eagle caught the dark approaching shadow and the hint of pressure in the clear air. Beating his wings he did what he knew to do against any peril: rise to meet it.

The impact was terrible and total. The sky, for Zucker, smashed in a blinding moment into darkness as the eagle hurtled through the canopy. Though still technically alive, the pilot was blinded, his nose spread like a pat of butter across his forehead.

The eagle's blood, bones and feathers were distributed nearly as finely as an aerosol mist across the cockpit—though the skull and upper bones of the wingspan had compacted into a ball of bloodied whiteness and driven like a cannon ball into the pilot's belly.

In his last second of life, the pilot, drowning in the blood being hammered out of his body, seemed gracefully to tilt the aeroplane until its under-wing caught the sun. When it hit the side of the canyon it was at forty-fve degrees to the rock.

The fireball of orange and black boiled into the silence of the rocks, and the thunder of it rolled ten miles between the walls, the echoes of the first impact easily drowning the lazy, tumbling clatter of the fragments dropping into the river far below.

The only memorial to the accident, thirty seconds after its occurrence, was a star-shaped stain of black and silver high up on the wall of the canyon, and a small brush fire in the tumble-weed and scrub at the base of the cliffs, where a hurtling engine had carried enough of its fuel connections flaming behind it to the ground to ignite the dry stems. And a lot of feathers still drifting down.

That, and an absence on screens back at the base. The pen-traces now drew pure, simple straight lines up the paper. It took Control two minutes, not three, to conclude the worst had happened and a pre-arranged security perimeter clamped down like an iron ring around the event. When North-West Aero-space lost a machine on test they had ways of keeping the fact close to their chests. Immediately, to the world beyond the green-glassed walls of the air control headquarters, the news went out that Zucker was on a "fly-on" mission: would be landing someplace else.

And indeed, that was more or less true.

Nevertheless, it was from this event that the fortunes of North-West Aerospace began to pick up. It was as if this totally unexpected, unfair disaster, on top of everything else, was the blow on the base of the spine they needed. It hurt, but it got them back on their feet. The President of North-West got the news in half an hour. He was about to board his flight to Canberra when the airline jeep rushed across the tarmac with the coded message.

Instead, he returned to the airport and told his aides to

organize a flight to Washington. When, one hour later, he was on his way there, the aides were left behind. They now had one plain task to fulfil, and the cases of evidence and propaganda destined for the President's mission in Canberra were flown on in his absence with the other nine North-West executives hurriedly assembled for the mission. The President's personal staff had now, in the light of this new but still private piece of bad news, to arrange a meeting between Eber Carroll and Secretary of State, James ("Jim") Parker. It was time to appeal for help from the top.

"When can you get it?" said Daniel as soon as Celeste had left. His eyes flickered away from Bridge's appraising stare.

"That depends. I need to know some things first."

"Go on then."

"Well, let's start with money. That's a nice simple one."

"You mean *I've* got to pay you?"

"Who else?"

"Well . . . your people."

"I haven't got any people."

"North-West Aerospace."

"Never heard of them."

Daniel thought about it. Bridge helped him out.

"I overheard two people talking in a café. How's that for a working agreement."

"So, I've got to pay you."

"Fifty thousand francs," said Bridge generously.

"I can't get that quickly."

"Then I know someone in Basle you can borrow it from. But he'll charge you twenty-five per cent interest, and if you don't pay him then he will be round to collect. He does the finance for East German refugees coming over the Rumanian border."

Daniel smiled. "You wouldn't recommend him."

"Not really, no."

"You're very businesslike," said Daniel with distaste.

"I am businesslike. I don't usually deal with amateurs."

Daniel stood up. The man's eyes chilled him. He began to walk about the room.

"I'll get the money."

"Right. Now let's get on before your girl gets back. You want this for Friday. Or before. What do you want to do a thing like this for anyway?"

"My affair."

"It's my affair too if I'm taking any risks. Now you'd better understand this, Mr Levitte. You're not buying something off a shelf. If this thing is going to happen it's going to happen because you and me co-operate. All the way. So the first thing is you telling me why you want to do this. You're rich, you've got a beautiful woman. What the hell is it about? Are you Red or something?"

Daniel laughed. "No, I'll show you what it's about. *Who* it's about." He got the Super-Celeste brochure from the record rack where he had filed it. "See that man? That's my father. Great man, my father. Maybe you can meet him. If you're my bodyguard for the week you can come to my sister's funeral. I'd like you to see the monster."

"Yes," said Bridge, "I might do that. You want to blow up this plane because you don't like your father? That's a hell of a thing to do. I don't like my old man much. He used to kick me downstairs till I got big enough to kick him back. But even so."

He picked up the brochure and studied the hard, obsessive face of Henri Levitte.

"Well, I suppose it's up to you. I strangled all of my father's pigeons once when I was nine. Go on."

"The day Jean-Paul died I rang my father. I wanted to find Marie-Thérèse. You see she and Jean-Paul were—into a thing together. Had been for years. And that bastard wouldn't speak to me. He could have told her before she got in her car. She killed herself in it."

Daniel poured himself another drink, the bottle clattered on the rim of his glass.

"As far as I'm concerned he killed my sister. It wasn't just doing that on the phone. He'd fucked up her whole life. And mine. And Jean-Paul's for that matter."

"Tell me about him, Jean-Paul. He was having a thing with your sister. Did you mind?"

"You don't want to go into all that, do you?"

"Yes," said Bridge, "I do. He's dead, isn't he. Your sister's dead. That's a pretty high accident rate for one week. What do you know about Jean-Paul's death?"

"Why should I know anything?"

"Well you might. Maybe you had it in for him too."

They looked at each other across the table. Neither spoke for thirty seconds. "Look," said Daniel, "the three of us grew up together from kids. My father kind of adopted Jean-Paul. His own father had died in the last days of the war, before he was born. You know what the three of us used to plan all the time? We were going to build our own boat and sail away somewhere that old bastard would never find us. I can't talk to you about this."

He shook his drink round in his glass and finished it.

"Go on," said Bridge. "I don't mind listening."

"He didn't treat us like kids. We were just three more of his bloody machines. Marie-Thérèse's job was to look after Maman. You can meet her too. He made her into a total invalid. Jean-Paul's was to be the next Henri Levitte. Of course, I wasn't good enough for that. He used to tell me that about twice a week since I was three."

"Sounds a good reason for you not liking Jean-Paul much."

"No. It got us closer together."

"Why didn't you all clear out?" said Bridge.

"Yes," said Daniel. "You wouldn't understand that, would you? I don't know. I think it's what I meant about him treating us like his machines. We belonged to him. He'd always got some way of keeping his hands on us, doling out money, promises. I was going to have a job in the company—that's another story too. And Jean-Paul, if you're interested, he started making love with my sister when she was about sixteen. It went on for about five years before father found out. He really went wild. Two of his machines having it away with each other. Just about the worst thing he could imagine. So he bought Jean-Paul off. He fixed a marriage for him, made him an allowance to look after the rest of his family, gave him a chance to fly Euro-Aviat aeroplanes. A good move. It's what Jean-Paul always wanted, the flying."

"But he went on with your sister."

"Yes. They bought a little apartment together. Went there when they could."

"So he took the money and the marriage and the career and went on with your sister anyway. That seems fair enough."

Bridge picked up the brochure again and looked at the profile of the Euro-Aviat boss. "I reckon a man like your father would have been delighted to know that."

"They took a lot of care he didn't. We had to be good at learning to keep secrets since we were kids. If we wanted a private life." Daniel laughed bitterly. "Actually, it did look as though it could come unstuck a few months back. Jean-Paul used to sleep around a bit anyway. I think he had a few funny tastes on the side. His wife, Estelle, was beginning to wonder about some of his nights away. She threw a real fit about three months back, apparently. Threatened she'd get divorce detectives to follow him round and then go and tell Henri."

Bridge dropped the brochure. "Divorce detectives?" he said calmly.

"Nothing came of it," said Daniel.

"I think I'll have one of your filthy drinks," said Bridge.

"Okay. I'll get you a glass."

He poured Bridge a stiff measure of the clear yellow liquid, and Bridge watched it turn milky and obscure as the water followed.

"How do you know nothing came of it?" he asked.

"You mean if she'd gone round to my father with that sort of stuff? The sky would have fallen in."

Bridge swallowed the drink in one gulp. "That's right," he said.

"Anyway," said Daniel, "that's the happy family history. Three kids. Two of us dead. If you want to know why I'm into this thing, that's why. My sister is dead. My best friend is dead." He spread his hands almost apologetically.

"Now, let's talk about the bomb."

"All right," said Bridge, "let's talk about the bomb. But do you mind if I say one thing? It can be easier to take out a man than a machine."

"Maybe," said Daniel, "I've thought about that too. I couldn't do it. This machine *is* him anyway. It'll do."

Bridge stood up, went to get a note pad from his case and started explaining.

"Okay," he said, "you want to blow the plane. I've got to get you something that will get through the security on the base. So it's got to be small."

"There won't be any security on me," said Daniel. "That's the whole point. I can just walk through with it. No-one else could."

"Don't count on it," said Bridge. "That place will be crawling with security after what happened to the pilot. I'm making you a letter bomb. It'll have a strip of plastic on one side you peel off and then an impact adhesive underneath it. Is this the colour of the plane?" he pointed to the brochure. "That's right," said Daniel, "the famous Euro-Aviat blue."

"Well that's the colour we'll package it in. What you have to do is stick it on the plane. If you're flying the thing it's reasonable you'd walk round it, right?" He studied the picture of the Super-Celeste again.

"How the fuck *are* you going to fly in this thing?" he asked. "It's a single-seater."

"Not this one," said Daniel. "This is a trainer."

"Anyway," said Bridge, "it isn't going to fly." He looked at the sleek outline of the plane. He could see Daniel's point. If you wanted to hurt someone hard, you could do it by breaking up something as beautiful as this. "It's a pretty machine," said Bridge. "A lot of people put in the hours making that. You're going to be popular with them."

"They can make something else," said Daniel. "Transport planes, civil aircraft. If you're going to get sentimental about it you'd better drop out."

"Now don't try and annoy me," said Bridge quietly. "I work for the money. If I took time to worry about my clients' hang-ups and morals I might get an ulcer."

Daniel was angry too. "You were the one who wanted to hear about it. I apologize if I bored you."

"You don't bore me, Daniel. Let's get on."

"Why has it got to go on the outside of the plane?" said Daniel. "It would do a lot more damage inside, wouldn't it?"

"Sure," said Bridge, "but we've got to detonate this thing, haven't we. We can't carry something with a time clock in it. Far too bulky. You want something that goes off exactly the moment you want it to go off. So what you are going to have is a little transistor radio. It'll be a real one, too, if anyone wants to turn it on to see. But it won't just be a radio. It will be a transmitter—like they use to control model aeroplanes. When you're ready, you can press the FM switch and it will transmit to blow the bomb."

"Even so," said Daniel, "why can't the bomb be inside the plane? Somebody could see it stuck on the outside."

"Yes. And someone could just notice you climbing up a ladder to get inside," explained Bridge patiently. "So we just have to take the chance no-one is going to notice you strolling round the *outside*. There's plenty of places they *won't* notice—if you put it on as late as possible."

"Where do you recommend?"

"It's up to you," said Bridge. "What do you want to do to this thing? Do you want to bend it for a week, or do you want to blow it for keeps?"

Daniel looked at the picture of the Super-Celeste. He said: "Well, why not just tell me the options."

"Okay," said Bridge. "I'll give you three options. Only just remember one thing. The transmitter is highly directional. Wherever you put the packet you've got to be able to get in a clear sight-line to it. You'll have up to 75 yards' range. Now, you see this thing here?" In the picture, directly below the cockpit, a small, slim fin broke the smooth underbelly of the plane. It looked like the diminutive keel of a sailing boat.

"That's either a UHF antenna or a TACAN aerial," said Bridge. "It's easy to get at. Our packet is going to be about seven inches by five so it will fit really nicely. Quite invisible from one side of the plane anyway. The rudder pedals and radar console will be directly above. It won't be much of a bang, because the bomb is going to blow straight off it, but it will certainly stop the flight."

"Okay," said Daniel, "I've got that. What's the next one?"

"Well, just behind that is the nose wheel. Right under the pilot's arse. When the plane is on the ground there are two doors that flap down. You'd do a lot more damage there because some of the blast would hit right inside the plane. You'd knock out the starboard control console, quite a lot of hydraulics for the nose wheel. You'd probably start a small fire. I don't know about this plane, but if you were lucky the belt feed for the cannon would be near enough. That could really start something."

5

"Inside the doors of the nose wheel," said Daniel. "Right. Go on."

Bridge moved his finger farther back down the plane. Beneath the belly of the plane below the fifty-five degree backward sweep of the wings there was a fat, torpedo-shaped pod.

"That's one of the missiles," said Daniel, "they haven't put those on yet."

"It isn't one of the missiles," said Bridge. "That's the centreline fuel tank. There's about a thousand litres of fuel in there. Now when the plane is on the ground, and the wheels are down, the main wheel leg door is going to be down too, right? That's going to come down over that tank. If you stuck it in between that door and the tank then you'd blow the whole plane. But I wouldn't do that in the hangar, unless you want to roast Henri Levitte and the French President and everyone else."

Daniel gave no hint of anything he might be feeling. He went on studying the plane's profile with fascinated absorption. Then he said: "This packet. The bomb. If you don't think I can walk in with it—How do I get it in?"

"Well," said Bridge, "that's why they're called letter bombs. They look like letters. Okay, you're taking a risk with the transmitter. If there's a thorough security check someone might open it up and take a look. They'd have to be pretty good to see what the wiring meant. But they might do it. They might just fiddle around with it. I wouldn't risk it."

"Start it transmitting?"

"That's right."

"And I'd have the letter in my pocket?"

"That's right, and it's not the only risk."

"What else?"

"Well. You've got to get to the position when you can be walking around the plane with a transistor in one hand and a bloody great envelope in the other. That could strike somebody as curious. You'll be in a flying suit. There's going to be about three or four loyal employees stripping you down to your jock strap and dressing you up again. They're pretty complicated, these suits. You've got to have a good reason to be carrying a letter round with you. So what you've got to do is write a letter to your father. That's reasonable. You're going up in the sky on a test flight and you want to write a note to your papa in case you don't come back. That'll be nice, won't it. You can write his name on the packet."

"But I'm not going to give it to him," said Daniel. "And what happens if there *is* a screen, like they have at airports. Isn't the packet going to show something up?"

"No," said Bridge. "Because the packet you are going to take with you is going to be a letter for your father. If anyone opens it, that's what they're going to find. The letter you take in is just a letter. Anyone gets suspicious about the radio, starts fiddling with it, starts checking you out, all you've got is a letter."

"I don't understand," said Daniel.

"Well," said Bridge, "the screens they have at airports. They put men through them, things show up in their pockets. But they don't do that with women's handbags. They just look through women's handbags. We're going to have two envelopes, Daniel. The one you take in is just a letter for your father. I presume Celeste is going to be there on the day, right? The one Celeste takes in is the bomb. You're going to tell her to have it with her on the base and give it to your father after you take off. And when you meet her on the base you're going to say, 'I've written another letter Celeste. Give me the one you've got and take this one to him instead'. You understand that? If they sort through Celeste's handbag, which even I doubt: nobody is going to take a chance of opening a personal letter. People could get suspicious about you Daniel, but not her."

"I don't like doing that," said Daniel. "She's not involved."

"She'll be all right. She wouldn't open it if you told her not to, would she?"

They both heard her key in the lock.

"She's back," said Bridge.

Daniel frowned. "Okay," he said. "I don't like it. Maybe we can think of another way later. You go and get the stuff together."

The members of the Defence Review Committee in Canberra were surprised to be summoned so early on Tuesday morning to attend on the American ambassador. Many were still needing a few hours more peace and quiet to recover from the Darwin Day celebrations of the night before.

The usual blinding sunlight, and the abrasive tones of the American Ambassador Leo Zanelli (who had not been given this appointment for his mildness of manner), were a rough start to the new day.

Zanelli shed no time in diplomatic courtesies. He had been up all night picking up the pieces of Murray's bungled remarks and taking his new briefing from Washington.

"Do you mind telling me why you people are so keen to buy a machine that hasn't even lifted its ass off the ground?" he demanded. "Why we aren't being given the courtesy of serious consideration?"

"Are you summoning us here to tell us we don't have a sovereign right to make up our own minds how we choose?" said Don Laird. Zanelli looked him over. The old Queensland politician was one of the closest to the Australian Premier, Zanelli knew.

"You're damn right you don't have the right to treat us like shit," said Zanelli. "Not while we are providing you with your missiles."

"I wasn't aware they were a gift," said Laird.

Mackenzie decided it was time to contribute his piece too. Before, in the present ugly mood, this crude American tried to spell out Mackenzie's niche in North-West's payroll.

"I think you Americans have always been at liberty to defend the Pacific if you chose to do so," he said. "The fact is that you've pulled out of South East Asia and put the burden on us. Which, as Mr Laird says, we have paid to take on—that means we buy where we choose."

"All right," said Zanelli, "I'll spell it out. You make a decision for the Super-Celeste next week and watch what happens to you. We'll see to it we bring you lot down. We'll make every inch we can out of this. We'll see to it the Australians know the following facts about this deal. One: that you turned down a superior plane which you could have bought through trade credits. But you prefer dealing with the Japanese trade-wise. There's still a lot of Australians don't agree with that policy. Two: that we would have let you build this plane at Mascot and Fishermens Bend. Thus trebling the size of your own aerospace industry and putting it into a world class for the 1990s. And three: that as a result of your hostile decision to buy the Super-Celeste the United States is reviewing its policy of supplying you with inter-continental missiles. You accuse us of being soft on China. Well, you just see how soft we can get."

Zanelli's words had the effect he desired. The Australians stared at him as if he had just announced World War III.

Zanelli stood up. "That's it, gentlemen. I'm sorry to be so rough. You just need to be shaken out of your fancy dreams down here. Every man, woman and child in America has contributed to the cost of those missile bases you're building in the Northern Territory. And they're fed up with the shit about us pulling out of South East Asia. North-West Aerospace needs that order from you. It deserves that order from you. And you need to place it. Now I suggest you tell that to your distinguished Prime Minister, who was too busy to see me this morning, which is why I asked you instead."

And he stamped out of the room.

It was Mackenzie who was delegated to tell the old warlord, the Australian Premier, the bad news. By general agreement, the Review Committee felt that enough was enough. That the limit had been reached in rocking the boat. They knew the old man's determination to buy the French plane; his desire to announce a swift decision so that any generous offers from the Americans would look like so much window dressing after the window was broken. But the committee had been convinced by Ambassador Zanelli. Without missiles, Australia would be back to the soft, vulnerable underbelly days of the seventies. He *had* to see sense.

"*And* there's ten top men from North-West arriving this evening," said Mackenzie. "They'll be spreading all the dirt in the book. I don't think you can go on with this."

The old man took Mackenzie's arm and led him over the lawn. They sat down in the shade of a eucalyptus, on white chairs before the pond and foundation where the Premier liked best to work.

"I don't think they'll spread much dirt in your absence," he said. "It wouldn't look good, would it, if the Americans started making trouble while the Review Committee was abroad doing its job."

Mackenzie frowned. "But we are not abroad."

"You will be," said the Premier. "You're all going to fill a long-standing invitation to fly to Paris and see the Super-Celeste in action on Friday." He paused to let it sink in. "I'm convinced about that plane, Mackenzie. I don't *want* this country relying on American missiles *and* planes. The Americans would never dare pull out on the missiles. I don't want any confrontation with them this week. I just want all you people out of the way and they can cool their heels until you get back. Mackenzie, I don't like the way these Americans do business. I don't like all this pressure and dealing and blackmail. We're buying our own defence of this continent, not paying the Americans to do the job for us. When you get to Paris, Mackenzie, you want to take good note of that man, Henri Levitte. When I met him first he was a lad of twenty. He flew here in a little plane he'd practically built himself. That's what aviation is about. It's about brave, tough, dedicated men, not all this political crap. That's the sort of thing we want in this country. That French plane, Mackenzie, is a beauty. It's a thoroughbred. I know a bit about planes. The Americans made this plane by getting a committee to sit on it until they come up with a flying trash can. Now this man Levitte is an individual. The plane is an individual. It's the product of one single-minded vision. It's honest. I like things and people to be honest."

He stood up. Mackenzie began to feel nervous. Nevertheless, the Prime Minister walked him back to the house with his hand on his elbow. Then, at the door, he said: "And when you get back, Mackenzie, I want your resignation from public life. I think it's time you retired to your property in the Snowy Mountains. Or maybe you'd like to get a job full-time with North-West Aerospace."

It was dismissal—final and complete. He tried to say: "I haven't done anything for these people."

The Premier looked at him in contempt. "I think that makes it worse, Mackenzie. I think that makes it worse. You haven't done a day's work for either master."

By nine that Monday evening in Paris, the police had received fifty sightings of the missing Claude. The fifty-first was the neighbour of the apartment that Jean-Paul Petit had acquired for his liaison with Marie-Thérèse. Marcel Derivat, who as a reward for his cleverness in tracking Claude thus far was in charge of the boring task of sifting the sightings, wearily put the fifty-first identification down as a low priority. The woman had sounded a typical nosy neighbour, and the address was unlikely as the haunt of a professional prostitute, even a high-class one like Claude. Derivat wished he had time to find out more about the excitement in the main operation room, but his superiors were keeping their discoveries to themselves. All he knew was that another girl had been persuaded to talk and had linked Claude with Hassin, a formerly well-known employer of call-girls who had recently mysteriously retired. During the afternoon the police had reached Hassin's room, broken the door open and found the dead Arab. The scrap of paper identifying the terrorist group from Algeria was of great interest.

Personally, Marcel Derivat thought this convenient clue almost too useful to be true. "It's not in their style," he had said to his chief. "Why didn't they claim the first killing?"

"Your phone's ringing," said his chief. Frustrated, Derivat went back to his narrow office and picked it up. It was the nosy neighbour again. This time she had seen a tall, blond man going in next door. She said she was going to barricade the door. Derivat promised her someone would call round. He noted the time. Ten-thirty. He wrote down the address. And wrote "Tall blond man sighted by neighbour entering apartment". Well, the place was on his own way home. He might as well call in and set everyone's mind at rest. Derivat was tired. He had been awake thirty-six hours and he wished for a little gratitude. Give it another half hour, he thought, and he'd pack it in.

Crispin Bridge was also feeling the day had gone on long enough. Twenty-four hours ago he had been drinking quietly in his Deptford flat, looking at travel brochures. Now he was, for the second time in the day, in a strange Paris apartment.

He had been over it thoroughly. It was a small, drab place, furnished with chintzy chairs and rickety antique pieces picked up cheaply in flea markets—an imitation of a home. A few trinkets of the dead lovers remained. The drawers were empty of papers, clothes and the rubbish of daily life. It was obviously a place to come to occasionally.

Bridge lay down on the unmade bed and rested his head on

the bright red night-dress left strewn across the pillow. He recognized that it was Claude's. There was no food except the rind of a congealing steak on an unwashed plate and an opened tin of haricot beans. He ate these, spooning them out of the tin as he lay on the bed. His jacket, its side pockets bulging with the two blue envelopes that the bomb-maker MacSweeney had completed for him an hour before, hung on a chair nearby. His gun under the pillow.

MacSweeney. God in Heaven, that had been a terrifying few hours. If he'd known how far downhill MacSweeney had gone since he'd first rescued him in Belfast he wouldn't have gone near him, he thought.

The little Irishman was living over a horse butcher's shop in a stink of drink, horseflesh and damp mattresses. Maybe that was just as well, because underlying the other stinks was the faint, sweet smell of MacSweeney's line of business—explosives.

"Jesus, MacSweeney," said Bridge, as he entered the bomb-maker's den, "don't you even keep the fucking door closed?"

MacSweeney was sitting cross-legged on the bed, studying a racing paper under a dim bare bulb.

"You don't want to worry about it," he said, not looking up. "I've paid my subscription for the year."

"What subscription?"

"To the fucking cops, who else?"

Bridge stepped cautiously into the room and sniffed the air in amazement.

"The cops know about you?" he said in alarm.

"I dope horses for a living," said MacSweeney. "It's nice to see you again."

MacSweeney. Five foot tall, still wearing his black beret; his face lined in grooves which no soap could reach. Not that it had much chance to.

MacSweeney owed Bridge his life, such as it was. There was no doubt that, when Bridge and his SAS patrol burst into Mac-Sweeney's bomb factory in Belfast, there should have been an unfortunate accident to MacSweeney there and then, to save everyone the embarrassment of an arrest and the expense of a trial. But Bridge, in his own way, had an instinct about people: he knew MacSweeney was different from the other IRA he'd met. On instinct, he had pushed him into a lavatory before the rest of the patrol arrived up the stairs—and told him to stay there.

The hunch had paid off. At the time, Bridge had wanted no more than a line of supply to a few of the guns coming over from America to the Republicans. He didn't intend to leave the SAS without some protection. It was a bonus to discover that MacSweeney was an artist in his own right: the little man from Armagh really didn't care a damn about politics. But he loved explosives. He loved making bombs, for their own sake. He was a craftsman.

"I've not done it yet," said MacSweeney. "I want your help, you see." He got off the bed and looked cautiously into a blackened tin mug. "Will you be having some tea? Something stronger?"

"No thank you," said Bridge quickly.

The little man went to his table and pressed a switch that cast a pool of bright light on the white oilcloth. It was the one oasis of cleanliness in the stinking room.

"Now then," said MacSweeney. "You want a big one." He spoke as if he was encouraging Bridge to buy a prize turkey.

"I told you what I wanted," said Bridge. "Get on with it."

MacSweeney was over at a small refrigerator. As he opened the door, three bottles fell from the top and smashed on the floor. MacSweeney kicked them aside.

"You're not drunk are you, MacSweeney?" asked Bridge.

"I'm never drunk," said MacSweeney, taking a foil-wrapped packet out of the refrigerator with caution. "Mind you, I'm never quite sober either. It's no fun being a fucking exile you know."

"Yeah. Well it's maybe more fun than being dead. Is that the stuff?"

"That's the stuff. And you wouldn't appreciate it. You thank your stars we didn't have this in the old days. You know where you'd be now Bridge? You'd be blowing down the Falls Road in fragments a millimetre across. You said you wanted a big one?"

Bridge looked at his watch. "Come on MacSweeney," he said.

"No, no, no," said MacSweeney. "You should know what you're getting here. I want to keep a good client. The last man

I did business with blew himself to pieces you know. Along with a bank."

MacSweeney laid the packet on the white oilcloth and unwrapped it with gentle fingers.

"Now look here," he said. "Cut yourself off a small morsel."

He offered Bridge a stained kitchen knife.

"A small one," he said. "The smallest you can."

Bridge cut a crumb from the faintly bluish dough beneath the lamplight. MacSweeney looked at it. "Cut that in half," he said. "Let me."

Under his fingernail he picked up the tiny point of dough and wrapped it carefully in an inch square of silver foil. Then he lit a candle in a saucer, picked a hooked piece of wire from a corner of the table that was six inches deep in rubbish, and threaded the silver packet on to the end of the wire.

"Now get over there," said MacSweeney. He dangled the small glinting package in the flame and Bridge watched the foil go white, then red.

The bang was louder than a pistol shot. The glare scarred the back of his eyes.

"*Jesus*, MacSweeney! What *is* that stuff?"

"Whatever it is," said MacSweeney, "You don't want to be around when it blows. That's the only point I'm making."

"Come on," said Bridge. "What do I have to do?"

MacSweeney, with the pride of a conjuror, pulled a drawer out of the table and reached in for a plastic wallet of felt-tip pens. The kind you can buy at Monoprix for a few francs. The ink core from each of the fifteen pens had been removed, and stuffed with the blue dough.

"Now," said MacSweeney, "what I want you to do is to hold these while I thread the other through it."

He was holding what looked like a ball of steel wool, but brighter.

"What's that?" asked Bridge. He held the wallet of plastic pens in both hands as MacSweeney had told him.

"Mag," said MacSweeney. He tore off a quarter-inch and dropped it into the candle flame. It blazed up with a split second's blue brilliance.

While Bridge held the bundle of pens, MacSweeney threaded the wire wool around their caps.

"It's a bad invention, this plastic stuff," said MacSweeney. "I mean, it could get in the wrong hands. You know, these little plastic pen cases are better than a steel drum for this kind of explosive. Did you know that?"

"MacSweeney," said Bridge, "I'm not proposing to start World War III. Can you tell me what sort of damage we are going to do here?"

"Don't worry," said MacSweeney, working on it. "Don't be in fifty feet of it, that's all."

Bridge watched him as he heated up a small electric soldering iron and attached a sheet of transistors to a tuft of the wire wool.

"You can lose a few fingers doing this," said MacSweeney. "Others wouldn't bother to solder it. But for you, nothing but the best."

Then he attached the tuft of wire to the rest of it threaded round the plastic pens, taking each strand at a time in dextrous, though dirty fingers.

"There you are," said MacSweeney. "Now you want a dummy one as well and a radio detonator. I'll tell you myself, that's a good job. That's all plastic, you know. Apart from the circuit. You'd be bloody unlucky to have that picked up in a metal detector."

Now, later, in Claude's flat, Bridge felt himself beginning to doze, so forced himself up and turned on the television positioned at the end of the bed.

When the news came on to the screen he turned up the sound. The usual crowd of international disasters had pushed his own topics of concern off the map. But at the end of the bulletin there was a glimpse of the Super-Celeste and the news that Daniel Levitte, only son of the founder of Euro-Aviat, would fly in the plane on its first trip on Friday; then profile pictures of the two men. The agencies had not been able to trace a single picture of father and son standing together.

Bridge lay back. In the course of the day, he reflected, he had collected quite a packet of money. He liked activity and money. Pure and simple, both of them. Pressing money into the hand of the Arab he had been able to kill—he smiled when he remembered it. He liked the feel of adrenalin pushing round his body. It made him drowsy and awake at the same time. He hoped

Claude would return. For more than one reason. There were quite a few explanations required from Claude. And he also remembered her body. He dozed again.

Marcel Derivat, around midnight—there had been three more calls to deal with since Claude's suspicious neighbour phoned— parked his car in the dim suburban street and peered at the small apartment blocks and single private houses. Most had grey stucco walls fronting the road and wire mesh fences on top of them. Shrubs and trees bristled over the walls to drop malicious pellets of rain from the ends of branches. There were few numbers visible on the garden walls and Derivat got thoroughly wet tracing number thirty-five.

The front door swung open to a cold, grey concrete foyer that smelt of cats. There was a lift, but he took the stairs. Apartment four couldn't be far up. He was so convinced, after fifty calls, that this was another name to cross off the list, that he felt no hint of alarm—even in the middle of the night, by himself. He knocked at the door of apartment four.

Bridge, like a cat, awoke at the knock and sprang from the bed. The gun was in his hand. "Open, please, it's the police," said Derivat.

Bridge put the gun under the pillow, smiled, and walked to the door. The "please" told him all he needed to know at this stage. He opened the door and let the damp young man enter.

"I regret troubling you so late," said Derivat, "but we have reports of a lady in this apartment we wish to interview. If you could just identify this picture." He pulled the profile of Claude from his pocket. Bridge looked at it. He shook his head.

"It's a little like my wife," he said, "but she's not here."

"Well, that's the usual thing," said Derivat with a pleasant laugh. His eyes flickered round the room. "This is your home M'sieu?"

"That's right," said Bridge.

Derivat noted the empty tin of beans on the bedside table.

"And where is your wife, M'sieu?"

"She is visiting her aunt."

"Well, there we are. Do you mind if I just walk round and then I will leave you in peace. I am sorry to trouble you."

"Of course."

Derivat walked straight to the bathroom, took a glance round and opened the bathroom cabinet. It was empty. He shut it softly and returned to the living-room.

"You say you live here? You seem to have very few things—no toothbrush, no shaving things."

Bridge thought: what a bright little bastard *you* are.

"I'm moving in the morning," said Bridge. "Actually, my wife and I have split up. She's taken everything, you see. It just happened."

"I'm sorry to hear it," said Derivat. He glanced at the night-dress on the bed. Then back to Bridge.

"Your wife takes your toothbrush and razor, but leaves her night-dress? That's a little strange, M'sieu."

"It's a strange world," said Bridge.

Derivat sat down, rested his elbows on his knees, his chin in his hands and began to consider the tall blond man very carefully indeed. He'd seen his chief doing this. It unsettled people. Bridge shrugged. He didn't seem unsettled. Instead, he walked to the bedside table and picked up the tin of haricot beans.

"I drive commercial vehicles. Fruit and vegetables."

"You have a slight English accent?"

"I'm English."

"You speak very good French for a driver of camions."

"And what is your name?" asked Bridge pleasantly. Derivat told him. Bridge nodded.

Bridge fished out the remaining haricots with his fingers. To do so he had to bend the jagged lid of the tin, which had been opened with a cheap cut and thrust can opener, wide open.

"Do you ever drive your fruit and vegetables to Les Halles?"

"Sometimes."

Derivat leant back in his chair and began patting his stomach. His handsome, rather pointed young face was bright with pleasure. The imitation of his chief's style of interrogation was impressive. Then he noted the tin of beans, held so easily in the Englishman's huge hand, and the first cold twist of peril struck him. His chief, he realized, did not interrogate suspects, alone, at night, in their own premises.

"Would you put that down?" said Derivat firmly. To his relief, the man put the can down.

"I can hear your friends coming up the stairs," said Bridge.

Derivat turned uncertainly to the door. A second too late he said: "I expect they are."

He was still turning his head back from the door when Bridge leapt on him, seeming to smother him like a huge cat falling over a mouse. The death was almost silent. The woman in the next apartment woke, however, at the single high gurgle. She lay awake for a while, angry. Now that creature next door was keeping her up with her sexual carrying on, she thought. In the morning she would make a *written* report to the police. You couldn't get satisfaction anywhere these days.

"Shit," said Bridge, by way of an epitaph.

He knelt down by the dead young man and turned the corpse's surprised face upwards. This wasn't a killing he had reckoned on. He regretted it.

Bridge didn't kill out of malice—except possibly that single aimed shot into the kidneys of his patrol leader back in the SAS. And he knew that complications swarmed like flies round a corpse. He hoped that Claude would arrive. She wouldn't like it, but she was going to have to help him get this body out of here.

Bridge dialled Derivat's station—he had found his identity from his wallet. He reckoned a straightforward enquiry after young Marcel should tell him if anything was getting Derivat's colleagues worried. They weren't worried at all. Derivat had gone home, they said. He would be back in the morning. He would, too, thought Bridge as he thanked them.

He heard the new step on the stairs. Claude was moving like a moth. Her hands were shaking so much with fear that she had scarcely been able to pay off the cab. All the way back from central Paris she had been terrified the driver had recognized her and was about to drive her straight into custody. She had never been on the run before.

As she fumbled softly at the door of the apartment, Bridge rolled the body into the only hiding place—under the bed.

He stood back from the door and let her open it. She opened her mouth to scream and he leapt at her, stifling the cry in her throat.

"Jesus," he said, "don't do that."

She dropped on to the bed, her mouth and eyes wide open, dark hair plastered with rain and sweat on her cheeks.

Bridge realized she was terrified of him.

"It's all right," he said. He crouched down beside her, put a hand on her knee. She did not change her expression but pushed it feebly away, staring at him in dumb horror.

"Come on, Claude. Get yourself together. I'm going to get you out of here."

She pulled the thin coat round her, began shivering again.

"Why did you kill him? Why did you *kill* him."

"Who?" he said, surprised. Then he realized she meant Jean-Paul Petit.

He said: "Do you want a glass of water?" There wasn't anything else in the damned place anyway. She nodded. When he got it to her, her hand was shaking too much to bring it to her mouth. He fed her with it like a child.

"Good," he said. "Good. Claude, do you want to get away? Yes? Right? Come on, talk?"

She nodded.

"That's right. God, you do look a mess!"

She looked as if she hadn't eaten for days, for a start. The police might have a job recognizing this haunted face as that of the plump, sleepy cat-girl from Marseilles.

"*Why* did you kill him?" she said more steadily, reproaching him. "Mother of God!"

He pulled out his wallet. "Look, Claude." He took out the pack of money Rose had given him this morning and split it in half. "Take that. That'll make you feel warmer. That's yours. I'll get you out of Paris tonight. Promise."

She took the money. She began to watch him attentively, like a calf that has just smelt the abattoir.

She said: "He said you were just going to talk to him."

"Who said?"

"The man who paid me. The detective."

Bridge sat down by her on the bed.

"Listen, Claude. Something has gone very wrong. Somebody's got us into this thing and they're going to try to put it on us. They're after you, right? There was a cop here tonight."

"Oh dear God," she said, shaking again.

"It's all right. He's gone. Now look, Claude, we're going to sort it out. What is this detective thing? What detective?"

"I can't tell you. Hassin would kill me."

"He's not going to do that. He's dead."

"Oh dear God," she said.

"Just stop the prayers, Claude. We've got to move. This started with Hassin, didn't it. Tell me about that."

She suddenly dropped her head in his lap and started to weep. She was soaked to the skin. His hands slid clammily against the wet dress over her smooth shoulders. "You're going to be dead of pneumonia before the morning," he said, "and you're soaking me. Come on, Claude, calm down. I'll get you dry, only go on talking."

He eased himself from under her, took one of the flannelette sheets from the bed and unzipped her dress. She did not protest. It calmed her. She allowed him to undress her and to wrap her in the sheet and dry her. She began to shiver less and talk more.

"Hassin said they wanted pictures of me and Jean-Paul. You know—*that* sort of picture. For a divorce. He said it was all quite okay. They were just for the divorce case."

"That's a pretty mucky thing to get into, Claude."

"I've got to live," she said petulantly. "I should have known though."

"Known what?"

"Jean-Paul wasn't supposed to be one of my customers. Hassin was the manager for the *Club Hippique*, you know?"

Bridge nodded. The *Club Hippique* was the name for the ring of girls that was ultimately and discreetly run for North-West Aerospace's interest.

"They took the pictures. *I* didn't get any money," she even managed to laugh. "I went to Hassin for the money and he said he'd never made any arrangement about any pictures. He hit me. He said if I'd been sleeping with Jean-Paul he'd report me to his boss."

"He did, too," said Bridge.

"I know, I got thrown out of my place. I had to freelance. Why did he do that to me?"

"He's not very bright," said Bridge. "He got the pictures. He got paid. Then he thought he could get some more money out of it by trying to blackmail the *Club Hippique*. That's when you and I met. I came to Paris to sort him out. What happened then?"

"I was on my own. I guessed you'd come to do something to Hassin. I thought you might look after me."

"I am," said Bridge.

"I wasn't doing too well. And then *he* came to see me."

"Who, Hassin?"

"No, your friend."

"Tell me about him."

"He was very polite. Very distinguished. He had pictures with him. The ones they had got of me and Jean-Paul and some more, too."

"What were those?"

"Jean-Paul and some other woman. He asked me if I knew her. He wanted to know if we did things together, all three of us."

"Did you?"

"I don't know who she was. He kept giving me money. He said he was from the divorce detectives. But he was so angry. It was strange. He hid it but I could see how angry he was. He had such eyes! Then he said Jean-Paul's wife didn't want to go on with the divorce. He said I could help. He said that all I had to do was to make a time to see Jean-Paul again and he would get a friend of the family to meet Jean when he came out and confront him with it. He said I'd be doing Jean-Paul a good turn."

Bridge nodded. "Go on," he said grimly. "*He* suggested the time, the date?"

"Yes."

"Why do you keep saying he is my friend?" asked Bridge.

She appeared not to hear.

"And that was strange," she whispered, remembering the moment. "When I wrote the date down he didn't say anything. He just looked at the pictures, especially the ones of the other woman. Then he set light to them. It was horrible. He held them in his hand, his right hand, and burnt them, and the flames went right down to his fingers and set the matches in the box alight. I could see he had really burnt his fingers."

"Are you sure?" said Bridge. He sat alongside her. "Matches? Like this. Not a lighter? He was holding the box?"

"Yes, I told you."

"Okay. Why do you keep saying he is my friend?" said Bridge again.

"Well, I tried to complain to him about Hassin. If he was from the divorce detectives maybe he could get me the money I was supposed to have had for the pictures. He knew about Hassin. He said, 'Oh Hassin has been dealt with'. And I said, Did Mr Mayflower do it?"

"You said *what*?"

"That's your name isn't it? That's the name you gave me."
Bridge looked at her in amazement. "When?"

"The last time we met. When you came over to see Hassin. You said if I had to go to a new address I could let you know by writing to you at the post office."

"Jesus wept!" said Bridge.

So he *had* been unfair to Rose. *He*, clever Crispin Bridge, had put himself into all this. Single-handed. He tried to imagine how he could have been that stupid. Well, it hadn't looked dangerous then. You come to Paris, knock a small-time black-mailer around a bit, take a fancy to a bird who is going to be working on her own and unlikely to be of any interest to any-one. Of course, if Rose had told him who was the client in Hassin's dirty pictures he would have been more careful.

"What's the matter?" she said.

"It's all right. Then he said he knew Mr Mayflower, I suppose."

"Yes. He said you'd given Hassin a good telling off and you were just the man to talk to Jean-Paul. But he didn't know where you were."

"So you told him. You told him the post office."

It was all very plain to Bridge now. Divorce detectives sniffing around until they get wind of Claude. Then a deal with her manager to get evidence. Then when they go back for the pictures the manager is sitting around in fragments explaining he has been knee-capped by a top professional hit man. The kind you can hire in the usual way favoured by the Corsicans and even the Triad nowadays—written instructions, cash in advance and no questions asked. And Rose and Bridge stupid enough to think Hassin was just taking pictures for his own amusement!

"Wasn't he your friend?" asked Claude.

"No," said Bridge briefly. "Now listen Claude, this is more of a mess than I thought. You've got to go back home. And stay there."

"I haven't got a home," she said.

"Yes you have. Marseilles. Anywhere in Marseilles."

"They'll be looking for me there."

"No-one looks for anyone long in Marseilles," said Bridge, "There's thousands of girls like you down there. With the money I've given you you can get a job in a café and stay out of sight."

"I bought an airline ticket this morning," she said mournfully, "I spent all my money on it. I haven't got a passport."

"You *are* a silly cow," said Bridge. He looked at his watch. "It's two o'clock." He sorted through the timetables he kept in his head. "There's a train at six. We can get your dress dry by then."

"Come with me," she said, "please."

"To Marseilles?" he was genuinely astonished.

She let the sheet fall from her shoulders and put her arms round his neck.

"Why not?" she said softly. "They're after you too. We could look after each other. You could get work as a waiter. We would have a nice life. I wouldn't sleep with anyone else."

He kissed her forehead. "You're sweet," he said, "you really are. But I'm afraid I've got to have one of those talks I'm so famous for. With whoever the bastard was who set us up for this."

"You come along later," she said confidently. "I'll find a nice room. It's a good idea going to Marseilles. Down by the harbour. It's fun there."

Bridge smiled again. Anyone who thought that stinking town of cripples and criminals was fun must have had a rough life elsewhere.

"Why don't we go to sleep?" she said. "I'm so tired. I'll make the bed."

"Leave the bed alone," he said.

"Come on," she said. "A little sleep," she took her arms from his neck and began to undo the buttons of his shirt.

After a few moments he pulled the blanket over them and dropped his head on the pillow. His hand ran gently down her large breasts and the curve of her belly, and stopped in surprise as she parted her legs.

"What's this then?" he asked.

She laughed. "That was poor Jean-Paul," she said, "he liked me to have nothing there. He said he liked me like a little girl."

Bridge said nothing. He explored the soft flesh, shaven of its pubic hair.

She sensed the sudden shiver that ran up his spine, and stroked it appreciatively.

"Look, Claude," he said, "it's nothing personal. But I think we ought to sleep." Bridge wasn't over-sensitive. But there was a dead man under the bed looking up at them, and the touch of that shaven flesh made him feel there was a dead man in the bed with him. Tired though he was, it was not easy to sleep.

The Levitte family, he thought, might make and fly good aeroplanes, but their sex life was something like playing blind man's bluff in a morgue. He wasn't surprised he would be meeting Henri Levitte tomorrow in a bloody graveyard. He was looking forward to that. He hoped he would have a chance to shake the great man's hand. And to find out if the flesh on the end of his fingertips was dead and scarred.

David Callaghan, global sales director of North-West Aerospace, shook Melvyn Murray's hand and motioned him back into the conference suite of Canberra's Lindemann Motel. The nine-man delegation from North-West Aerospace followed them in. None of them looked happy men. They'd arrived one way round the globe, via a tedious delay in Fiji, to discover the Australian Defence Review Committee had just set off in the other direction, via Singapore, for Paris. The point was not lost. By Wednesday evening the tabloids would be running the story "Air Men Find Bird is Flown". The papers enjoyed rubbing on the salt. They would find space (after strong suggestions from the DoD press office in Canberra) to retell the saga of the last aeroplanes Australia had bought from America.

"We have been caught on the hop right the way through this business," said David Callaghan as soon as the party had sat down. "Everything's been done too late. I've got to remind you, Murray, that it was you who said we only needed one man in

Australia on this trip—yourself. You should have known they were planning their decision."

"Well," said Murray, "you go ahead and scapegoat me. If it makes you feel any better. I hear you've turned that bastard Mackenzie over to the wolves, by the way. I'd have liked to do that myself. You could have given me that pleasure."

"We're not here to give you much pleasure, I'm afraid," said Callaghan. "What do you think we feel like, coming here and learning from the press the entire DoD had just left for Paris?"

"They didn't buy their tickets from me," said Murray.

"It's not just an embarrassment to us," Callaghan pressed on. "It's an embarrassment to the President by this stage. And I mean the President of the United States. You can guess how Carroll feels. These bastards flying off like that: it's an insult, after all."

"Look," said Murray, "the first thing *any* of us knew of this was Monday morning. I got to Canberra. And Mackenzie says the whole thing is cut and dried and the only thing that'll stop it is if the Frogs fly their machine into the Eiffel Tower. I'm quoting. The fact is the Australians don't want to buy American. Well, that's tough on us, but for Christ's sake you can't take it out on me."

But they could. They could and would. Just as it would have been taken out on Ackermann, thought Murray. It seemed a long time ago since he had spelled the same story out to the French Hun.

"Well, what about that story, then," said Callaghan.

"Which story?" Murray gathered his thoughts.

"The Super-Celeste flying into the Eiffel Tower."

The men in the room leaped forward attentively.

"Well, what's going on in Paris," said Murray acidly, "I have no idea."

"I know," said Callaghan softly, "I've spoken to Rose in Paris myself. But the initial approach came to you, Murray. Come on. I'm interested. You know this Daniel Levitte. He rang you first. What do you think?"

"He's a crazy young man. I refused to get mixed up in all that."

"Fine," said Callaghan. "I'm sending you to Paris tonight. If you want to stay with this company you'd better start getting mixed up with the Paris story. We're angry, Murray. We've come a long way to find nothing but a fuck-up."

Murray looked at the other men. He knew how they felt. He couldn't blame them. You invest ten years' effort and not just money but ten years of your life building a killer aeroplane, and then the customer takes off to look at someone else's.

"Maybe you'd like me to go and blow the plane up myself," he said. "It's one way of doing business."

"Personally I'd really like just that," said David Callaghan. "So far as I'm concerned I'd like to see the Australian Defence Department and the Super-Celeste and that old Henri Levitte going up in one lovely ball of fire. Because if we lose this game, Murray, we're going to lose all our friends at the White House. Let alone NATO orders for the next six years. You know that we can't really afford *not* to let the Australians have missiles." He let it sink in, then continued: "Right, now we've got to get on with our job. We're going to have a press conference at six. Then we release pictures of our plane flying and we start promising the goodies. The trade deals, the sub-contract to build at Elizabeth, the missile problem, the lot." He stubbed his cigarette out viciously.

"It's not going to look good with these buggers still laughing, but we're just going to have to take the smiles off their faces. And *you* can get to *Paris*, Murray. Talk to Rose and make sure he plays a good game. He's a secretive little bastard. That's his job. But I want you to make one thing clear to him and his outfit. Till now we've been playing round with this Daniel Levitte thing. I don't know if there's anything moving on it or not. Well, we're going to stop playing around. If the Australians are going to stake everything on watching that plane fly, then let's be honest. If there's some way to stop it flying, *stop it*. And if you want to know why we're so keen, Murray, I'll tell you, we just lost an F-24. Fucking maniac pilot flew it into a canyon. No one knows, *yet*."

"I understand," said Murray, "it really is the week for human sacrifices, isn't it." He got up and walked straight out, slamming the door. In twenty swift minutes he had been blamed for the whole débâcle, and given the dirtiest of the pieces to sweep up.

Bridge woke on the moment of 4.30 am. Like the air timetables in his head, he had an internal clock as accurate as a musician's sense of perfect pitch. He slid from the bed, opened the door of Claude's apartment and listened. All was quiet. He returned to push the button on the bedside lamp and look at the peaceful Claude, her face smooth in sleep. It was a shame to wake anyone into the mess and misery of the morning she would have to face. Bridge thought: he'd killed this woman's last lover, her pimp, and a policeman who was looking for her—all in the last two days. None of which was her fault. Perhaps, he thought, that was why he cared about her.

"Claude," he said, "wake up."

Her eyes rolled at the room, collecting scraps of bad memories together. She smiled at him in the end.

"The dress is dry. Dry as it will be anyway. Come on. We've got to get a train."

"To Marseilles," she said, "I remember."

He picked up the phone. There were many radio cab firms in Paris. Some of them less inquisitive than others. He dialled.

As the dial sprang back he said: "Claude: you know I said a cop called earlier. You remember that?"

"Oh yes," she said, "that's right, you did."

"Well," said Bridge. "He was going to take you away. Put you in prison. Accessory to the murder. You understand?"

She stood up, naked. She looked frightened again. "Why did he go away?"

"He didn't," said Bridge. "Hallo? Cab for 35, Rue Troyat. West of Neuilly, off the—you know it? Good. Apartment Four. We've got a problem—a guest we have to get home. He's drunk. I mean he's okay. He won't mess up the cab, but he's drunk and asleep. That all right?"

"What do you mean?" said Claude as he put the phone down.

"I'm sorry Claude. I had to hit him."

"Where?" she said. "Where is he?"

"Don't you worry. When the cab comes, you go and chat to him. I'll join you."

"Oh God," she said. "There's no end to this. Where is he?"

"Come on. Get your dress on. You're going home. Just take it easy."

"To Marseilles," she said.

He helped her dress. Slid the still damp cloth over her shoulders.

"And you *will* come," she said. "You will come. A beautiful, simple little life together."

"Claude," said Bridge, "how old are you?"

"Twenty-seven, why?"

"If you'd wanted a simple life, you'd have started it by now. It's not that difficult."

When the man with the cab rang the bell he sent her down. He checked the room briefly, but accurately, then hauled the dead Marcel Derivat from beneath the bed. All was well. Bridge hunched the dead man over his shoulder and started to drag him down the stairs. The toes of his feet trailed like dead vegetables behind him. Claude was already in the car. The driver stared phlegmatically through his windscreen. "Many thanks," said Bridge, making his voice thick. "Too much of a good thing. Come on Jules, in you go."

"Mind he doesn't mess up the cab," said the man. "Where to?"

"St Ouen," said Bridge, "I'll tell you when."

Claude looked fixedly out of the farther window. Marcel Derivat jogged his head companionably against Bridge's shoulder. He kept the body wedged upright. The rain started coming down again. The driver turned his radio on. Half way across the bridge that carries a feeder road above the northern ring motorway just beyond St Ouen, Bridge told the driver to stop.

"He's waking up," he said, "I reckon he wants to be sick."

"Told you so," said the driver. "Get him out of here."

"Okay," said Bridge. "Drive down to the end of the bridge and I'll catch you up. Walk will do him good." He bundled Derivat out of the door and shut it swiftly. "Go on," he said, "drive off or he'll want to get back in. I'll be with you."

The driver glanced suspiciously at the figure being propped up on the pavement. Bridge was holding its forehead and talking to him. Then the cab moved off and stopped a hundred yards down the road. It was a black, dead hour of night. From the parapet of the bridge there was a fine view of the glistening motorway, well lit, almost empty. The camions were the only vehicles out, on their way to the various markets. Their multiple tyres hurled the surface water from the black roadway into clouds of oily spray. Bridge tucked the second fragment of Arabic script into Derivat's inner pocket. Then with one easy lift he tipped the dead man over the parapet into the first gap of the traffic below and walked quickly back to the cab.

"Where is he?" said the driver.

"He's crazy," said Bridge. "Said he wanted to walk. Come on let's get to a metro."

The driver pressed on. He took care not to look at his customer, even in the rear mirror. But when they disembarked he said: "That was an expensive trip, M'sieu."

Bridge smiled, and paid him ten times the sum on the clock. At the station, he bought her a return ticket to Marseilles.

"And when am I coming back?" said Claude bitterly.

"Not till this runs out," said Bridge, "but it all helps. Anybody asks you, you're going to see your sick grandmother. Cry, carry on. Tell them she hasn't long to go. You go to Marseilles on a single ticket and no luggage and they'll get curious. Use your head a bit, Claude, and look after yourself."

"Will you come?" she said pleadingly. "Later? The Hotel Algonquin will know me. Down by the harbour."

"I might, too," said Bridge. "And there's this, Claude." He showed her the picture of Henri Levitte on the Euro-Aviat brochure. She was in the train. Like lovers parting. Strip lights shone up the photograph. "The man who came to see you, who said he was my friend. Was that him?"

She looked a the picture, frightened again.

"I don't know," she said. "Yes. Could have been. I'm not good on faces."

"He burnt his fingers. You're sure of that."

She nodded.

"All right Claude. Go and get your hair combed out. Look after yourself."

Night, nearly morning, a train, long, already pointed to the south.

"You *are* English aren't you?" said Claude. "When you say goodbye, kiss your hand. Would you?"

Bridge got back to the Levitte apartment to find Celeste angry as a scalded jaguar.

"There were reporters and TV people here all night," she said. "I thought you were looking after Daniel. Where have you been?" Her black dressing gown—and nothing inside it but herself, thought Bridge, was stitched with green dragons.

"Looking for Claude," he said.

"Did you find her?"

"No. What were the reporters here for?"

"About Daniel flying in the plane and me walking out of the session yesterday. Daniel's father's gone mad about it. With both of us. He's been on the phone. He doesn't like Daniel pushing himself forward. That's what he said. That man's going to drive Daniel crazy," she said, quietly and urgently, "I've got to have a talk with you about this. Later. I think you could help."

"Where is he now?"

"Dressing in there for the funeral. You're coming too, aren't you? You'd better get ready."

"I haven't got much to wear for a funeral," said Bridge.

Daniel, hearing his voice, came into the room. He looked stretched into the final state of exhaustion, thought Bridge. And probably packed with tranquillizers too.

"Thank God you're back," said Daniel. "I've got to get on to the air base tonight. My father wants me locked up for the week, out of harm's way. Something I said on the TV interview has set him off." He looked enquiringly at Bridge.

Bridge nodded to him briefly. "I expect your father likes to get everything ready well in advance. Like me."

Daniel searched his face, and got the message he wanted.

"So you're going tonight," said Bridge. "And when are *you* going, Celeste?"

"Friday morning."

"Did you find that girl you were looking for?" Daniel asked. Bridge shook his head.

The phone rang. It was the caretaker below to say the car had arrived to take them to the funeral.

On the way, Celeste said: "I'm frightened of meeting that man. Why *did* you say that to the TV, Daniel?"

She was now wearing a black woollen dress with a high waist.

She looked alarmed. Bridge suddenly saw the bedraggled Claude in comparison.

"What did he say?" said Bridge. Daniel was not talking to anyone.

"Oh it was the usual trouble," said Celeste. She took Daniel's arm. He made no response. "They wanted to know if Daniel was going to be back with Euro-Aviat again, taking charge if his father retired. He said that was a hypothetical question."

"That sounds pretty harmless," said Bridge.

"Well, that's what it's like. Henri said remarks like that knocked millions of francs off the share value of Euro-Aviat."

Bridge looked at Daniel Levitte with some sympathy. They were on the steps, in a cold wind. A cat took the chance of the open door and slid into the building, evading the closing door by a hair's breadth.

"*Would* you like to run Euro-Aviat, Daniel?"

Daniel laughed. "That's right," he said, looking sidelong at Bridge. "That's my big ambition in life. Didn't I tell you?"

Within half an hour they were standing in the crowded cemetery of St Sulpice. There was now a light powdering of snow on the ground, and the florid marble of thousands of memorials to the bourgeois dead of Paris stretched round them into the mist. Plastic flowers inside dirty glass domes on many of the graves gave the place the look of an iced wedding cake that had been left out in the rain. The grave for Marie-Thérèse lay open at their feet. Clods of newly-dug earth littered the snow round its rim like black bile. The priest chanted on, a drip of mucus at the end of a sad nose. Bridge looked occasionally at Henri Levitte, gaunt, white-faced and propping his heavily drugged wife on a stiffly held elbow. And occasionally, too, Bridge was aware of Henri Levitte's hostile, quizzical glance in his own direction.

Immediately after the ceremony, at the gates of the cemetery, while the huge black cars eased into line to take them away, Henri Levitte summoned Daniel imperiously to one side.

"Who is this man? What do you mean by bringing a total stranger to the funeral?"

"I've asked him to look after us for the week," said Daniel. "I expect you have your own security people, Papa. And I have Celeste to think of."

"You ought to buy a dog," said Henri Levitte. "Don't you see that it is an extremely insulting thing to have a man like that breathing into the grave of your own sister?"

"I didn't think of it like that, Papa."

Bridge stepped forward. "Can I introduce myself?" he said. He stretched out his hand. Levitte looked at him with frosty disdain. He did not stretch out his hand. Let alone remove his glove. He merely raised his right hand to remove his glasses and give Bridge a hard and hostile stare.

"Well, everything's all right now," said Bridge to Daniel. "I'll leave you now, sir."

"Wait a minute," said Henri Levitte. He went on looking at Bridge with interest. "Have you been in the army, young man?"

"Sir?"

It seemed that Henri Levitte did not really require an answer to this question—just an opportunity to look thoroughly at this bodyguard his son had acquired. Bridge returned the gaze. He tried to return it with all his usual blue-eyed blandness, but the older man frowned slightly. He turned back to Daniel.

"Let me make it quite plain, Daniel," said Henri Levitte. "I don't subsidize you to keep servants. If you're frightened about yourself I'll see to it you are looked after."

Bridge smiled and saluted Daniel. "Don't worry, sir, I'll find my own way back. It's a pleasure working for you."

It would be, too, he thought, as he trudged the long road along the cemetery's black railings. It was going to be a real pleasure to knock God Henri Levitte out of the sky. Bridge could take a lot of aggro, except from anyone that came over with the commanding officer bit.

The jumbo-jet dipped a port wing as the pilot corrected his course over Alice Springs and the sun climbed swiftly to pour on to Ackermann's face. He looked down. Though at this altitude the usual delicate flower of an ice crystal had formed on the window, the heat down below on the burnt brown desert was almost tangible. The long line of the Macdonnell Ranges scarred its way across the otherwise totally empty landscape.

In the end, no less than forty Australian aviation men were on board the French airliner. Ackermann, with clearance from Paris to bring along practically anyone who wanted the trip, had been amazed at the speed and enthusiasm with which the party had filled up. Apart from the Defence Review Committee there were delegates from the Army Aviation Corps, the Government Aircraft Factories, the Department of Supply, the RAAF and the Defence Department.

Ackermann felt pleased enough: like a big game hunter coming home with a fine bag of man-eaters. He also felt like a courier on a package tour. He strolled about the vast, bus-like interior shedding goodwill and conversation.

It was not, however, going to be a relaxing trip. The Australians had, literally, been thrown up into the sky at a moment's notice. In the long flight ahead, most of it in the dark, flying away from the sunrise, there was plenty of opportunity to put a great number of unanswered questions in Ackermann's way.

The men from GAF had fastened like limpets on to the American Ambassador's offer to allow the American plane to be built in Australia. Would the French make a similar offer? Their factories, as Ackermann well knew, were running out of orders for the Mark Two Nomads, Australia's own home-grown machine, and were facing one of the recurrent and painful troughs that afflicted the industry every decade. And then there was the traditional "blue versus brown" competitiveness between the RAAF and the Army, each eager still, despite government action to end the bickering, to circumscribe each others' air role. And then there were the simple enquiries about the kind of entertainment that would be laid on in Paris. Ackermann went on being cheerful and expansive. He had forty well-built Australian males on board and he knew Paris had a reputation to keep up in lavish entertainment.

By the time they had lifted out of Hong Kong, Ackermann was exhausted. A dry-as-dust armaments expert was asking him why the Super-Celeste wasn't installing a Hughes AWG-12 fire-control system. Fortunately, the cabin crew dimmed the lights and turned on the night's feature film. It was another of the science fiction horror movies now in vogue. Ackermann watched the opening sequence as a rocket lifted gracefully from its pad and then exploded colourfully in mid-air. He closed his eyes peacefully and removed his earphones. Perhaps not the most tactful choice of films, he thought, but at least it would keep the Australians quiet for a while. It would be good to see cool, grey, wintry France again.

At Dreux, by a miracle the weathermen had been promising with more optimism than conviction, the front of high pressure that had been standing over the Atlantic moved in. The last snow fell even as the skies cleared, and every man on the base looked up with delight as the few flakes fell from a powder blue sky.

Henri Bosco, flying the Super-Celeste's immediate ancestor over the chosen route, swept in low over the base. He gave a victory roll as the sun, for the first time in a month, glinted on his wings. Behind him, the sky split at his noisy passing. The drivers of the little Euro-Aviat supply vehicles stopped to look up at the unaccustomed brightness and to watch Bosco climb back into it. Bosco grinned with delight, so far as that was possible with a force of 3G dragging his eyelids half-closed. At the top of the climb he fell off it steeply and plunged almost vertically down.

The mechanics around the Super-Celeste went on with their work. There was only one slight problem remaining: a fractional loss of pressure in the cylinder which lowered the nose wheel. Perrault crouched down with them as they worked. They assured him that everything was going to be fine.

"If it stays like this for weather," he said, "we can have our shoot up."

At the far end of the base a target was waiting. It would be an extra treat for the spectators. The twin cannon, 30-mm Oerlikon-Buerle KCAs, firing Hispano-Suiza projectiles could between them deliver 600 rounds in a single second of air-ground firing.

Perrault patted the team leader on the shoulder, stood up and drove off across the concrete to see how the more cosmetic preparations for Friday were going. It was never going to be possible to make Dreux look like a carnival, but the VIP reception area was surely going to look more cheerful than usual.

Refrigerators for champagne, blue carpets, potted palms were rolling in.

Perrault's driver stopped obediently as a military car flashed him to halt. The soldiers saluted and opened the boot, lifting the spare-wheel cavity lid and feeling into its farthest recesses. So far as security was concerned, Dreux was by now a fortified settlement. Every man on the base wore a plastic identification tag, with a colour photograph of its rightful possessor and his thumbprint. By the evening, with two clear days still to go to the day of the flight, the base would be to all intents sealed off. The last bottle of champagne and the last tub of flowers would be moved in. On Friday the official party and the press would enter by a route that was bounded by a perimeter of steel-tape fencing on either side, leading direct to observation areas whose boundaries were less visible but equally stringent. Not a mouse could cross the electronic curtain around the plane without the security controllers being aware.

Perrault watched the huge activity in progress; the Euro-Aviat delivery vehicles scurrying like demented beetles across the vast concrete expanses of the base, now drying in the welcome sunlight.

Andreas, the catering manager, gripped his elbow. "The salmon, M'sieu Perrault. It won't arrive today. I have told them, I have screamed at them. What can I do? *Please*, M'sieu, may I let them deliver it tomorrow."

"No," said Perrault. "No exceptions." The list of materials that would be allowed entry after the base was sealed tonight was already drawn up. "You know that, Andreas. We're going to be lifting the lid off every *vol au vent* between tomorrow and Friday."

Andreas waved his hands in despair. "I should get a job as a chef in a prison," he said.

"Yes, well," said Perrault, "if you try and bring in so much as a spoonful of soup after tonight, that's where you'll be." Andreas knew he meant it. Jolly, relaxed Perrault had put Dreux into irons since the death of Jean-Paul. Dolefully, Andreas went off to replan his menu.

In Paris, the funeral lunch was hitting problems too. The dining-room in the Rue Frédéric might have been created with such an occasion in mind. Like the profiles of corpulent opera singers, the heavy red velvet curtains bulged at each side of the long windows, restrained by silk ropes at their waists. Henri Levitte's wife, Hortense, now sipping wine on top of her drugs, had become foolish. More foolish than usual. She suddenly launched into an emotional speech: a sideways glancing blow at the melon on her plate had sent it reeling on to the damask tablecloth, but she made no attempt to re-collect it.

"I'm very, very, very, very frightened about Daniel flying in this machine," she said to Celeste. "But I do hope his father will *understand*. He is so talented, isn't he, Henri? I do hope his father will *understand*. I think it's time Henri started to think about retiring and leaving things to Daniel a bit more." She nodded and smiled, then wiped her mouth with her napkin. Her voice tinkled into the silent room.

Henri Levitte snapped his fingers and the servant hastened to remove the plates.

Celeste said: "Hush, Maman."

But Hortense, her face deadly white against her extravagant black lace mourning dress, wouldn't be hushed. "Now my poor Marie-Thérèse is gone I want to see my dear son happy. Why won't you give him a place on the board, Henri? Can't a bereaved mother ask you that? I know you've been thinking of it."

Daniel's toes curled in horror at the cheapness of it. His father made no reply, but began to break a bread roll into dust, until the servant had left the room.

"I'm sorry we have to deal with this foolishness again," he said, "but I suppose this is as good a time as any. Now that Marie-Thérèse is dead, her part of the inheritance will go to Daniel. I'm sure Daniel will be glad about that. I expect his living expenses will continue to increase. But I presume he is not seriously talking about interfering in the affairs of the company again. I am afraid the company is not a charitable concern. I'd much rather Daniel used his talents doing all the things he is so good at."

Daniel nodded politely. And with equal politeness he said: "I do hope you did not object to the television interview I gave last night, Father. Naturally, the interviewer wanted to know if this flight marked the beginning of my joining the company again. I simply said the company's best interests would continue to be served."

"Very good," said Levitte. "Just so long as you appreciate that there is no chance we are going to repeat past disasters. Personally I would love to be able to look forward to my own son continuing my work. But you have no respect for me and my world. And there's no point in pretending otherwise. If I do make any arrangements about anything to do with the company, it will be for the good of the company."

Hortense clattered her fork on her plate. "How can you *say* that Henri, when the boy is risking his life flying in your aeroplane."

Henri Levitte said: "You should have married a green-grocer, Hortense."

It was no good. Daniel could take it all. He had heard it too often before. But it was not possible to eat at the same time. He pushed his plate away. Fortunately that diverted his mother. "You must eat, Daniel. You must keep up your strength."

Poor Daniel, thought Celeste. They would continue, both these two dreadful people, treating him like a child until the day they died. It was so unfair. She'd met Daniel after his disastrous spell of employment in the Euro-Aviat organization. He had been taken on to assist in employee welfare—a post designed to bring him into maximum conflict with his father in the minimum time. He had listened sympathetically to a union case brought him from the company's insulation sub-contractor in Lyons (a matter of lung damage to employees handling asbestos on contracts for Euro-Aviat). Henri Levitte had personally stopped the compensation that Daniel had arranged. The sub-contractor was responsible for his own men, and Euro-Aviat was not—as he still liked to remind Daniel—a charitable organization. As usual, the father had been harsh but right: to accept responsibility for sub-contractors' misfortunes would have set a disastrous precedent. The affair had had some publicity. It had been on that occasion that Rose first decided to put Daniel on his file.

The meal settled into a frigid silence, punctuated by the noisy sips Hortense took from her wine glass. Daniel wondered if his mother was becoming an alcoholic. The room was over-heated, the table over-cluttered with silver and china. The meal, brought in from the usual caterer, was cool and tasteless. Daniel wondered how much longer he could stand the stuffiness of the room and the gloom around the table.

Finally, Henri Levitte said, "It is going to be good weather, they say. Friday is a very important day, my dear Celeste. I am so happy Daniel is flying with the plane. I'm so happy our most important creation has *your* name." He patted her hand. She looked at her hand as if it did not belong to her. Involuntarily her knuckles clenched white.

"And now," said Henri Levitte, standing up brusquely and throwing his napkin on to the table, "I have work to do. I must see whether our Australian guests are going to be well entertained. We seem to have stolen a march on our friends at North-West Aerospace. Everyone is coming to Dreux."

The ghastly meal was really over at last.

"Oh there *is* one small thing," said Henri. "Celeste. By all means telephone Daniel at the base if you like. But—I shouldn't really say this even to you—every call in and out is being monitored. So if Daniel wants to say rude things about me, remind him of that. After poor Jean-Paul's death, the least we can do is keep the utmost security at Dreux."

Crispin Bridge enjoyed his midday meal. It was high time to eat. It was also high time to *think*.

He chose a warm, aromatic restaurant in the 18th arrondissement and then chose his own style of repast. *Vichyssoise*, two omelettes *aux fines herbes*, a huge dish of beans in white sauce, a green salad and three apples.

The chef was intrigued by this vegetarian Englishman. "It is good for the stomach to take a little meat, M'sieu," he suggested. "You ought to enjoy the foods of France while you are here."

Bridge looked at him and smiled peacefully. "Well, you can bring me some cheese," he said. The man bustled off and brought back a vast wooden board. In fact, he prided himself on his cheeses. "Let me recommend you a nice cheese," he said helpfully.

"Don't bother," said Bridge, "I'll have half of that one."

"*Half* of that?" said the proprietor. The disc of cheese was nearly two inches thick and eight inches across.

"That's right," said Bridge, "half the *Trappiste de Belval*."

The man looked at his customer with new respect. "Ah," he said, "M'sieu knows about cheese."

Bridge leant back. He was relaxed and content—and tired. Otherwise he wouldn't have bothered to show off. Keeping a low profile was one of the rules of the trade. But he hoped the job was nearly over. It should be.

"It's a good cheese," said Bridge. "Made at the Abbey of Belval in Picardy. Best of the monastery cheeses. Nice glossy rind. That's how you can tell it." Along with timetables, Bridge collected cheeses. The proprietor cut him half this one and left him to it. He would not, as a result, forget the interesting blond Englishman.

Which was a pity, from Bridge's point of view. The last message on Marcel Derivat's pad had been the nosy neighbour's sighting of a tall, blond man entering the apartment next door. This particular restaurant, Le Trou Normande, was the particular favourite eating place of the local police—and their increasingly large number of guests—who had now set up a Major Event HQ for the so-called Algerian terrorist murders.

Bridge ate and thought. He took it step-by-step. Because somewhere along the way, he was beginning to think, there was something very odd. Somewhere along the line he was being asked to believe the nearly unbelievable.

Rose had got him to fix Abdul Hassin. Nothing unusual there —normal line of business. Dirty little villain gets the notion of trading off some dirty pictures of a North-West call-girl and a Euro-Aviat pilot. And gets dealt with.

Right, we know all that.

Well, so Abdul also tried the same blackmail deal with the pilot—or his wife more likely. Reasonable too. The wife goes raving off to solicitors for a divorce, and private eyes go back to Abdul to fix some real nasty evidence. Believable too.

From here on, though, Bridge was not so sure. Would you believe Henri Levitte himself had got into the act at this stage, gone to see Claude and arranged a highly professional way of ridding himself of Jean-Paul Petit?

True, thought Bridge, it was a weird family. And if Henri Levitte *had* found out his beloved protégé was still into Claude *and* Marie-Thérèse (and once detectives started prying into him they'd have doubtless found all that out), then he could well decide enough was enough. But having met Henri, he couldn't imagine him doing it himself.

On the other hand, if you *did* want to have a member of the family murdered, what better time than the very day he was supposed to be flying your brand-new aeroplane?

Would a man like Henri Levitte go to that sort of length? Obviously his *son* would.

Bridge cut the rind off his cheese thoughtfully.

Why not get the money from Daniel, hand over the packets and go? No reason. There *shouldn't* be any reason. He'd walked into a crazy family, busy slaughtering each other like old-time Mafia. These things happened.

Bridge shook his head. He didn't believe a word of it.

He finished his meal at leisure, took the time from a fat-bellied grandfather clock ticking by the hearth, then strolled in the welcome sunlight to the nearest telephone booth. You could almost believe it would be spring soon. The warm air of Paris, carrying the smell of fish and old milk, in streets like this anyway.

He reached Rose. Rose sounded shrill. "What in hell have you been up to?" he complained. "I told you not to go crazy. Why haven't you rung in?"

Bridge smiled. "You want it both ways Rose? I thought you told me to go home."

"I told you to leave the Arab alone for a start," said Rose. "You're damn right you're on your own. We don't touch that sort of thing. That policeman wasn't you too, was it?"

Bridge scratched an index nail down the yellow paint of the booth. "These Algerian terrorists get everywhere," said Bridge. "Now look Rose, you know fucking well I wasn't going to go home. You know that and I know that. Not till I tried to find out who put that pilot job on me. Okay, that's the way you work. That's fine. You don't know anything about anything. You don't have to tell me how clean you are." He paused. Rose kept silent. "All right," said Bridge. "I'll just say goodbye, nice knowing you. Then you won't have to know anything that might keep you awake."

"Hold on," said Rose quickly.

Bridge listened.

"What *about* Friday, then? Is it on or off?"

"Oh, *Friday*. Yes. It's on."

"You're sure nobody's going to get hurt?"

"You keep asking that, Rose. I heard you."

"Yeah, well I know you, Bridge. Just remember this though. I *paid* you to go home. You go off and take another fee from that screwball son, I don't want to know."

"That isn't why I stayed in Paris," said Bridge.

"Well, don't stay any longer. Hand over anything you have to hand over. Then go. When are you planning to leave?"

"I'll take the 21.15 flight to Brussels. Tonight. Why?"

"Do you want cover?"

"Yes, thanks." Bridge told Rose the passport number and name he would be travelling on, the address in the passport and the profession, salesman.

"Hold on," said Rose.

"Now what?"

"Nothing. I write slowly. Okay. If you need it, ring M. Dumas. 233 5897. You've been selling him a new call system for his radio cabs."

But Bridge wasn't really listening. Not to Rose. He was suddenly trying to listen to something starting in his own head. He didn't know what, yet. Something as near and as far as a name you know perfectly well and can't retrieve from some corner of memory. But this wasn't quite something like a name. And with it went that odd feeling at the back of the neck you have in a dream when you are in an empty corridor and there is a footstep behind.

"Now," he heard Rose say. "What *did* you find out about the Petit job?" The voice was dry, distant and high.

"Nothing," said Bridge.

"Really?" said Rose, "but I thought you—. And Claude? Where is she?"

"Rose—there's a couple of men outside the box. I don't know where Claude is."

"Okay," came the answer quickly. "Take it easy then. If there is any trouble, leave me to sort it. Your kind of sorting— people don't seem to live too long. And listen, Bridge. Don't take a gun. Don't take anything but yourself. And if anyone does pick you up, just stay quiet."

After he had rung off, Bridge didn't move for a while. He thought that maybe, if he didn't move, the thing he was looking for in his head might surface by itself. Then he noticed there was indeed an old woman tapping patiently at the glass to get in. Politely he held the door open for her and walked all the way back to Celeste's apartment.

There was no chance for quiet thinking there. Nor sleep. Celeste rushed to him as he opened the door. She was still in that demure black dress, but barefoot, and her hair fallen sleek and free on her shoulders.

"We *must* talk," she said. "Now. While Daniel's out."

"Where is he?"

"He's down at the bar on the corner. He's starting to drink again. He wants you to meet him there."

Suddenly she started weeping, and sat on the bed; wrapped her arms about herself and rocked to and fro. Bridge looked at her in alarm. "Come on," he said. "Now what? Do you want some of that jasmine tea stuff?"

She looked up and smiled.

"Funerals suit you though," he said.

"Who *are* you?" she said.

"You know all about me."

"Wait a moment," she said, "and I'll stop."

He made the tea. A nice, cosy little scene too in the circumstances, he thought. A real English teapot, yellow with mauve flowers.

"I don't know who you are," she said, "but I know you can help Daniel. I know you can. You met his father?"

Bridge nodded.

"He's obsessed with his father. He just can't grow out of it. He's got to get free of him. How can I go on living with it all? I want Daniel. I want to live with him. I want to have children. You know—it's terrible but—you know what I keep thinking? Jean-Paul's dead and Marie-Thérèse. I keep thinking if only . . ."

She started weeping again.

"Drink your tea," said Bridge.

"I wish *he* was dead," said Celeste.

Bridge said nothing at all.

"All right," said Celeste. "I'll tell you what else I keep

thinking. I've got this feeling you and Daniel are up to something together. Are you? Well, you wouldn't say, would you.
But if you wanted to help Daniel, the best way to help Daniel
might not be what Daniel wants. I mean—"

Bridge crouched down on the floor in front of her. "Come
on," he said, "look at me. You and Daniel and Jean-Paul and
Marie-Thérèse and the old man. You think I can sort all that
out? I'm just here today and gone tomorrow. In fact I'm gone
tonight. Daniel goes to the base tonight. So I'm going home."

She leant forward and gripped his wrists. "You can't do
that," she cried. "I can't stay here on my own."

"Well," he laughed. "Friends, relations. You want me to
stay here with you?"

"You must," she said. "If you don't, I'm going. I'm just
going. I won't go to that damned place on Friday. I won't, I
won't."

Bridge stood up. This wasn't good.

"If you can't stay here on your own, get someone to come
here. Or go and stay with someone else."

"I'm frightened," she said, "I need to be in my own place.
And I don't want to make a fool of myself with friends."

"Look," he said. "I've got to deal with Daniel. The bar on
the corner on the left?"

She nodded. "You must help me," she said. "I don't know
how you can, but I know you could somehow."

He looked at her beautiful green eyes.

"Turn left out of the door," she said, gesturing with a
graceful hand, "then left again."

He went on looking at her. Until she frowned slightly.

"Celeste," he said. "Henri Levitte. Is he left-handed?"

"What a funny question."

"Think," he said.

"It's not the kind of thing you can remember. Why don't
you ask Daniel?"

"I'm asking you."

She thought. "No, he's not," she said. "Of course he's not.
I can remember watching him telephoning. He has a large
gold ring. He's not left-handed."

"Thank you very much," said Bridge. "Listen, can I telephone."

She nodded.

He took the phone into the kitchen and stubbed the dial fiercely. "Louis?" he demanded. "Paul here. Check out Orly for eight hours tonight. Don't ask why. Just drive out and ring me." He gave Louis, the fellow assassin of Jean-Paul, the number to ring. To Celeste he said, when he had put the phone down: "Maybe I'll stay for a bit." He picked up the plastic shopping bag he had already packed with what he now needed.

In the bar Bridge was sorry to see that Daniel Levitte was hitting the drink with some energy. Bridge sat down opposite him, moved the three-quarters full bottle of brandy firmly to one side and waited. Daniel went on making patterns on the table with the wet base of his glass: ring overlapping ring, then smudging them out with his fist.

"You haven't got time for that," said Bridge. He took the glass out of Daniel's hand and put it back on the table.

Daniel looked up. He was drunk already, thought Bridge with disgust. But careful drunk.

"I am sorry to have kept you waiting," said Daniel, "we had to go to see the grandfather." He seemed to brighten up. "And what did you think of the great Henri Levitte? Well on form today."

"If you say so," said Bridge. "Now listen, Daniel. Listen hard. I *did* find Claude. I found a lot else. You remember you said Jean-Paul's wife was thinking of going for a divorce? Well it looks as if she did a bit more than think. Suppose someone showed your old man pictures of Jean-Paul with Marie-Thérèse, with Claude—that sort of thing. You know your father. You may hate his guts, but you know him and I don't. Now would a man like your father be so angry with Jean-Paul— after he'd done everything for him, made him a top pilot, all that? *How* angry would he get if he found Jean-Paul was still screwing your sister?"

Daniel slapped the table in anger.

"All right, not screwing, having their whatever it is. And keeping it *quiet*."

"They loved each other," said Daniel. "You know what that means?"

"That's right," said Bridge.

"Yes, that's *right*," said Daniel. "But you wouldn't know at all, would you? You know what all this is about? Really? They loved each other. They're dead. None of the rest matters. A week ago they were alive and walking about. Real people. *Real!*"

"Christ! Try and concentrate Daniel. *Would your father be so angry with Jean-Paul that he'd get Jean-Paul killed?*"

It worked. Daniel Levitte put down the glass he had just picked up again.

"What?" he asked quietly.

"It's what Claude was saying. About your father. Would you believe your father went to see her? Would he do that? Himself?"

"Who killed Jean-Paul?" said Daniel. His eyes were hard on Bridge.

"I'm asking you."

Daniel picked the glass up again and swallowed.

"Machines," he said.

"What?"

"My father only cares about his machines. People? He treats them like machines."

"Daniel," said Bridge, "I'm trying to talk about facts. Sober up."

"So am I," said Daniel. "My father killed my sister. I told you that."

Bridge gave it up. He wouldn't get any more sense out of Daniel, that was plain. He beckoned the waiter, got a glass and poured himself a large brandy. He'd run out of people who could make sense of it. It was his job now. Daniel went back to making his rings on the table. The bar was dark. Back in the seventies someone had tried to make it into an English pub. Now the mass of mahogany and cut glass, brought over from Lambeth and installed in Paris, was looking as authentic as the real thing. A fly paper from last summer hung from the yellow ceiling. Fly papers were chic last year. Everyone in Paris had them, in the smart hairdressing salons, even the restaurants. Like the cult of Russian posters at Celeste's studio. It's the all-real style. If there are real flies: catch them on a real fly paper.

Bridge looked at the fly paper a moment and the dried
6*

particles of tissue stuck, at the end of a brief flight to somewhere else, upon it. He knew this was the time to decide. Fuck
it, Bridge told himself, get the money and get out. Don't go to
Orly, do it the way you did in '73: a single ticket to one of the
Normandy ports, a quick knife through the canvas winter cover
of a thirty-two footer and no-one to see a small boat drifting
into the channel at three in the morning. Then a four days'
quiet sailing to Dale in Wales and open the sea cocks 200 feet
from the shore and come in on the dinghy. Why stay?

"Well Daniel," said Bridge. "What about the money?"

Daniel Levitte took a fat envelope from his pocket and pushed
it across the table.

"Fifty thousand," he said. Bridge took it, rubbed the thick-
ness of the packet in his fingers.

"Good," said Bridge. "Did you write a letter for your
father?"

Daniel nodded. Like a drunk conjuror beginning a trick he
took a white envelope from his inside pocket and handed it
over. The envelope was sealed.

"Do you want to count your money?" asked Daniel,
insultingly.

"No," said Bridge. "But I want to know what this says."
He waved Daniel's letter.

"You can read it," said Daniel.

Bridge stood up. "Where's the loo?"

Daniel nodded to the back of the bar.

"Stay here. And don't drink. I'll bring you your new toys.
And you'd better stay sober and learn how to use them."

"Wait a moment," said Daniel. He looked cunning. "Leave
that money here. You might just disappear."

"Jesus," said Bridge. "It's lying there in front of you,
Daniel."

"So it is," said Daniel. "Sorry."

He didn't look up. His head was bent over his game with the
glass. Bridge set his plastic shopping bag down again, dropped
Daniel's letter on the bar table and sat down himself.

"Well, why don't I have my treat here?" he asked. He tore
the letter open and fingered through the three pages of tight,
angular writing. Daniel, he knew, was alert now and watching
him again.

"My dear Father. Maybe I am writing to you, not from a grave, but from the scattered pieces of your beloved aeroplane. So this is a letter from all your four 'children'—this machine, this Jean-Paul, this Marie-Thérèse, this Daniel. Can you imagine how glad we are?"

Bridge flicked through the other pages, running his finger down the middle of the lines.

"Well?" said Daniel.

"That's fine," said Bridge. "I'm glad you started with a maybe. Anyway, I just wanted to know you weren't landing me in any shit."

The two men watched each other until Daniel shrugged.

"Oh yes," said Daniel, "I'm sorry. I should have remembered. Doesn't matter to you, any of it, does it. 'Land you in the shit'. No, that's right. Letter isn't about you. It's about me. Forget it."

Bridge folded the letter. "You want to kill yourself, Daniel, nobody's stopping you. I asked you all that yesterday and you didn't want to talk about it. So now I'm doing what you pay me for."

"I want to kill myself?" said Daniel. He lit a Gauloise, breaking three matches to do so.

"It doesn't read like much else," said Bridge, "but I'm not asking."

"No. You *ask*," said Daniel. "You want another drink? You want me to pay you overtime to listen? No, I forgot. You're not interested. You told me to write a letter—there it is. I don't know why you find it so boring, though. I find other people very interesting."

"You're drunk, Daniel. Anyone as interested in yourself as you are, you've got all the audience you want. Now shut up and listen. You remember the places I told you to put the package?"

"Yes."

"Well, do yourself a favour and leave it at that. Just hit the fucking plane if that's what you have to do. Now, I'm going to the loo. I'm going to fix up those two envelopes and the radio."

He got up again and grabbed his plastic bag. Much more from Daniel Levitte, he thought, and Daniel Levitte wouldn't even make it as far as the air base.

Bridge locked the lavatory door, stuffed paper in a hole drilled through it, and sat down. He took the small transistor radio out of its polystyrene box in the shopping bag and checked that it was switched off. The frequency, he knew, had been cemented on line. Then he unscrewed the back with his fingernail and dropped four slim batteries into place. Very carefully he closed the device up again and put the radio on the floor. Then the envelopes. It was no problem to tell them apart, since Bridge had already sealed the explosive pack with old-fashioned red sealing wax. He inserted Daniel's letter into the other, and, with his cigarette lighter, melted enough wax to run neatly across the seal. He lightly pressed the base of the lighter into the wax to distinguish the one envelope from the other.

Then he rejoined Daniel Levitte. The whole operation had taken less than two minutes.

He passed the radio across the table. "There you are," he said. "Top right hand corner there's an AM switch to FM. Switch it on to AM if anyone asks you. Then switch to FM and pull out the aerial and you've got a transmitter. As soon as you point the aerial inside seventy yards you'll detonate. Got that?"

Daniel nodded. "And on AM it works as a radio?"

"That's right. But don't use it. You need everything out of those batteries."

Bridge glanced round the bar. The booth they were sitting in was as dark and unobserved as it ever would be. "And here's your letter to your father. Write his name on it. Now. And under it put 'To be opened after take-off: urgent'."

"What's this stuff?" asked Daniel.

"Sealing wax."

"That's a pretty weird idea."

"It's a private letter. If they do get interested in it, on the security side, don't make it easy for them. Tell them it's private. Make a fuss. When Celeste brings the real thing in in her handbag they won't be so ready to make another fuss. The other thing is, of course, that the one I'm giving her is sealed up too. Because we don't want Celeste opening the bomb to read your letter."

"You have to give her—*it*? The real one?"

"Damn right I do. Don't tell her about it. I'll say you left it with me. The less time she has it in her hands the less time she has to get curious. Now write on that envelope too. Same words."

He wrote. The packages seemed to fascinate him. He picked them up apprehensively.

"You're sure this fucking thing won't go off in my pocket?" he said.

"No," said Bridge, "it won't do that. It goes off if you open it and if you beam its signal at it."

"I don't *want* Celeste having to carry this," said Daniel. "Why don't I just take the real one in with me?"

"I told you. They'll maybe screen you. But they'll probably just look in *her* handbag. And if they start fiddling with the radio you don't want to have the bomb near you anyway. That's the first reason. The other is having a good reason to carry that envelope around with you while they get you into your suit. You've got to be able to say exactly why they can't be nice and helpful and deliver the letter themselves. You're waiting for Celeste to arrive with another letter. Just tell them all about it. You wanted to write a last letter to your father in case you didn't come down, and you wrote one letter and then another one and you've changed your mind. They'll soon lose interest."

"Yes," said Daniel, "I expect they will. If you're anything to go by." He smiled. He seemed more relaxed now. He touched the packet again and stroked it.

"Well, they'll be thinking of other things, won't they?" said Bridge gently. "Like ten years of building an aeroplane, and hoping it's going to work a treat, and whether they're going to sell it to the Australians. Crap like that."

"That's right," said Daniel. "I hope they are. It's not my firm, is it? They fired *me*. It'll be really nice seeing some of those smug bastards' faces again. I want to shake their hands and listen to them saying how nice it is to see me again. Right! I've sobered up. Let's get out. Leave me to have a word with Celeste. In fact I'm going to be collected in an hour's time. I presume you are not coming to watch the show on Friday?"

"Yes," said Bridge. "I'll be building a nice quiet alibi somewhere."

The glass doors of the bar swung shut behind them. The evening was clear and hard, the temperature hovering on zero.

"And Daniel," said Bridge, "about alibis. Just in case you ever thought you might like to mess me into this. Anything like that. You don't know my real name, and you don't know where I come from. And if you try to start putting anything on me you're not going to catch up with me. But *I'll* catch up with *you*. You or your kids if you have any or whatever. Now that's a promise. That's the way I work."

"I know," said Daniel. He didn't look at all drunk now. His eyes were a little too wide open, too much staring into his dark world. But then all the Levittes had such eyes. "We won't be seeing each other again," said Daniel. He laughed. "Be kind to Celeste, won't you? She likes you. She likes me. Good judge of character, isn't she? Well, there we are." He nodded, smiled again with one side of his mouth, and walked back down the street. Bridge called him back. "Daniel," he said. "Put it on the nose wheel. That's the best place. That'll do you fine." Daniel nodded again and left him.

The sunlight was already lost on the street level. Only the chimneys, roofs and skies above were still enjoying the un-expected gold of a clear February afternoon.

And in another part of the sky the Australians in their 747 were sleeping on their way towards Europe.

With dusk, at Dreux, the security perimeter began to come down to ring the beautiful blue aeroplane with a circle of safety. An anthropologist from another planet would have realized at once that the Super-Celeste was a goddess of some kind. She was attended by her priests. She was pulling towards herself, with mystical powers, worshippers from all parts of the world for some special ceremony. Probably, if other human religions were any guide, some ritual of sacrifice.

PART FOUR

"If you do that again, sonny, I'm going to break your neck," said Melvyn Murray. He was crushed behind a barrier with 300 other people in the steam bath of Bangkok airport. The 747 taking him back to Paris had sprung an oil leak. The offending child had bought one of those battery-powered devices that gives out a peal of derisive, maniacal laughter. Again and again and again.

"What you say to my boy? What he say to you Kev?" said the bull-necked New Zealander father: hot enough to start a fight.

"I told him to can that fucking noise," said Melvyn.

The New Zealander raised a quivering fist—then the scene broke as the baby-voiced Thai announcer informed them that the repair had now been made but by international aviation law the crew was due for a ten-hour rest period.

Melvyn just stood looking at the empty destination board. He shook his head three times very slowly. Sweat trickled down his brow and stung his eyes like tears.

Everybody comes to the time in their life when enough is enough. "I'm fifty-three years old," thought Murray. As it had gone, so it had gone. A week ago: on top of the heap. The super-salesman whose comings and goings filled an inch or so at least every month in the diary columns of the world's aviation magazines. Known for his cool and his command. What had he said to Ackermann? *You'd do the same for me.*

Fifty-three years old. Three marriages. The third now no more than a civilized arrangement for the sake of a trio of insolent, greedy, adolescent offspring. Standing in a stinking airport on his way to Paris. Not to sell anyone a plane but to encourage a little creep called Rose to blow up somebody else's.

A decision had been taking shape in his mind ever since he had slammed the door on his colleagues in Sydney. Like an oil bubble coming up through water. This was no good any more.

Why had he taken Ackermann to Wiseman's Ferry? To offer another middle-aged salesman a bribe? No. He had invited himself to Wiseman's Ferry. To meet himself. "No-one in the world knows we are here," he had said to Ackermann, he remembered. It was a lie, as they both knew. It had been there that Daniel Levitte had telephoned him.

When you get to the crossroads, and decide to take the fifth way out, you still have to go to somewhere. Murray's life style had made so many places in the world familiar to him that he had no kind of personal geography, not the way most men do. There was no one small town whose every corner he knew. Nowhere his heart was lodged. He just knew pieces of it all. Had it been himself or Ackermann who had said, looking at the wide, brown river at Wiseman's Ferry "I could have bought a farm here"? It didn't matter.

Melvyn Murray went to the British Airways desk, cashed in his ticket and booked a single ticket back to Sydney. There was a flight within the hour, but he did not take it. Instead, he checked out and took a cab to the Europa Hotel, where he booked two calls. The first to Rose. The second to Hermann Ackermann's office.

The call to Rose reached him at 10.15 at night. To the moment. To the exact moment that Crispin Bridge was due to fly out of Orly back to London. It was because of that that Rose was still in his office. What he had not imagined was that Vic Wild would have stayed on too.

Rose spent many hours in his office alone. He sat at his desk, the rest of the building empty, apart from the night cleaners. The pool of light from the desk lamp soaking into the black leather of the desk top which was always, at the end of the day, clean of papers and dust. Rose used to rub the desk surface clean himself. And then he would often sit there alone. Hour after hour.

Sometimes, Wild would pass the building late at night, on way back from a film or restaurant, and see the light still on. Why had Wild stayed on tonight? Victor Wild had enough instinct to know there was something in the air, too. He had a gut feeling. He knew the deal with the Australians was in a ruin. He knew—though not what it was—that there was something else.

Rose sat at his desk tonight. A silence had developed between himself and his colleague. Instead of sitting, as he normally did, with an empty surface in front of him, Rose had put a few papers before him. From time to time he sucked the fingertips of his right hand.

The phone rang in the outer office. Murray had got to the official switchboard number and not to the one on Rose's desk. Rose, already angry at Wild's staying on, let his colleague pick up the phone, then heavily pressed the buttons that would transfer the call, record it, and allow Wild to listen in.

THIRD CONVERSATION TAPE 4DZ79 22.15 hours PARIS

MURRAY: Am I through to you, Rose?

ROSE: Nice to hear you, Murray. Where are you?

MURRAY: Bangkok. I don't know what you've heard. Everything's crumbled in Australia. They're all on their way to Paris to see the Frog fly.

ROSE: That's tough for you, Murray.

MURRAY: That seems to be the idea. You're talking to the corporation scapegoat.

ROSE: Sorry about that.

MURRAY: Yeah. Well I've got a new mission. I'm supposed to come to Paris and lean on you.

ROSE: Come again?

MURRAY: You remember the young man who came to me. The one who wants to do a demolition job.

ROSE: Yes.

MURRAY: Well, this corporation has run out of alternatives. I am supposed to come to Paris and see what you're doing about it.

ROSE: Whose idea is that?

MURRAY: The whole team.

ROSE: Good Christ!

MURRAY: Well. What *is* happening on it? Anything?

ROSE: *Are* you coming to Paris?

MURRAY: I don't know, Rose. My job's selling aeroplanes. I'm sitting here getting drunk and thinking of retiring. This project—the one we're talking about—this is supposed to be Melvyn Murray's chance to help himself out of the shit. So what goes on with it? Is it fixed up?

ROSE: No, Murray. I haven't been able to do anything on it.
MURRAY: You haven't?
ROSE: Too far out.
MURRAY: Well, you can wave North-West goodbye for me, Rose. There's not much point in coming to Paris to watch the funeral. The dingos buy the Celeste and we go back to bicycles. Jesus, Rose! If you could have stopped that thing on Friday I'd still have a job and the firm would still have a machine to sell. You do know that, don't you?
ROSE: I don't know, Murray.
MURRAY: Well, have fun. And if anybody asks, my letter of resignation is in the post.
END TAPE THREE

Murray laid the phone back, went to the window and looked at the dance of lights from Bangkok, far below his hotel room. He stripped the top from the second bottle of Scotch he had ordered and poured himself a half tumbler. "Stupid little bastard," he said. The reception rang him to ask if he now wanted his next call put through. "No," said Murray. "It doesn't matter now." By now Ackermann should know he could afford to collect the money and win anyway. North-West would never dare ask for it back.

Rose waited for Wild to come in from the outer office where, obviously, he had been listening in. Rose checked the time again. It was a pity about Wild. But it had to come. It was going to be time to have it out with his colleague.

Wild stood in front of the desk, his arms hanging loose, waiting for Rose to look up and face him.

"That's one of the best men this corporation had," he said.

In the isolated pools of light, in the silent office, the hum of the central heating in the background, Wild sounded louder than life.

"I've always thought so," said Rose. He sat at his desk, neat, calm, his small, plump features totally without expression.

Wild stripped off his tie and flung it on the desk.

"Jesus!" he said.

Rose picked up the tie, folded it neatly and laid it on the farther edge of the desk, ready for Wild to take away.

"So why didn't we do this job?" said Wild. "Will you mind just telling me that, Rose? Are we really paid to sit here and watch the whole fucking programme go down the plug? Christ, Rose. All that screwball needed was a nudge in the right direction. All *we* needed. What's the poor sod Murray going to do now? What happens to North-West? You realize you've just thrown the whole game away?"

"Sit down," said Rose.

Wild had never, ever, seen Rose angry about anything. He saw it now. He picked up a chair and swung it noisily. He sat down, tilted his chair and put his feet on the corner of Rose's desk.

"Get your feet off there," said Rose.

"I'm going to tell people about this one," said Wild. "I am really going to see to it. You're not acting for the company, Rose."

"No," said Rose. "That's not what is going to happen. Now listen, Wild. I want you to do some thinking for a change. Right? Melvyn Murray. North-West salesman. He's got a kick in the teeth from the corporation. He's bitter as hell. He's thinking of resigning. He's told to come to Paris and he doesn't. He calls me instead and asks what's happening. On the phone. You know what happens to people when they get bitter and think of resigning? They start thinking about their future. They start thinking of kicking the old firm straight back in the balls. Come on, Wild. Just work it out a bit. You mean I should tell Murray 'don't worry old friend, we're seeing to it that plane blows up on Friday'? How much do you reckon that information is worth to a man who's been put down by his colleagues and is getting drunk by himself in a Bangkok hotel? What you want me to say to him? 'It's a big secret Murray, promise you won't ring up your pal Ackermann and tip him the story'? Did you know Murray had authority from his office to bribe Ackermann with a life pension to ease up on this project?"

"No," said Wild. "I didn't." He took his feet off the desk. And began to pay attention.

"I'm sorry, Rose. If you're right about that. But you don't take me into your confidence. See it from my side. We work together, for Christ's sake. And anyway, that's a side issue. The point is, *we should have done the job.*"

For fifteen seconds the two men looked at each other.

"Or are you saying we *are* doing the job?" asked Wild.

Rose's desk phone rang. The words were few. Wild heard a man's voice say simply, "Nobody came."

"Okay," said Rose, "I'll let you know."

"Is that what you're saying?" asked Wild.

"Wait a moment," said Rose. He went to the door and locked it. "Is the front shut?" he asked.

"Doubt it," said Wild, "cleaners in."

"Yeah. Well that's a pity."

"Expecting visitors?"

"We might be. Unfortunately."

Wild stood up and went to look from the window. The street was empty.

"Don't stand around there," said Rose.

Wild came back, quickly. "So something *is* on," he said.

"I'll tell you Wild. I want to tell you something you ought to know by now, anyway. Or maybe something you seem to have forgotten, because it's the first fucking thing *I* learnt in the CIA."

"Go on."

"You act in private. If necessary you even die in private. You ever carry a suicide pill on a mission? I did ten. And in those days it was cyanide. A lousy way to go. Do you think I work for this corporation so they can say 'Look at that good job Rose did'? I don't want them to *know* the jobs I'm doing. All that crap about 'You and I work together': *I* work for them. *You* work for them. We do it in private. We keep it so private that *no-one* knows. Like my year when I went to work for someone else? You still haven't got enough sense to understand me?"

"I'm sorry, Rose. I got it wrong again."

"Yeah. And I've had a week of you sitting on your ass, and giving off a big stink of resenting it. And that's bad. Because I've had enough else going on without that. Did you ever imagine we'd have this scene where half the corporation actually knows about this thing from Daniel Levitte? People ringing up actually saying 'Are you going to blow up a plane?' The way you serve a corporation in this game, Wild, is to protect them from their own stupidity. *If* anything happened to that plane on Friday, that is going to be nothing to do with

North-West. Not a whisper. It never happened. We got a call from the young man and we told him to get a shrink. And we wrote to his girl to tell her. Remember? It was your fucking idea, no less."

"Do you want me to apply for a transfer?" said Wild. "We've done pretty well for a few years, Rose. Maybe you're right. I'm not a professional. That sort of thing—is too lonely for me."

"For Christ's sake," said Rose. "Don't grovel!" He cocked his head and listened.

"Cleaners in the corridor," said Wild.

Rose nodded.

"I won't ask you any more," said Wild. "I haven't been too bright."

"That's right," said Rose. "But you're going to hear some more anyway."

"Why?"

"Because I may not be around."

"Okay."

"It's not okay," said Rose. "This job. I think it's going to turn out it was *not* a good idea."

"I'm not asking any questions, Rosy. Tell me what you want to tell me. Is there somebody out there?"

Rose seemed not to hear him.

"Wild. If I end up dead—shut *up*, don't say anything—there's a man you are going to have to look out for. He's called, for our purposes, Crispin Bridge. He shot the pilot. He's fixed up Daniel Levitte. I don't think you're going to find him because I don't think he's going to come looking. Not after he's found me."

"That Englishman? The one I saw months back? You really did that, Rose? God Almighty! The *pilot*? Petit? You had that done?"

"I didn't say that, I said he did it."

"Where is he now?"

"I'll tell you where he should be. He should be at Orly, dead. Police had a marksman there."

"The police know all this? Rose: the whole thing is going to break round us!"

"Not *the* police. A police. One of the Specials. Roget. You know him. Bridge murdered an Arab and a policeman. Nobody asked him to do that."

"The truth is going to come out," said Wild.

"Jesus, Wild, what do you think truth is?"

"Look," said Wild. "If there's a man out there, you and I don't have time to swap philosophy, for Christ's sake."

"We have time," said Rose. "Let me tell you about the truth, Wild. Stop twitching around. Bridge isn't going to shoot the fucking door in. You remember those old ladies used to go out wearing clean underwear in case they got knocked down by a bus?"

"You're not making much sense to me, Rose."

"I'll get there. Look at this office. This is our clean underwear. Right? Anybody raided this office and took it to pieces for a week they wouldn't find a thing here, would they? There's no files, there's no papers. Everything we do—everything we really do—where do we keep it?"

"In our heads. Except for your tapes."

"That's right. In our heads. You ever work for Nixon when you were in the club?"

"No."

"Okay. You remember the great thing they were looking for all the time in Watergate, all those shining knights in Congress? The smoking gun. Remember that phrase? That's the other notion of truth. Something you find lying around in a heap. And that one's just for criminals who leave the corpse buried in the window-box. I'll tell you how you and me and Nixon ran the truth: *it's in the head*. It's a collection of different stories in different peoples' heads. And if your head gets blown off, the truth gets blown with it. You ever hear of the doctrine of Credible Deniability?"

"I'm not a great thinker, Rose."

"Two years after Watergate. *Two years*. When everything was supposed to be cleaned up and shining again, the doctrine of Credible Deniability was official United States diplomatic practice. You know what it meant? It meant if a diplomat could safely say with his hand on his heart that something didn't happen then he was allowed to say that."

"Yeah, but Nixon: they found the smoking gun. They found the tapes. And *you* make tapes, come to that."

"And I *really* rub them out. Shall I tell you about those Nixon tapes? All the millions of words written about all that stuff. No-one ever made sense of it, all those fucking journalists and congressmen. Shall I tell you that those tapes were about? Truth is in the head, right? It's nowhere else. You do a job and you cover your tracks. Then you cover the tracks you make covering the tracks. You launder the money. You get a man to do a job and he doesn't know who he's working for. And the job he thinks he's doing isn't really the job he thinks he's doing. And the people you get the job done for don't know you're doing the job for them. And if the job goes wrong there's no way anyone is going to put that picture together again. Because it never was together. Bridge couldn't be sure he was working for me when he killed the pilot. North-West didn't know the pilot was going to get killed. The pilot didn't know he was going to get killed. The girl who got him on to the target didn't know what she was doing. Right?"

"I thought you were talking about Nixon."

"I am. That man *knew* about truth. He knew it was something in the head. And if you're into things on the scale he was then you need one hell of a big head to hold it. You know what those tapes of his were? He was just trying to make his head bigger. He really regarded those tapes as part of his own private head. Just memory. Now. If you've got a fact in your head and you forget that fact there's nobody can blame you. That's what that game was about—bits getting rubbed off the tape. Okay. That's where he got off line. He believed you could forget this and that and it never happened. He was too bloody honest— that was his trouble. He could have wiped everything off, any time. Nobody could work out why he didn't. I'm telling you. He made a simple, logical error. He thought that because he had made it all up anyway it belonged to him."

"Beyond me, Rose. Where *is* this Bridge, do you reckon? I mean—him we can't forget."

"God knows. But wherever he is, I'll tell you this: there's still no way it is ever going to be laid at North-West's door. And you don't have to tell anyone in the Corporation that we did the job for them."

"They wanted it done."

"No they didn't. Did anyone ever tell us to go and do it?"

"Murray just did."

"And if anything went wrong with it and you and I admitted doing it, what would happen to us?"

"The Corporation would turn us over to the police. I know that."

"Right. So remember that. That's your insurance. We didn't do it."

Rose put on his neat black coat and patted the shoulders free of a few grains of dust. He looked like a little pink-faced lay preacher off to the boys' club.

Wild picked up his own tie and ran it through his fingers.

"What *do* you work for, Rose? I mean: it's not like carrying a cyanide pill for the American way of life. North-West Aerospace is a business. You going to go out there and deal with some killer and maybe get killed and you don't even mind if nobody ever knows what you've done for this damn outfit?"

"It's not a damn outfit," said Rose. "It's one of the biggest aerospace industries in the world. It has a plane that has taken ten years to build and there's hundreds of thousands of people depending on selling it. You've always made some fun of me going round to the conventions, meeting these people. And I know they don't want to meet me. But I've worked for this lot just as much as the pilots and the designers and the rest of them. Any human outfit, Wild, there's shit to shovel. The cheap bastards are the ones who build a bit of glory out of burying men like me and Nixon when their whole nice, clean life depends on *having* people like us keeping it clean for them. You religious, Wild?"

"No," said Wild, embarrassed.

"Maybe I am," said Rose. "Maybe someone does have to shovel the shit for all those nice, clean family men in Texas building nice, clean aeroplanes. Think about it, Wild. This plane doesn't fly on Friday and 70,000 Americans get a living for the next ten years building F-24s. It could happen. Jean-Paul lived a dangerous life anyway—okay, he wasn't shot down in a nice, normal war, but what else are we fighting except a war between economics in Europe and the US? He was flying a killer plane and we are flying a killer plane. Why's anyone go to war except to win? What are they trying to win except the chance to live a decent life earning a good screw?"

"One last time," said Wild, "stay here the night. I can get a gun. *Something*."

"No thanks. You're not so young any more either. And this man is a good one. He has an SAS training behind him. You'd never see him in a hundred years if he decided to come for you."

Wild shook his head. "I think you're in a state, Rose. I think you're not making sense."

"Anyway," said Rose, "I want to find out how the hell he found out."

Wild ducked back from the door as Rose unlocked and opened it. He heard Rose's steps fade into the corridor, and the hum of the elevator coming up the building to collect him.

For the first time in his life, he went to Rose's desk and opened the drawers. As he expected. They were empty. He should have known, he thought. All those hours Rose spent up here alone. The man was going out of his head. A man who thinks Richard Nixon was Jesus Christ?

"Tell me the truth," said Celeste. "What is this thing about a letter you have for me?"

Bridge noted the girl's tension. There had obviously been emotional farewells. He'd left Daniel a clear hour to make them.

"Later," said Bridge.

"I'm not going to open it. He made that clear. I have to give it to him on Friday. So give it to me now."

"*Later*," said Bridge. "He told me to give it to you later."

"He seemed so upset."

Trust Daniel to make it all hard for everybody, thought Bridge.

"Did anyone telephone me?" he asked.

"No. Are you staying here?"

"That depends. Depends if this man rings me."

"And on me," she said sharply.

"Of course," said Bridge. "But I thought you'd said you wanted that."

She was looking very, very beautiful. Her hair rumpled, her dress not buttoned at the throat, as if she had put it on in a hurry.

She shook her head. "Yes, I want you to stay. I'm used to having strangers in the house."

"What do you mean by that?"

"You and him. Why do you have to have secrets all the time? Will you get me a drink?"

He poured her a Cinzano.

The phone rang. She moved to it, then turned to him questioning.

"Take it," he said. "Anybody asks if I'm here I'm not."

She picked it up. Bridge moved to stand close to her so he could hear the voice. He was very close to that beautiful sweep of tumbling hair, and its fragrance. When he recognized the voice he took the phone from her.

"Go on then," said Bridge. It was Louis.

"I've been there. You're right. Just one of them. Roget. He takes on this sort of thing. You want to know where he is? Up in the rafters ready for a single from seventy degrees and no ricochet."

"Can you take him?"

"Sure, but what are we starting on?"

"Nothing we can't finish. I told you there'd be only one. Right? This is one-to-one deal. You take him and I'll take the other."

"You sure? Who is it?"

"The man who gave us the trip to the vegetable market, Louis."

"Bastard. You've been lucky."

"Get on with it, Louis."

He put the phone down. Celeste looked puzzled. "Vegetables?" she said.

"That's right. I buy and sell things. I do deals."

She smiled. "Do you ever tell anyone the truth?" she asked.

"Oh yes," said Bridge. "I'm different. I always tell everybody the truth. Things only start going wrong when people don't tell *me* the truth. I'm staying, by the way."

Her eyes widened. "Why? I mean why suddenly?"

"Because I've got somewhere else to go before I go where I have to go after I've been somewhere else."

She laughed. "That's not saying anything."

"Yes it is."

She finished the drink and asked if he wanted another. He shook his head.

"And while I'm here," said Bridge, "if anyone wants to know if I'm here, I'm not."

Celeste felt the drink and the fatigue of the day going to her head and her limbs. She felt she was floating, that she needed something she had long gone without.

"You are my imaginary companion are you," she asked, "someone who never happened? I do wish I *did* know who you are. You're like Daniel because you are full of secrets and, my God, you're not like Daniel because you seem to know what to do with them, whatever they are."

Bridge checked his watch. He reckoned it would be half an hour, twenty-five minutes to be safe.

"I'm going out," he said. "I'll be back in an hour."

"There's one thing you should know," she said. She was angry he was going out. She was very cool now, no evasions.

"If you stay here with me, whether anyone knows or not. You sleep there and I sleep here. There's not going to be any of that."

Bridge smiled. It was the first time she'd ever seen anything in his eyes except that strange camera.

"Want me to tell you the truth?" he asked.

"Yes?"

"We'll see."

He was gone before she could say anything, angry or otherwise.

Rose, waiting for the elevator to arrive, watched the numbers of the floor flicking left to right, listened to the hum of the box approaching. The svelte aluminum doors trembled slightly, then slid open in front of him. The elevator was empty, apart from a dust-pan and brush left by a cleaner. The doors hushed shut behind him and the box went back down to the street, with Rose inside.

The foyer was empty too. The typewriter on the receptionist's desk was shrouded in its grey hood. The glass doors to the street were bolted top and bottom. So, obviously, the concierge was in the building already. Well, the concierge would just have to come down and bolt them again.

Rose stooped, clearly visible in the strip light from the cinema opposite, and unbolted the foot of the door. There was a letter on the mat, addressed to him. He recognized the printed device on the envelope. It was from the printers of the brochures the office turned out in official working hours. Rose picked up the letter and laid it on the cover of the receptionist's typewriter.

When he swung the door open, the cold from the clear night moved in like a wall.

At any time, there are those who find the Champs Elysées a lonely place. Even in midsummer, the empty August of Paris, there is something too wide, too remorseless for the individual in its long sweep uphill. And in the huge windows the display of goods seems chilling—a cold display of wealth directed not at the passer-by but at some world audience a long way from street level.

For Rose, as he walked with small, precise steps to a corner he did not know if he would reach, the night was exhilarating. His mood was, as it happened, much like that of Daniel Levitte who was, at this moment, being driven towards Dreux in a company car, a fat blue envelope against his heart.

In Paris, the clear night was holding good. Small breezes, changing direction minute by minute, dabbed like fingers at Rose's impassive cheeks.

Crispin Bridge joined him at the corner.

"Keep walking with me," said Bridge. "If there's anyone else around with you, you'd better tell them to lay off. I've got a gun on you."

"Bridge!" said Rose. "Of course there's no-one else. I thought you were flying out tonight."

"Well, I got put off the idea," said Bridge. "They've got some trouble at Orly. Policeman fell off the roof, I'm told."

The two men walked in silence, turning out of the well-lit main street of Paris and towards the first, darker, *rond-point*. Rose hesitated.

"Walk," said Bridge.

"What do you mean, a gun? What do you think I've done, Bridge?"

"Oh, I think you know, Rose. I think you know. Don't worry. You're going to stay alive."

Rose felt the chill grip his spine. He sensed it was one of Bridge's well-used devices. How he would say, with all the warm assurance from that simple, ruddy face under its crop of blond hair: "don't worry, you're going to stay alive".

"What would you like, Rose? Would you like a coffee. Would you like something stronger? You choose."

They were passing a restaurant. It seemed well lit.

Rose said: "I'd like a meal, Bridge. I feel really hungry. Why don't you be my guest?"

Bridge smiled. "That's a good idea, Rose. You mean here? You'd like to sit down in the middle of the restaurant under the big lights? Well that's a good idea."

The floor waiter, seeing the two men hovering, padded discreetly to swing the door open for them. They needed customers. The place was nearly empty: too empty, in fact, to give Rose much cheer. The waiter took their coats and offered them a quiet side table. Bridge said: "No, we'd like to sit in the middle. Over there."

"Of course, m'sieu." Even better for business. Anyone passing by would now see the restaurant was well occupied. The waiter beckoned his associates. A leather-bound menu the size of Shakespeare's first folio appeared.

Normally, these two men would not have been an answer to any restaurateur's prayer. Rose, who stayed rigidly with steak and french fries, despising French food on principle—and Bridge, with his doctrinaire diet of fresh vegetables and cheese.

"Have a proper meal," said Bridge. "You work too hard, Rose. And you must let *me* pay. You keep paying me so much money and we don't want to waste it, do we. I'm not in a hurry. Are you? I've got time to kill." He smiled at the waiter, who nodded encouragingly.

"Bring me two large Pernods," said Bridge. "While we think. Put your hands on the table, Rose," he added swiftly.

Rose laid his hands on the white linen.

"Not my drink, Pernod," said Rose. "You'll have to help me out."

"You'll drink it," said Bridge. "I don't like it either. I'd say: let's drink it for Daniel Levitte, who liked it."

The wine waiter poured the yellow liquid out and Bridge added the water to make the luminous yellow cloudy.

Bridge raised his glass. "And here's to Jean-Paul Petit, and Abdul Hassin. Wait a moment, Rose. And to that young policeman, Marcel Derivat. And what's this man tonight? Roget. That's quite a collection, Rose. Now why did you want to add me to the heap?"

Rose drank, and grimaced. The first waiter was back for their order.

"My friend's going to start with a dozen *escargots*," said Bridge. "And I'll have an apple. *Oui ça:* an apple, a fresh apple."

Rose reached for a handkerchief to dab his forehead.

"Show me your hands, Rose," said Bridge. "Keep them out here. You've burnt your fingers, Rose, haven't you?"

"An accident."

"Bloody ironic one too. You really overdid it, didn't you? Burning up the evidence."

"I swear to you I didn't place a gunman at Orly on you," said Rose. "I'm not responsible if the police are looking for you. You *know* that."

"Yes, you're a clever little bastard, Rose. *I* know that. And I believed the whole bloody rigmarole. And I like the way I found out. I like that too."

"What?" said Rose. He fumbled with the snails, then pushed the plate away.

"Eat them," said Bridge. "All up. Nice little slimy creatures. They should go down a treat." He watched Rose manipulating the shells.

"You're left-handed, you see," said Bridge, watching him. "That bit you did burning up the pictures, when you were making out to be Henri Levitte for poor Claude's benefit. It was very good, very impressive. I mean, she remembered it very clearly. But anybody who is left-handed holds the box in his right hand and the match in his left. So if you are holding pictures in one hand and a match in the other—you see? And Henri Levitte is not left-handed. You *are* a sinister little bugger, Rose. There's one snail left. Eat it."

Rose gagged, then did as he was told.

"So why the whole charade?" asked Bridge. "I wonder. I suppose you thought—once you got the bright idea of getting the pilot killed, it would be worth really covering your tracks on that one. I suppose you got the idea once Abdul had come up with his filthy pictures. Is that the way it went, Rose? You thought the police would get to Claude eventually, right? And she'd tell them about this old man coming to see her with the pictures and asking after me? Not a bad idea, Rose. Not a bad idea at all."

"I admit all that," said Rose. "But what in hell did you expect me to do if you got caught, bail you out? It doesn't mean I tried to get you killed, tonight."

"*I* think you did. I don't think you wanted to get me killed after the Petit job, mind you. But then the thing really started to take off, didn't it. You'd hit on a real pile of worms in the Levitte family. A real love nest. You'd found out enough about that bunch to know it was *just* possible Henri Levitte would do something as crazy as getting the man who was screwing his daughter put out of the way. Unlikely. But just possible. Probably just likely enough so that if the story came out they'd throw me in prison and bury the story to protect the honour of France. Or decide I'd made it all up anyway. Because after all, if I said I'd been working for *you* you'd have denied it. They'd probably decide I hadn't been working for either of you. Either way you'd be clean out of it."

The waiter reappeared. This time Bridge ordered Rose a dish of baby squid cooked in oil.

"So what happened next? Daniel Levitte gets in touch with you. Because in all your fucking around and inventing things you had actually hit on something very true. You'd found out that that family really does loathe each other. Suddenly you had one of them on the doorstep actually asking for help to clobber another one. His lovely daddy. So you thought—'Why not? Let's do it all over again.' Keep the original story intact; get me back to Paris. Tell me you hadn't asked me to do Petit. Good thinking Rose."

"I still didn't fix you to get killed tonight."

"But I keep telling you: yes you did. Because once things had got this complicated, then you had to start tidying up. Pilot dead, plane blown up. Police bound to get to Daniel Levitte—whether he goes up with the fucking plane or not. You wouldn't want me around, Rose."

Rose looked with horror at the mess now placed deftly under his nose. The tentacles of the squid curled prettily about the plate, their tiny suction plates still clearly visible.

"This is a bit childish, Bridge," said Rose.

"You said you were hungry. What in hell did you do all this for anyway, Rose?"

"What do you mean?"

"Getting people killed at all. That's a bit outside your brief, really, isn't it?"

"Yes," said Rose. "Outside my brief. That's one of the phrases. Bridge: nobody in the firm I work for asked me to do that. But *you* ought to understand that, Bridge. Pilots get killed, planes blow up in the normal course of events. It was my decision alone. I was just helping them to something they really wanted."

Bridge smiled. Rose looked pathetic. As if finally, in front of death, he wanted *someone* to understand.

"I can imagine," said Bridge. "That's why I'm not an officer with a pension. *And* it's why I'm not in an army prison. Nobody didn't want him dead."

"And I didn't," said Rose eagerly.

"You're going to say you didn't want me dead again," said Bridge. "Well don't bother. I really *am* not going to kill you Rose."

Rose laid down his fork and looked at him, with more of an appeal for rescue than ever.

"You gave this thing to Daniel Levitte? You got him a bomb?"

"Don't worry about the details. You're going to get your big day on Friday. No doubt about it. The bigger the better. Because that's my insurance for staying alive. You're not going to be able to afford to get me killed, Rose. Not between now and Friday. Because between now and Friday I'm carrying a taped confession and a written confession from you, Rose."

"You haven't got that."

"We will. We'll go back to your office and make it."

Rose shrugged.

"And *after* Friday those two confessions are going to be lodged somewhere they'll stay lodged until I die. And when I die they will come out. And they will have so much detail in them they'll put you and your firm away for ever. You did all this so far to save your fucking aeroplane? Well now you can spend the rest of your time saving *all* your fucking aeroplanes.

Eat your little octopus things, Rose. That one there for a start. The one with its tentacles in a twist."

Rose shut his eyes and swallowed it whole.

"I don't want you dead, Rose," said Bridge. "I mean, where would my money come from? The money you are going to send me from now until I start drawing my old-age pension."

"This is just blackmail then?"

"That's right. More sensible than the pleasure of wiping you out, Rose. And if I were you I would stay out of this sort of thing in future. Your mind's too tricky. The arrangements that come off are the simple ones."

"Bridge, listen. The police must be after you. I mean—in any case. What are you taking this so personally for?"

Bridge ignored him. "That man at Orly: Roget. He still works on his own I hope? Or used to until tonight?"

"That's right. He acts on special information. You know the system."

Bridge knew it. It is an arrangement unique to France. The idea is simple: a small group of police marksmen that operate on a one-to-one basis with accredited secret service representatives. When there is someone that really needs taking care of, these people will do it. It may leave a few major crimes unsolved (in the sense of no-one coming up for an expensive trial and expensive stay in prison afterwards). But then that helps save money—and the man with a bullet in his back is not going to be committing more crimes while the legitimate police are still plodding after him. And for the secret services it is a safe and tidy way of getting rid of embarrassments.

"Come on Rose. I'll get the bill. Then we can go to work. And remember. From this moment you are going to *need* me to stay alive."

The two men walked silently back to Rose's office.

They spent two hours at work with the tape recorder there before Bridge was satisfied with what he had got.

Bridge then left the building first, by the rear exit.

Celeste was not asleep, but wearing her Thai silk night-dress. She pulled a Chinese dressing gown around her shoulders as Bridge approached.

"*Now* where have you been?"

"Why is the phone off the rest?" he asked.

"I don't want anyone calling. Or coming round. Friends or reporters or anybody. I've told the caretaker you're the only one to be let in."

"Daniel might ring."

She shrugged. "They're monitoring all the calls out of the base. And anyway—" her eyes were full of tears. "He's off by himself somewhere. He'll just have to find his own way back if he wants to."

"You're feeling sorry for yourself."

"I'm *not*. It's that damned family. And that horrible aeroplane. You don't have to live with it."

"You're feeling sorry for yourself. Come on, make me some coffee."

She smiled.

They sat down together on the chaise-longue. She bent forward, her hair falling over her cheek, studying the disc of black coffee in the bone china cup.

"What *do* you do?" she asked. "Where do you live in England?"

"In one of those little thatched cottages with roses round the door."

"Oh yes? With your wife and six children?"

"Seven."

"No, tell me."

"Why? I live in a concrete apartment block in south London. It used to be my mother's."

"You know a lot about *us*."

"Don't know anything about *you* at all."

She stood up, and went to fetch her little box with the luggage label in. The one she had round her neck when she came out of Vietnam as a child.

"That's me," she said. "I've been trying to collect something else ever since. And now they've even taken my name away and given it to an aeroplane."

"I told you to stop feeling sorry for yourself."

"Do you *want* to make love to me?"

"Yes."

"Why do I want to make love to you? I don't . . ." She stood up again. "You know, I feel—" she said, "I feel he's gone away to some other woman. I dream about that aeroplane as if it's another woman."

"You also think too much," said Bridge. "Come here."

"If you don't think," she said, "you get into trouble." But she came towards him, warily, but gracefully, like the practised model she was. The wide belt of the Chinese gown slipped open, and he could feel, without touching her, the silk of her skin beneath the silk of her night-dress.

"I like things and people very simple," he said.

"Oh, you should have met that poor girl Claude," she said. "She was simple."

"Yes," he said, "I liked Claude." It was the second slip he'd made in the whole business. But his blood was rising. She seemed not to notice what he had said.

"*Why* are you staying?" she said. "It's not just me, is it?"

"Maybe," he said. "I'm beginning to feel part of the family."

They began to fuel up the Super-Celeste at five in the morning of Friday, February 22. It was one week, to the hour, since Jean-Paul Petit had woken from his last sleep. Daniel Levitte watched the process. The blue Euro-Aviat fuel wagons moved softly in, their white hoses raised like questing snakes in search of the fuel inlets. Only the three fuel cells ranged centrally along the aircraft's spine would be filled. The largest, of over a 1,000-litres capacity, lay just aft of the seat reserved for Daniel Levitte.

Daniel circled the gleaming aeroplane. Those attending it gave him a curious glance or two. A security guard checked his identity tag, comparing with a cold stare its colour photograph against Daniel's face.

In fact, most of the men resented his presence. It was a close community he had intruded on.

The machine seemed to be hungry for the air. To Daniel, the powerful sweep back of the wings gave him the feeling it was already being restrained from flight.

Daniel Levitte approached the plane, bending down to look up into the well into which the nose wheel would rise. No-one paid him any attention. Behind him, a red wagon drew up silently: all the service vehicles in the hangar were electric. This one contained the 30-mm shells. The twin cannon they would pour from were two small, watchful eyes in the fuselage: the first points to break the totally smooth skin of the Super-Celeste's sharp end.

Daniel straightened up to let the two white-coated men get on with their work. He hunched his coat round his neck and began to walk down the hangar. The transistor radio jogged against his thigh.

The place was brilliant with light. He walked past the area to which the machine would be wheeled for the official reception before the take-off. Incongruously, on the dead grey concrete, this area was carpeted and bounded by white silk ropes.

Then he stepped past the guard at the small exit for personnel and into the cold of the pre-dawn.

It was 5.15. Six hours and forty-five minutes before the flight.

There was a scarf of fog over the air base, curdling and drifting between the buildings and the roaming vehicles of the guards. Yet, if you looked straight up, you could see a few swimming stars. Daniel had gone fifty feet from the building when the headlights of a truck swung on him and bore down, horn blazing urgently. He stood still, the light smoking in the fog.

"Right, stay there," shouted the driver as he swung down from the truck. He came at Daniel with his gun waving. His partner, a huge policeman, equally armed, followed.

"What's your business?" He gripped Daniel's lapel to see the identity tag.

"I'm Daniel Levitte."

"Yeah? What are you doing here?"

"I'm flying in the plane later."

"What are you doing out here?"

"I'm just walking."

The driver silenced his companion: "You're the son of M. Henri?"

"That's right."

The first interrogator wasn't impressed.

"You walk around here by yourself you're liable to get eaten by dogs. Let alone shot. Whoever you are."

"Easy, Jean."

"Well, now you know I'm here, you can let me get on with my walk."

He turned from them and paced towards the perimeter fence. Behind him he heard the two men arguing.

"I *know* who he is. Fucking waste of time is who *he* is. What's he doing here?"

"You'll find out when he takes over from the old man. You want to be polite to these people, Jean."

Daniel walked in a straight line to the perimeter fence. A few wind-tormented shrubs had been let grow here. Daniel took the transistor from his pocket and felt the ground below the thickest of them. The earth was dusty and chill. With his bare hands he scooped a small hole and buried the radio in it.

At 07.00 hours the Australian delegation was woken in Paris. For some, it was all too soon. Despite the long flight to Paris, most had been busy the night before enjoying the traditional pleasures of the city. For some, the pleasures had been of an *extremely* traditional kind. Ackermann had spared no effort in his role of courier. This morning, the Australians came down to the reserved dining-room laid for their breakfast, and he was there to welcome them. For each, he had an identity tag for the air base and a comprehensive PR kit on the Super-Celeste.

Senator Mackenzie, swallowing iced orange juice to combat the dehydration of last night's drinking—which had entirely failed to take the edge off his gloom—turned the glossy pages. No doubt about it, on paper the Super-Celeste was designed to do everything but sing. Speed, ceiling, endurance ahead of any rival. The finest long-range dogfighter in the world. Mackenzie scanned grimly on, then closed the pages.

He looked up to see the bland Ackermann at his side.

"All it has to do is fly," said Mackenzie.

"We have transport at eight," said Ackermann. "You have a comfortable night?"

"Yes thank you," said Mackenzie morosely. "I slept like the dead."

All over Paris, people were getting ready for the trip to Dreux. The Premier's helicopter was again in position to lift him there for 10.00 hours. The press and TV reporters had to make their own way—Levitte had never been any friend of the media, and laid on no free trips even for this occasion. Yet, most of the press had done the old man proud: "Monsieur Aviation" as one paper had it, "Reaching for the sky with his newest brainchild." Several papers carried pictures of Daniel and Celeste, arm-in-arm by the Seine. The picture had been sent out from Euro-Aviat's press office with heavy emphasis. *Paris-Matin* put the picture on its gossip page, with the caption: "The new machine bears her name. And he is flying with it! Is a new generation of Levittes ready to take to the skies of France?"

It was this page that Henri Levitte's most trusted director, M. Perrault, now laid, without comment, under the nose of his boss.

"I am sure this is the right time, Henri," said Perrault.

Levitte glowered at the page, then pushed it aside. The two men were eating their breakfast in the small executive block at the heart of the air base. Purple velvet flock wallpaper peeled from the old concrete walls of the wartime control tower.

"You *know* it is the right time, Henri. Now is the time people can believe it."

"What people?" said Levitte angrily, "this trash?" He gestured at the paper, scattering crumbs from his croissant over the page. There were times when Perrault could discern the old man's grip beginning to change. From the stubbornness of an iron will that had sustained him all his life into the yet more harsh stubbornness of intransigent old age.

"Not them. The tax collectors," said Perrault loudly.

He waited. Henri Levitte looked quickly up as the sound of a piston-engined plane hummed into the room. He still kept a few around for transit jobs. And the real reason, many believed, was because it was still to that droning sound rather than the shriek of his sophisticated jet engines that he warmed most. Just as he had kept the old World War II air base for his office.

"You know what it's about, Henri," said Perrault. "You're going to be with this place for a long time yet. I expect you'll outlive me if you want to know. But if you don't hand over your control five years before you retire—"

"Or die."

"Or die, if you insist, then we are going to have this place taken apart in tax commitments."

"And who's going to believe I'd hand it over to my son? Apart from these fools."

"Everyone. He's flying the plane. It's a reconciliation. And, really, Henrí, it *is*, isn't it? I'm very happy about it. It is marvellous that your son is flying today."

Levitte stopped eating and began to wipe his lips with the linen napkin. His dark eyes scowled on Perrault.

"The only thing that matters," said Henri Levitte, "is that *this* goes on. After I've gone. After you've gone. He thrust his chair back and went to look over the airfield. The fog had vanished, and the light was flooding clear on to the long vistas of concrete runway.

"We are building machines to defend France against her enemies. We are fighting the aviation industry of America. Now we have to fight these little—*weevils* who want to take it off us in *tax*. 'Nothing's certain except death and taxes,' said Jefferson, I believe."

"Well there it is," said Perrault. He was angry himself, but he knew how to hide that. "And fortunately there is one way round that. The French still believe in the family. Give your son control of it now, subject to the board's *executive* control, and you can keep all this together. You know Daniel doesn't want control."

"Doesn't deserve it, hasn't earned it," interrupted Henri.

"Good enough. He doesn't, he hasn't. But it is now *credible* you can give it to him. No-one is going to think it isn't reasonable—I'm talking as a lawyer."

"Better get him up here," said Henri. "Before the Australians arrive."

Perrault breathed out with relief. He rang the silver bell set into the mahogany table and dispatched the aide to bring Daniel in.

"And it is true," said Henri looking out of the window across the vast plain. "I don't want to go on taking all the responsibility for ever. You have done a good job on all this, Perrault. Since Petit died, you've taken a strong hold on everything here. You know that I want you to be the chief executive."

"And you know that isn't why I am pressing you now."

"Yes, I know that." The two men were silent, waiting.

The small aeroplane, having delivered whatever it had to deliver, was now turning into the sun ready to take off. The sun lit the discs of its whirring props. Henri Levitte looked, wistfully, across the air base towards it.

"I *would* have hoped my son . . . you know that . . ."

"I think you always wanted your son to be like you," said Perrault gently. "And that doesn't often happen. But he's doing his best now, you know. And after all, we've called the aeroplane after someone very dear to him."

"God knows what *she* sees in him," said Henri. "No. I'm sorry Perrault. If we make this arrangement then it is an *arrangement*. I don't want any encouragement to Daniel to think it means anything other than what it is. It's a tax arrangement. God knows I'll have his mother weeping enough tears of joy. Daniel Levitte is what you call a poor fish. He can have control on paper—all right, I agree to that. And you say we have five years to build in enough company law to see he never has it any other way?"

Perrault nodded. "Obviously it has to be done discreetly."

There was a knock, and Daniel was shown in.

In Paris, at the door of the restaurant where Crispin Bridge had demonstrated his knowledge of French cheese, the police hammered until the proprietor awoke. He came wearily to the door.

One of the police had been in the night before. He recognized him. One of the men from the dead Derivat's station. Now they all wanted to know more. A man with an English accent, a blond? The one you were mentioning last night?

"I never saw him before. I just told last night—I was interested. It was an anecdote."

"It's all right. He just ties up with something we heard. Something with Derivat."

"Ah yes, poor Derivat. He used to be in here often."

"Good. Now, tell us about this English man."

In Celeste's apartment, Crispin Bridge stretched across her sleeping body to reach his watch. Then he propped himself on his elbow to look at her. It had been a strange passage of hours, being alone in this place with her. He ought not to be here. He should have given her the letter and gone. It was crazy to stay here. Asleep, her hair spread loose as spindrift across the linen pillow, she looked nothing like anybody's notion of the top fashion model of all Paris. Nor like the elegant girl on Daniel's arm in today's newspaper. There was great calm in the fragile Eurasian face, and she looked very vulnerable. Yet it was the expression they had been looking for at that photographic session she'd walked out on. When they'd dressed her up and stood her in front of a mock-up of the plane with the scrawny kid. A refugee, a waif who had learnt to fight.

And yet she looked like Claude too, he thought. That puzzled him. He'd slept with a great many women. And he had noticed —as most men do—how *alike* women looked, at this moment, asleep.

It was half-past eight. There were three and a half hours before the flight. He put his finger to her lips. It had been good. Very strange and very good. She woke.

Over their strong coffee he said: "I've got to go. Look, I've *got* to go. So have you. Daniel gave me a letter for his father. He wants it given to him before the flight—just before the flight. He wants your father to read it once he's in the air. When you give it to him, will you do something for me? Give it to him and walk away. Get out of his sight. From what Daniel told me— it's going to upset him. Will you do that?"

She seemed not to understand what he was saying. "I won't go there by myself," she said blankly. "I *won't*, not now. You'll have to drive me there."

Jesus, he thought. Why in hell did I stay? He knew why he had stayed.

"Celeste—" he began. But one look at her told him she wouldn't do it, wouldn't get there.

Well, it could be the last place they'd look for him.

"Okay," he said. "I'll drive you there. But then I'm driving back. As soon as we get there. I've got work to do."

She smiled, "Thank you. I knew you'd help."

Daniel stepped into the light and faced his father. The windows, designed to give a commanding view of the base, back in the war, now transmitted the full strength of the rising sun. The old man's head was crowned into a blaze of light. Daniel blinked.

"Sit down," said Henri Levitte.

Perrault smiled at Daniel; went on crumbling the dough of a bread roll into fragments.

"Have you been down to see the Super-Celeste?" asked Henri.

Daniel nodded.

"I was up early," he said. "There was a strange noise."

"That's right. I understand it was a fan in the air-conditioning on Assembly Point Three," said Perrault. "Woke everyone up. Set up a resonance in the hangar. Well."

Daniel sat down.

"I'm advised," said Henri Levitte, "that this is a very good time." He looked and frowned at Daniel Levitte. The younger man seemed tired, remote and *untidy*. As if he hadn't gone to bed at all.

"We have to make some business decisions," said Henri. "They're not, may I say, very much to do with you. They're for the good of the company. And I'm afraid that's what I care about most in life, apart from your dear mother, as you may have appreciated. I'm advised, and I think it is right, that we make some new arrangements on paper for the future. I don't care much about paper, but it seems to rule our lives. I am going to sign some documents this morning, and I am going to announce before the flight that you are designated the titular head of this company and M. Perrault here is the executive head. You've obviously shown a spirit of co-operation in volunteering to fly today and I think we should take the spirit of things while it is right and make that announcement."

Daniel raised his eyes from the hands of Perrault and his work of turning the bread into dust.

"You're making me the head of Euro-Aviat?"

"In name. Nothing changes. I'm still alive and well. You must appreciate Daniel, that I'm very grateful for your gesture. But I don't think you want to stand in my shoes and I must make it plain you are not going to."

"But because I said I would fly today, that makes it possible for you to tell people this?"

"Of course. I said so."

"You make it very easy for me," said Daniel.

"I don't understand you?" said Henri Levitte.

"I mean I've always had a very easy life," said Daniel. "And I'm very grateful to you."

"Well, I'm glad," said Henri. "And now I'd better get down

to see how things are on the floor. I trust that Celeste is coming?"

Daniel Levitte stood up, smiled and shook his father's hand.

Perrault stayed on in the room after Henri Levitte had gone. After today, he thought, he would be the effective controller of everything in sight at Dreux, and in thirty other factories and establishments across Europe. Yet he felt sad. How many years had he played soft-man to Henri's hard-man act? It had become a close relationship. It had served him well. And now the old man was going.

Perrault knew that. It was easy to say "it is only on paper". As an accountant, Perrault knew it was the paper that counted. And yet it wasn't *that* he felt sad about. Perrault, cheerful, amiable, hid inside him an accountant's heart of steel where facts were concerned. But inside that kernel, private even from Henri Levitte, there was a heart he remembered from a youth, long lost studying philosophy at Liège. In those days existentialism had been all the rage. He thought about that, for some reason now, and the conversation he had just heard between the father and son. There was some term his professor had used: —*contingency*, that was it. Something the opposite to the way the Super-Celeste fitted the air like a hand to a glove. Something about people acting on each other, even touching each other, but not together.

Perrault, chief executive-designate of the Euro-Aviat empire, stood up from his chair to the full weight of more practical considerations. The first guests to the big show could already be arriving on the level and sunlit air base at Dreux.

The scene in the hangar, as the morning gathered pace, began to look more like show business. The plane, now moved to its place of honour, was surrounded with banks of flowers. It even began to look faintly ridiculous.

Perrault had orchestrated the morning's events personally. To hold the main speeches and celebrations before the flight had struck some as a temptation to providence. But if the unimaginable happened and the plane was in any way damaged on landing, it was more sensible, Perrault argued, to exhibit it intact beforehand.

His hearers knew what he meant. And they knew what

Perrault meant by the unimaginable. Appalling as it would be if the Super-Celeste never returned, it would at least be just slightly preferable to have drunk the champagne first.

At the main entrance, the security staff—twenty-five in the regular employ of Euro-Aviat; thirty drafted in from *Securitat-Smith*; fifteen from the French police branch established after the student riots of 1980—they were all almost overwhelmed by the pressure of arrivals. Although the Defence Minister, air-force chiefs and the Premier himself were now spinning out of the sky in a clatter of helicopters, there was a flood of action to handle.

Bridge had been counting on that. Two hundred yards down the arrow-straight road from the air base he made Celeste pull up. He'd insisted she drove, to calm her. They were driving Daniel's sports car, a recognizable target. But no-one, Bridge knew, had tailed them from Paris.

"What is it?" she asked. She was calm now. She had been very calm too when she had telephoned Euro-Aviat's Paris offices to refuse the special chauffeur-driven car available to her. And whatever she thought about the events ahead of her, she had certainly dressed to dominate them. Her hair, immaculately coiled about her head, gleamed in the low, cold sunlight.

Bridge scanned the road ahead. Blue flags hung from the concrete guard house that marked the break in the long wire perimeter.

"Well," said Bridge, "that's it. You can walk the rest." He slid the letter from his pocket; gave it to her. "Remember what I said. Give it to Daniel. And will you promise me one thing, Celeste. As soon as that plane starts moving, will you take yourself off to the bathroom, and stay there. Will you promise me that? In your state, you can't stand the strain. Will you do that for me?"

"Yes, Crispin," she said.

It was the first time she had used his first name. He frowned. Though it wasn't his real name, it belonged to him.

"You *must* come with me. Please. I'm so frightened. I don't know why."

"I can't," said Bridge. "Henri Levitte *and* Daniel told me to stay away. I've done my job and I've got paid."

"Oh yes?" she said angrily. "And last night? That was doing

your job too was it? Do you think I normally behave like that?"

Suddenly she slammed the car into gear and in a flurry of gravel accelerated to the gate of the air base.

She braked hard up against the red and white barrier dropped across the entrance and waited. Euro-Aviat's security chief had taken over the checkpoint in person, and now, politely, asked them to step out.

Celeste, immediately recognized, was the cause of a flurry of cameras from the pressmen mounting their own guard on the air base.

The security guard saluted, then turned with more curiosity to Bridge.

"You were given passes, Mam'selle?"

"No," said Celeste. "They were with the chauffeur in the official car. But I wanted to drive myself."

The man hesitated. "And this gentleman?"

"He has been looking after Daniel and myself since the pilot died."

"I see. You are a sort of bodyguard, M'sieu?"

"That's right."

"English?"

The man's eyes narrowed.

"That's right."

The guard was joined by a policeman, who looked carefully at Bridge.

In the distance, another helicopter droned out of the sky from the direction of Paris.

"Well, I am sure you can see we have our own security arrangements here," said the chief of the guard. He was a sly, sharp-eyed little man.

"None the less," said Celeste coolly, "I insist he stays."

The guard hesitated, shrugged slightly.

"May I have a word with M'sieu in the office, and Mam'selle, may I ask you to pass through the screen there. I am afraid we have a rule to look at luggage, handbags and so forth."

"Of course."

With a firm hand on Bridge's elbow the guard and the policeman ushered him into the small room in the guard house.

The place had been built to stand against machine-gun fire in World War II. The walls were very cold, and very thick.

"May I see your papers M'sieu? And I think you have a gun?"

Bridge passed both papers and gun across the cheap wooden desk.

"And a licence to the gun?"

"It's there."

"I would prefer it if you accepted that your duties are not required on the base, M'sieu."

"I'd agree with you if you hadn't just lost a pilot."

The guard looked at the policeman.

"I see." He approached Bridge and searched him thoroughly for further weapons. "Well then, if it is the wish of Mlle Celeste, I must issue you with a pass. And we will keep your—things— here until you leave."

Bridge smiled grimly at him and left the guard house with an easy step.

As he did so he asked himself: "What the fuck are you doing here, Bridge?" Still: there was plenty of time.

The policeman tapped the phone until he got to the air base's hard-pressed switchboard. "It's a Paris number," he said. "As quickly as possible."

As he waited for the connection he said to the chief of the guard: "I think we should make sure about this one."

As he waited, a shadow fell across the room, as the huge and luxurious Mercedes coach that was bringing the Australians to Dreux passed silently into the compound.

It was 10.30 in the morning. One and a half hours to the flight.

Ackermann, summoned to Henri Levitte's office as soon as he arrived, was glad to hand his troupe of charges over to the professional care of the chefs and maidens in the refreshment marquee. "Quite amazing," he thought, as he watched the Australians happily falling to again on the food and drink. Still, he admitted that a Parisian breakfast must have come as a real deprival to men the size of the Department of Defence representatives. He watched his flock eating, and smiled contentedly. Poor old Melvyn.

Levitte greeted Ackermann warmly. It was the first time in his career that his employer had embraced him.

"You have done very well," said Levitte, "against a great deal of pressure. The Americans must have been feeling very annoyed."

"We kept it moving," said Ackermann. "I think if they had been able to get more time they would have brought a lot *more* pressure."

"Mind you," said Levitte, "don't think you did it *all* yourself. There has always been a personal understanding between myself and the Australian Premier."

"I appreciate that. And I presume you knew that matters were nearer to completion than I did."

"Well, Ackermann. There was nothing I could usefully let you know. And I didn't want you to slacken your efforts. Nor do we yet have any laurels to rest on. Today, I pray and trust, we can sign a binding commitment. After the flight."

"And how will things go in Europe?"

"It will fall in line. NATO will hardly be able to buy American again when we have a machine already coming off. You've made this a great day for us, Ackermann."

Ackermann smiled his gratitude for the compliment.

"And we must discuss commission percentages on NATO deals very soon," said Levitte quickly. "Now, would you like to bring the French and the Australian defence ministers up here and we can open a little champagne."

Daniel Levitte cupped his hands at the tap and dashed cold water over his face. His black hair stuck to his forehead. His hands were trembling. His mouth was still dry. Far away he could hear a band strike up. As he dried his face, the pilot came into his room, bringing Daniel's flying suit with him, looking like a deflated doll.

The band was louder with the door open. Daniel felt the real scene fading, shimmering into something remote. It was a circus: that was it. The marquee, the flags, the sky-blue aeroplane against banks of hot-house roses. And now music—and this serious man, the pilot Bosco, the veteran pilot, zipping him into a clown's suit.

Daniel tried not to look at Bosco. He felt it was important not to meet the man's eyes.

"There it is," said the older man. "Nervous?"

"A little."

"It'll be all right. First flights are something for the newspapers. That's what Jean-Paul used to say. Between ourselves, one aeroplane *is* the same as the next. It will fly."

Daniel nodded. Henri Bosco decided the man was dumb with terror. He clapped him lightly on the shoulder.

"Now we go and exhibit ourselves."

Daniel picked up the envelope.

"What's that?" asked Bosco sharply.

"It's a letter I want to give to my father."

"Put it in your nav. pad frame. On your knee. If you want to."

Daniel looked down. A plastic-covered panel was sewn on to the right leg of the blue suit. He slipped the envelope in and followed Bosco to the car that was waiting to take them across the tarmac to the hangars.

It was eleven in the morning.

The sun was high. Far beyond the base, the huge Normandy plains were dotted with the forest clumps that looked like spectators.

At the bunker by the gate, the phone rang sharply in the cold and damp of the confined wartime block. The guard raised a hand for silence as he listened, then gestured violently to the rest of the station staff. "Okay," he said. "We'll get him."

He dropped the phone and gave instructions: "But don't fuck up the event. Not unless you have to. That was Paris. Just try to get him quietly."

The President of France, with Henri Levitte at his side, was being introduced to the governmental figures in the Australian delegation. He moved slowly through the group, murmuring politely: an elegant, still handsome man, he brightened visibly when his eye fell on Celeste. In her high-necked, utterly simple woollen gown she did indeed look suitably dressed as a patron goddess.

"A beautiful aeroplane, a beautiful name, a most beautiful symbol," said the President.

"And may I introduce my son," said Henri Levitte. He beamed. He was the white-haired, kindly-looking chief of Euro-Aviat proudly presenting his triumphs.

"A very happy day for a very distinguished family," said the President. Cameras exploded around the group. Daniel and Celeste turned to look at each other. It seemed a long time since they were together. She was alarmed at the darkened, inward-seeing gaze. As if he scarcely recognized her.

"Are you all right?" she asked.

"Yes. What's *he* doing here still?"

Daniel had noticed Bridge, standing well back from the throng about the white-roped enclosure.

"He wanted to come. He has . . . been looking after me."

She feared that perhaps he had seen it all in her eyes.

Daniel's hand reached to the pad on his thigh. "Do you have a letter for my father?"

"Oh yes," she said.

"Give me the one you've got. And take this one: give it to him as soon as you can, once I'm in the plane. Give it to nobody else. Give it to him."

A microphone boomed a request for silence, and Henri Levitte led the way into the magic enclosure around the plane. Attendants swiftly rolled the ropes back.

"I love you Daniel," said Celeste. But he didn't seem to hear her. He took the envelope she gave him almost greedily. Then gave her his. "Give it to him," he repeated.

From his viewpoint at the back, Bridge watched the exchange of the envelopes. There was no sign of the transmitter, he noted. He'd been right about that, then. Daniel was determined to go all the way.

It was time to go. Bridge moved swiftly but smoothly, making his way as invisibly as possible through the throng to the exit. He was two yards from it when six policemen crowded into Assembly Point Three. They had guns in their hands. They spotted Bridge almost immediately. One of them stepped up to him, gun raised. "Turn round," he said. "Watch the dais. Move and I'll kill you."

Bridge turned round. He was glad he'd seen the gun. The policeman wouldn't fire it in here. Not unless he didn't mind about a bullet going straight through about six spectators.

Bridge turned attentively back to the dais.

It was 11.15.

The speech was brief.

"We have come here to see a change take place in our lives," began Henri Levitte. "This aeroplane is the finest machine ever to have been built on French soil. This machine is the fourth generation of fighting aircraft to have come from these factories. From now on, our lives will be a little bit safer. And—" here he smiled—"a little more prosperous so far as those of us in the European aviation industries are concerned."

The audience laughed appreciatively.

"And may I say something briefly on a personal matter. My beloved son Daniel is flying in this aeroplane today in tribute to the memory of a dear friend of this family, the pilot Jean-Paul Petit. And in tribute to the memory of a beloved daughter. There is, perhaps, always sadness at the edge of the moments of our greatest happiness. I am proud to tell you of the strength and common aims of this family. I am proud to be able, in France today, to say we are still a family company. Despite our size. It is in the spirit of the family that we have together created this aeroplane.

"I am proud to tell you that from today Daniel Levitte becomes the titular head and owner of this organization and M. Perrault, who is the most brilliant executive I have ever had the privilege to work with, becomes the executive head.

"And for myself, as I watch this beautiful machine in a few moments becoming airborne, I will remember how very different, how very beautiful, too, were those machines at the beginning of my long and happy association with the air.

"Our most distinguished guests here today include a number of friends and colleagues from Australia. That vast continent, which, like our own, must protect herself against those who may wish her harm. That is why they are here. They have come, not to see me, but our Super-Celeste. And our young and beautiful Celeste too perhaps. But they remind me, as I come to the close of my career—how long ago—how little *time* ago it seems that I flew, alone, across their vast and beautiful land. And if I had not been privileged to grace this new aeroplane with the name of my son's fiancée, then I would have called it after the name of that little aeroplane of long ago, *Eastern Light*.

"Today, I feel a huge circle of events has been completed. When you watch our Super-Celeste climb towards the light, and as my Australian friends watch, I would like you to remember, if you will, this rather lengthy pilgrimage of my own. And that desire we all have, to reach for the light."

For a moment, no-one spoke. The old man was known for his emotional speeches, thought Perrault, but this one was a triumph. For some reason he found his cheeks wet with tears. He turned to look at Daniel. The young man was looking at his father with eyes like cold stones.

For a moment the normally placid Perrault stopped breathing. It was not a look that he was ever going to forget. Even, instinctively, it rung a bell of warning in a corner of his mind—but then the tide of the programme's events moved on, and he had to turn back to the microphone to compère the throng below him.

As Perrault invited the audience to separate themselves into the colours of their official passes—reds to the flat roof of the executive block, greens to the press compound on the concrete outside—Bosco, the pilot, took Daniel's arm.

"Time to go and fly, Daniel," he said.

Daniel turned back to Celeste. She embraced him.

"Look after yourself," he said.

Suddenly, the end of the hangar split to show winter sunlight as the vast doors concertinaed open. At the same moment, a siren blew and the Super-Celeste, led by a single, diminutive vehicle, began to ease away towards this light, flanked on each side by its procession of white-clad attendants.

Bridge, sensing that now if at any time the solid guardians at his back could be, if only fractionally, diverted, took a sharp breath, and flung himself like a diver into the crowd. He wrenched at the ankles of those he passed, tipping them into a shouting throng where no-one would dare fire.

"You fucking stupid bastard," Bridge told himself. "Now get out of here."

He had already seen a door half-open behind one of the half-assembled Super-Celestes. There were thirty feet already between him and the cops, who elbowed after him through the protesting journalists. Bridge dived through the door in a scissors fold that scarcely moved it, then got on to his feet, sheltered his face with his arms and crashed through the window ahead.

As he zigzagged down the side of the hangar he heard the first shot rattling off corrugated iron above his head.

There were only thirty yards to the end of the hangar. He covered them in eight seconds, running straight now. He was right to do so. Euro-Aviat's security police were not up to this kind of action. Having wasted time firing from the window they now picked their way through the broken glass and then poured after the figure vanishing round the hangar's far end. They hadn't even got the sense to summon up *Securitat-Smith* men on the radio they'd been given.

When they got there, there was discouragingly little to see. Well, the entire population of the air base was elsewhere, watching the aeroplane moving into position for take-off.

Here at the windy, empty end of the base there was no cover for a cat.

"Shit," said the first cop to round the corner.

"Behind the water tank?" suggested the next to join him.

Guns raised, they converged on the rusting water tank. There was no room behind it for a man to hide.

"Inside?"

Its rim was six feet from the ground. One of them pulled himself up. The tank shifted on its mounting. Four feet of black, foul water lay below him.

"He must have made for the other end. Get back to the gate, François: take the truck. I'll raise them on the radio. And the rest of you just stay round that aeroplane. He hasn't got a gun. We know that. And he can't get out."

At the gate, the security chief rang Paris.

"Do you want a general alert?" he demanded. "The plane's out there. It's ready to roll. Do you want it stopped?"

There was an agonized silence for five seconds. Everyone knew the appalling risks. Sweat began to roll down the security chief's neck.

Paris baulked at a cancellation. Good. "Get on with it. *Find* him," he yelled.

Four more policemen, hurling themselves into the truck, stabbed a siren into a wail of alarm and screamed off back towards the hangar. Almost at once, the sound was lost in the first triumphant roar of the twin turbo-fan engines. Smoothly, the yellow triangular chocks were whipped from the wheels.

Daniel, every muscle clenched, sat shivering in his navigator's seat. They had handed him in like a parcel. Clumsily, he had settled into the black nest of the seat and let them strap him in. Once again, soundlessly, they had explained to him the controls of his zero-zero ejection seat. Now, the canopy closed around him, he felt in a comfortable, womb-like dream, totally embraced and warmed. The outside world came to him only through his earphones. He listened to Bosco and the flight controllers calmly exchanging their pieces of news. Wind-speed and direction, the checks on the hydraulic systems.

When the engines surged alive the plane seemed to tremble too, like a horse: the voices in his ears crackled more urgently. He turned his head. Across the concrete he could see the small police truck hurtling towards the hangar, a blue light flashing soundlessly. Then, nearly as gently as a ship on a launchway, the Super-Celeste began to ease towards the end of the runway: black lines on the perspex canopy shook the image of concrete disappearing below.

Dreamily, Daniel Levitte reached down to his knee and slid the envelope out of his nav. pad container. With gloved hands he began to work on getting a purchase on the sealed flap, so that he could, when he wished, rip the packet open.

Bosco's voice reached him. "You all right, Daniel? We're going to take her up in fifteen seconds."

Daniel nodded. He couldn't bring himself to talk to Bosco. The pilot frowned, but was too busy to bother with Daniel at this point. He aimed his machine down the runway like an arrow and waited for the final release from ground-control.

Crispin Bridge, hearing the roar of the plane as it hurtled forward, made his next run, reached the first six-foot wire mesh fence, swarmed up it like a cat and rolled over into the shadow of a fire tender on the far side. He was now in the service area of the air base. It was nearly empty, for the fire and ambulance crews were lined up, engines running, within reach of the runway. Raising his head he could see the plane streaking down the runway: its twin exhausts shimmering purple through orange in the middle distance, the hot air left behind shaking the concrete in a mirage. He lowered his head, breathing hard and shivering. He heard the truck scream round the corner. It was time to move again. It wouldn't be long before they saw the trail of wet from the tank to the fence. Ducking and sliding, keeping below the sight-levels of the press compound, Bridge made his way to an ambulance at the far perimeter. From the other side of the fence he had seen that its bonnet was up and a mechanic was working on it. The mechanic now stood, open-mouthed and gazing at the departing Super-Celeste as Bridge silently sped towards him. There was just one more fence between them, a defence perimeter too. Made of the newest thing since barbed wire—barbed tape. Handy stuff, flat on the roll; unwound it is a million razor blades joined end to end.

On the roof of the executive block there was a spontaneous cry of delight as the plane grabbed the sky. It was an astonishing lift-off: the blue dart on the runway seemed to burst forward as if catapulted, then stand almost on its tail to climb with a crash of sound that tore the sky in half. On the roof, Celeste pressed her knuckles to her mouth. She had *had* to stay and watch, mesmerized. She had to do it. As soon as it was all right, she'd do as Bridge had told her. But she had to *see*. She shrank as Henri Levitte put an arm round her and squeezed her breast: the old man was gazing into the sky, quite unconscious, it seemed, of anything but the sky, his hand gripping and squeezing her painfully, as he watched the Super-Celeste climb into the top of the great sunlit dome, a trail of white vapour suddenly pouring out from behind to mark its passage.

Daniel, his face distorted into a mask as the G pressures hammered him back into his harness, forced his eyes open. The plane reached the top of its climb and the grey-brown rim of the world swung back into place. The plains of Normandy tilted below them. Suddenly; brown and empty as a plate. Voices, crackling between the ground and the machine, were already high-pitched with pleasure and excitement. Bosco smiled and lifted the nose of the plane to the sun, just as Zucker, the dead American whose existence he had never known of, had lately done.

He could see the air base, flung down on the brown fields like a network of diamond fencing. The red fire tenders and the low buildings scattered across the concrete like toys.

"We've got ourselves an aeroplane," cried Bosco. "Can you hear me Daniel?"

Again Daniel did not answer, but he could hear Bosco asking

the men on the ground to try to talk to Daniel direct. Maybe the poor sod had fainted, thought Bosco. Could be risky; if you faint and vomit you can drown.

"I'm all *right*," said Daniel, briefly.

So. He had arrived. The whole thing had come together at last. Even down to the final ironic gift: the entire Euro-Aviat empire. Even that, given cynically, not a gift at all.

Daniel felt happy. He felt the sun blazing on to him. In a few moments they would be over Paris. He would have to wait. He wanted *them* to see it. He wanted it near enough for them to *see*, all those bastards down there. And high enough so that they would never know, never be able to piece it together, never know the truth. Daniel felt the thoughts spinning in his head as the plane itself rolled. Bosco was obviously beginning to enjoy himself. Below, the first crust-like suburbs of Paris crawled over the ground. Bosco, was descending. Yes, let them see it: the more they saw it the more the explosion would hurt.

What was it going to be like to die? Daniel took the envelope in his left hand and pressed it between gloved finger and thumb. The hammering scream of the jets below him pushed his thoughts into a kind of mechanical peace: he was part of the machine. He was its true pilot. Easy to understand the delight of the kamikaze pilots aiming themselves at the decks of American destroyers. Hurtling down to that final moment of— what would it be? Blood red, or white heat, or just suddenly silence, for ever? Daniel felt his penis growing hard, pushing against the embracing harness. His hands shook, his stomach was twisting in a protest of fear.

"Coming round now," he heard Bosco say. "Systems easy. She's beautiful. One low-level sweep over you then climb to fifteen thousand. Then I'll come in on the target. But if I miss it, too bad." His eyes roamed over the vertical and head-up display of instrumentation in front of him. It was going as good as he could have expected. On the ground they had been complaining about smoke, but that was their problem. That was asking too much for a first flight.

Daniel, sitting in the instructor's seat, was fifteen inches higher than the pilot—a vertical separation that had been copied from the SEPECAT Jaguar. The world was all visible, but far away.

It was the easiest way to die: he was already outside the rest of it. It was easy, even, to forget the pilot who would have to die too. He could see nothing of Bosco but the black loom of his head-rest. Daniel began to watch from the window to see the first sign of the air base at Dreux.

Another police truck now spilled out and swept through the crowd of employees who jostled and protested. The Super-Celeste was well out of sight, no longer there to entertain them. Keyed-up and awaiting her return, the employees, like the world's press, now turned their eyes and their emotion on the burly men pushing and searching through their ranks. "Fuck off," shouted one of the fuel-tender drivers.

So far, no-one had seen Crispin Bridge. Least of all the mechanic working on the ambulance. He now lay under a blanket inside that vehicle, snoring the deep sleep of a man who has been concussed. His face was covered with blood—not his, Crispin's.

Bridge, wearing the unconscious man's coat, went back to finish the man's job, clearing a blocked carburettor with cool and steady hands, though they'd been slit on the tape right through his coat sleeves. The police crew from the truck met at the wire fence and conferred urgently. "He should be here," said one. "If he's not here then it looks worse. Matthieu, Paul, get to the roof and show your guns. Ask the girl. It's too bad, they'll have to be frightened. You and I go over here. He could have climbed the fence."

On the roof, Henri Levitte emerged from the ecstasy he had been in as the Super-Celeste had climbed out of sight. He now accepted the congratulations of the Australian Defence Secretary and the French Premier. Indeed, as he walked about this roof top in the cool February sunshine he was all smiles. People clapped politely as he passed: it was a moment of triumph. The two official photographers allowed in for the occasion crouched to capture the embrace between the still pale-faced Hortense and her husband in his moment of glory.

"After touch down," said the Australian Defence Secretary, "you and I should go and sign a few arrangements, sir."

Henri Levitte shook his hand. Celeste, hesitantly, reached into her handbag for the letter.

The hand at her elbow was discreet, but firm. The police chief, still breathless, steered her towards the low black rail that edged the flat roof. "That man who came in with you. Have you any reason to believe he knew a woman called Claude Breguet?"

She looked at him in total surprise, trying to understand. "Who?"

"A prostitute. We know that Jean-Paul knew her."

"Claude?"

She remembered. She had remembered it and puzzled about it and then forgotten it during the night—Bridge saying, "Yes, I liked Claude."

"We think this man might have killed Jean-Paul Petit. He might be here to do something else."

Her eyes widened. "Oh God," she cried. "The letter? The letter he took with him?"

"*Who?*"

She broke from him and ran across the roof to Henri Levitte. "Quick," she cried. "Quick!"

The air base approached. Daniel, his mouth too dry to swallow, saw the pattern of buildings ahead, swinging slightly as, with a heightened whine from the jets, the plane lined herself up for the approach. It must be now. Finally, *now*. He waited until the horizon climbed up through the sky and he knew he was into the final descent. The Super-Celeste howled in triumph. They were riding out of the sky towards the ground, the wheels already sinking down. With a firm hand, Daniel gripped the envelope again in his left hand and tore the end apart in one clenched pull of nerve and muscle and will.

On the ground, the shock wave of the explosion felled everyone standing on the roof. Afterwards, even piecing it together from the memory of the survivors, it was difficult to record what had happened.

Suddenly, Celeste had run across the roof, holding a packet in her hand. She had almost stumbled between Henri Levitte and the French President and pushed the packet into Henri Levitte's hand. Someone remembered her crying: "Something dreadful is happening. Open this. *Open it.*"

Concussion erased the last second of memory before its strike. There was no-one who could fully report the truth of the next few moments. Henri Levitte, maybe irritated but alarmed, had taken the envelope and torn it open. The bomb, like a rose, blew the man and the girl apart.

Daniel looked down at the torn envelope in his lap. The G pressure was colossal. They were climbing again. In his earphones a clatter and shriek of voices telling them to stay in the air. "We've got a disaster here," said a voice from the ground. Daniel could hear the pilot swearing. There was no ground any more, just the dark blue sky. The shadows from a bright sun moved rapidly across his body. Daniel looked at the envelope. All he had done was open a letter. It was ridiculous. Voices shuttled to and fro in his earphones: "Take it around. Jesus —" The plane had not scattered in a cloud of metal in the cold air. The sun spun past him.

"Daniel, Daniel." He found a piece of paper in the envelope. "Something has happened down there. Your father." Was that Bosco? "We're going round again." He could still see the air base, as they banked: even cars in the park, like flies. A white vehicle, an ambulance maybe, racing to the edge of the concrete.

"Daniel, Daniel—" Bosco's voice was high, urgent. "Your father—" Daniel heard nothing. He took from the envelope a piece of paper with a brief note in a childish round hand.

On the ground, the bells sounded the emergency across the base. At the gate, the remaining police and private security staff were on their feet, looking at each other in horror as the siren of an approaching ambulance—lower, more strident than one of their own vehicles—brought them racing out of the old blockhouse. The barrier, the simple red and white pole, was still down. It was plain that the ambulance was accelerating, its blue light flashing, its horn adding to the siren. The policeman who had first rung Paris flung his weight on to the counterweight of the bar. It lifted: not quite far enough—the bar and the blue light shattered on impact and the ambulance swung in a forty-five degree skid through the gate and on to the road for Paris. Bridge, at the wheel, said: "Move over," quite quietly. In this kind of driving he was relaxed and amiable. If anyone had stood in front of him now he would have run them down and gone on without change of expression. In the distance, across the base, the men in the blockhouse heard other ambulances hammering towards the administrative block. "What the fuck has happened?"

Hermann Ackermann knew he was going to die. In his hands, to his amazement, he held pieces of his own gut. He sat, squatly, legs apart. It was his head that hurt: the explosion had thrown him against the edge of the roof, cracking his skull on the perimeter wall. Not badly—enough to jolt his eyes out of sync. "I am going to die," he thought. His hand was full of red and white entrails. He felt sick. Why am I feeling sick when I am dying? He decided to lie down on his back and look at the sun. He had seen the sun. How that sun shone at Wiseman's Ferry! You must not look straight into the sun: it is bad for the eyes. Ackermann looked at the sun. There was a weight across his leg. That didn't worry him. He didn't like the stickiness between his fingers. He rubbed his fingers together. The sun was huge and red: fading all the time, it grew larger none the less.

The weight on his leg was the corpse of the Australian, Mackenzie. MacSweeney had been right enough. It was powerful stuff.

Across them both fell Perrault, but immediately he rose again to his feet. He was deaf. His ears were blown off, he thought (they had not been). Perrault was bleeding from what was once his left eye. But he was on his feet and licking the blood, like a dog, as it trickled down his cheek. He knew his eye was gone. He too looked first up at the singing blue sky. The Super-Celeste was in sight: he could see. It caught the sun. He could still see that. He pressed himself back through the fallen limbs, pushing them aside till he reached his master and Celeste. Then he stood up. They too were lying. Almost in embrace.

He found himself—later he often wondered why—kicking Henri Levitte away from her. She was breathing. But he knew she was dead. As his blood fell like tears from his blind eye on to her, he closed her own. Then he fell himself, on his back, and before unconsciousness—it began with a feeling of cold and numbness in his feet—he saw again the aeroplane still circling in the sky.

"Get it down," Daniel told Bosco.

"Can't do that. We've orders."

"I'm giving them. Get this thing down. *Now*."

On the road to Paris, the ambulance stopped. Bridge opened the back, threw the unconscious driver into the ditch and jumped back in. Northwards, silent now, the horn switched off, driving north through small roads, towards the sea. He reckoned he could get fifty kilometres up the Eure valley road before the ambulance got dangerous. Far enough north to make them think he was heading for a channel port. Or anywhere except Marseilles. His hands felt pulpy on the wheel.

Daniel beat upon the pilot's helmet with both fists, over the back of his seat. "Celeste," he cried, "Celeste!"

Bosco leant forward to avoid it and, against his own terror, fastened the plane on a course to the airfield. He'd heard enough. From the ground: a bomb, and the cool voices of ground-control enquiring if by any chance there was another on the plane. Bosco realized he had pissed himself. He could feel the warmth. The old nightmare had come back. The time in the Sabre. His knees trembled. Voices from the ground and Daniel Levitte at his back. His mouth hung open, was dry.

For the next few moments the plane flew itself. In Bosco's mind there was a crowd of voices, horror and the memory of nightmares. *They'd blown up Levitte.* He'd heard that. *At any moment the machine would go up too.*

"Bosco?" screamed Daniel. "What in fuck are you doing? Fly it. *Down*."

Bosco grunted, his hands heavy in horror.

"Just get this thing on to the ground," said Daniel Levitte. "What in hell are you doing?"

"*Flight SC,*" said the voice from the ground. It was calmer now. Down there, they were beginning to get a grip on it. "We want to get you back now. But take it to 315, on the far perimeter, and we'll send you a tender."

"No," said Daniel. "Get it back to that block. Get it down now."

Bosco was in the grip of hysteria. He held the wheel with slack, open mouth.

"Listen," said Daniel. "There's no other bomb. Get this thing down where we took it from. Get it *down*. Who do you think is running this thing now?"

From the ground, Euro-Aviat's technicians watched the

plane slip sideways through the air, a knife of steel: for a moment they thought Bosco must have lost it. It was either a manœuvre that was going to end in fragments or a way of changing direction in a dogfight. Then they came in on the runway Daniel had chosen.

From the roof of the administration block, white-coated mechanics lifted the remains of Henri Levitte, gently, on to a stretcher.

"I'll kill you," said Daniel, as the plane levelled out. "I'll find you and kill you, Bridge."

Again, he read the note Bridge had put in along with the paper wadding: "You'll get your fifty thousand francs back two years from now."

By the time Daniel Levitte had reached the roof, the aeroplane only a hundred yards away, some of the mess had already been cleared. In a disaster it is the first thing people do, even with their fingers: start clearing it away. To get life back to normal. The walking wounded had walked. Some of the dead had been carried. But there were still a lot of people on the roof as Daniel leapt on to it. Those who could stand fell apart like the Red Sea as he walked through them. Beneath two sheets, side by side, lay Celeste and Henri Levitte.

Among the wounded, only Perrault, conscious again, had insisted on staying. A bright-red, bloodied pad held to his eye: but still on his feet.

It was he who told Daniel that both his father and Celeste were dead. Daniel put an arm across his shoulder.

On the ground in front of them, blood was still soaking into the grit of the roof-proofing. "Get yourself fixed up," said Daniel.

The police were now there in strength. It was one of them, in a later press interview, who recalled how impressive Daniel Levitte had seemed at that moment. A man still young, with the wiry hair of his father—black, not white—and "more in charge of events than any of us, despite what he had been through."

Yet only one other man dared to approach Daniel Levitte at this moment—afterwards identified as the Australian Minister of Defence. He had said, it seems, "Nothing I can say, friend. Except we have the plane your father wanted. I'm sorry for the bastards who did this. By Christ, get them. And count on us."

Daniel Levitte looked at the blood on the ground, spread out like the shape of a continent. So much blood.

"Oh yes," he said, "we will."

Then he walked to the low perimeter wall, against which Ackermann had been flung by the explosion to die. He'd met Ackermann once. "Who's that?" he asked Perrault. Perrault told him. "Yes," said Daniel, "Hermann Ackermann." He remembered him. The time he'd worked here before, he'd met Ackermann. Ackermann had been good to him. He was sorry. He looked down at the grey concrete of Dreux. So grey, so long and cold. There was nothing to cry for. Not yet. If ever. Celeste, Celeste!

He turned back from the aeroplane below. The Super-Celeste would protect Europe and Australia for the next ten years, he thought. Thousands of her.

He turned to the nearest man, who happened to be Perrault. He said: "Get that plane moved off. I want that looked after. Look after my Celeste."